KU-503-624

The Twelve Wishes of Christmas

RUBY BASU

ONE PLACE. MANY STORIES

This novel is entirely a work of fiction. The names, characters
and incidents portrayed in it are the work of the author's
imagination. Any resemblance to actual persons, living or
dead, events or localities is entirely coincidental.

HQ
An imprint of HarperCollins*Publishers* Ltd
1 London Bridge Street
London SE1 9GF

www.harpercollins.co.uk

HarperCollins*Publishers*
1st Floor, Watermarque Building, Ringsend Road
Dublin 4, Ireland

This paperback edition 2021

1
First published in Great Britain by
HQ, an imprint of HarperCollins*Publishers* Ltd 2021

Copyright © Ruby Basu 2021

Ruby Basu asserts the moral right to be
identified as the author of this work.
A catalogue record for this book is
available from the British Library.

ISBN: 978-0-00-847137-8

MIX
Paper from
responsible sources
FSC™ C007454

This book is produced from independently certified FSC™ paper
to ensure responsible forest management.

For more information visit: www.harpercollins.co.uk/green

Printed and Bound in the UK using 100%
Renewable Electricity at CPI Group (UK) Ltd

All rights reserved. No part of this publication may be reproduced,
stored in a retrieval system, or transmitted, in any form or by any means,
electronic, mechanical, photocopying, recording or otherwise,
without the prior permission of the publishers.

This book is sold subject to the condition that it shall not, by way of trade
or otherwise, be lent, re-sold, hired out or otherwise circulated without the
publisher's prior consent in any form of binding or cover other than that
in which it is published and without a similar condition including this
condition being imposed on the subsequent purchaser.

To dad and mum, for always encouraging me to try

Chapter 1

WELCOME TO PINEFORD

Sharmila Mitra stood in the bracing freshness of the winter air tracing her fingers along the words of the sign. Exhaustion after ten hours of travelling warred with the excitement and slight sense of unease she had ever since she found out she'd be spending Christmas in the quintessential small US town of Pineford.

'Are we going to take this photo or not?' her best friend, Penny, asked, waving her selfie stick.

Sharmila gave an exaggerated sigh. 'If we must.'

'We must,' Penny confirmed. 'Although whether I can get us both in the frame is a different question.'

'Perhaps you should squat a bit,' Sharmila replied, shaking her head. Good to know even a transatlantic flight hadn't affected Penny's ability to make a quip about their ten-inch height difference.

After several false tries, they finally snapped a shot they were both happy with.

Penny rummaged in her bag then pulled out a marker pen. 'Do you think we should increase the population by two?'

'I don't think staying here for less than a month qualifies,' Sharmila said, removing the marker from Penny's hand with a playful tug.

'The town is bound to welcome you with open arms as an honorary resident. Isn't that what happens in those romance movies you love?'

Sharmila gave her the side-eye. 'Or I'll be made into a skin suit. That happens in movies too.'

Penny wrapped her arm around Sharmila's shoulders, giving her a loving shake. 'That's the positive outlook I know and love.'

'I'm trying to be positive,' Sharmila said as they got back into the car. 'But it's strange. I guess I still don't believe this is really happening.'

'Why not?'

She shrugged. 'Things like this don't happen to people like me.'

'People like you? You're exactly the kind of person it should happen to. You deserve something good to happen after everything you've been through.' Penny squeezed Sharmila's shoulder. 'Who'd have thought that when you took pity on the lonely old man in your aunt's teashop, this would be the result? When was that? A year and a half ago?'

Sharmila inclined her head. Just like in the films she loved so much, a series of coincidences, or fate, had brought her to Pineford. To think, if she hadn't been helping out in her aunt's café while she was on a sabbatical, she never would have met Thomas Adams.

She wasn't even supposed to be working that day – she'd had plans to visit some nearby tourist attractions when her aunt called asking if Sharmila would cover for her in the café because of an emergency. It was only months later, she found out that it had also been a quirk of fate that Thomas had gone into the café that morning.

She could never explain what impulse led her to start talking to Thomas, particularly when, beyond taking meal orders and handling payment, she tended to avoid conversations with the café patrons. But something about his loneliness, his sorrow, and his distant expression spoke to her. He looked the way she felt.

If it hadn't been July when they first met, she wouldn't have had her much-loved Christmas in July movies playing in the background. Then they would never have bonded over their holiday stories and she would never have told him her secret wish to experience a small-town American Christmas.

Earlier this year, Thomas had asked her to keep this December free. She'd been curious, of course, but he refused to give her any details, telling her it was a surprise. She didn't think she would be able to take time off, especially since she would have only been back at work at the law firm for a few months after her sabbatical. Then fate again intervened when an opportunity came up for her to transfer from her firm's Birmingham office to their London headquarters. She had enough time before starting at the new office to take a long holiday in December.

And now here she was, in Pineford. It was like living in a fairy tale. If only Thomas were there to experience it with her.

'Are you all right, hun?' Penny asked. 'You haven't said anything.'

'Yes, I'm OK.' She gave Penny a small, sad smile. 'I was thinking about Thomas. I really liked him. We got on so well so quickly. You know, I'd been really looking forward to seeing him last July when he was supposed to visit England again. It was really disappointing when he didn't come. If I'd known he was ill, that he was dying, I would have gone to see him instead. I miss him.' She gave herself a mental shake. That was enough. Giving in to her emotions wasn't going to help. 'But this gift he left me, this holiday. It's huge, more than I could ever imagine. It doesn't make sense.'

'Oh, come on, Sharms! I've told you before. Everyone wants to be adopted by your family for your mother's curries alone. Didn't you tell me Thomas wanted you to call him "mama" because he wanted to be an honorary uncle?'

Sharmila chuckled. 'Yeah, and of course Thomas knew "mama" refers to a maternal uncle so he managed to tease my dad at the same time.' She gave one last glance at the sign before they drove off. She bit her lip. 'I can't believe I'm going to experience my first real Christmas this year. Like straight out of the movies.' She took a deep breath. 'Come on, Jeeves. Onwards to the inn!' she said, motioning to crack an imaginary whip.

If the old-style charm of Pineford Inn was any indication of the town, it was exactly right for her Christmas fantasy. The outside was picture perfect with its white-boarded façade and extensive wrap-around decking, with pillars interspersed between the balustrades. She spent so long taking photos and staring at the inn Penny had to drag her inside.

The reception area was a Christmas grotto. Sharmila's gaze went from the garlands festooned round the banister, to the mantelpiece, down to the logs already crackling in the fireplace. She tilted her head back following the height of the real fir tree as it almost reached the wooden ceiling beams in the lounge, red and green ornaments placed immaculately.

Exactly how she imagined it would be.

While they completed the check-in formalities, Sharmila and Penny were each offered a mug with a piece of cinnamon sticking out of it. She loved the welcoming touch; it suited the old-world atmosphere of the inn. She raised her mug and clinked it softly against Penny's. Almost in unison, they sniffed their drinks. She detected apple and spices. Could it be hot apple cider? She'd only tried the alcoholic version of cider before.

She took a sip, tasting the spices and notes of citrus. Perfect. This holiday was already getting off to a great start.

'Miss Mitra, Miss Calloway. I have your reservations right here. Two rooms booked for three nights, checking out on Monday morning.'

Sharmila cast wide eyes at Penny, her heart sinking at the news. Of course, it was too good to be true. She took a deep breath, then turned back to talk to the desk clerk. 'Is the booking only for three nights? My understanding was we'd be staying here for the duration of our visit – until the twenty-eighth.'

The clerk frowned as she stared at her computer screen. 'I'm sorry. The computer's showing a Monday checkout but let me go speak to someone. I won't be a moment.' She went into the back office.

'Don't you dare!' Penny warned when Sharmila's shoulders slumped.

'What?'

'I know how your mind works. You're thinking you knew this was too good to be true.'

Sharmila lips quirked slightly, despite her panic, at how well her friend knew her. 'Well, can you blame me? When there's a problem as soon as we arrive?'

'You have to be positive. The world isn't as bleak as you think it is. It'll all be fine, you'll see.'

'Well, sorry if that hasn't been my experience so far.' She closed her eyes briefly. Her words had come out much sharper than she intended. The last thing she wanted to do was alienate Penny.

Sharmila may have passed on the chance to come to Pineford if it weren't for Penny, preferring in recent years to stay firmly inside her comfort zone. But Penny had encouraged her to seize the opportunity, and say yes to the trip, even offering to join her without a moment's hesitation. Penny's presence meant everything to her.

Without Penny's optimistic outlook on life over the last few years, Sharmila wouldn't have been able to handle her grief. She looked up at Penny, expecting to see hurt or even anger in her friend's expression but all she saw was love and compassion.

'I'm sorry, Pen,' she said, reaching out to hug her.

'It's OK, Sharms. You know I understand,' Penny said, returning her hug. 'After losing Hari suddenly and now Thomas. You've dealt with a lot. But you have to stay positive. Thomas wanted you to stay in Pineford until the end of the month. I'm sure everything's been arranged. Do you have the email from the lawyer? Why don't you check what it said?'

'Oh yes.' She dug into her carry-on, pulling out a folder.

Penny chuckled. 'I can't believe you're still printing off emails and boarding tickets.'

'Got to have contingencies,' Sharmila mumbled as she rifled through the folder. 'What would happen if the network went down or there was no Wi-Fi or I broke my phone? You'd be sorry you made fun of me then. Ah, here we are.' She read through the email. 'Actually, it doesn't specifically say we're staying at the inn the entire holiday, only that rooms have been booked here for our arrival.'

'See, I'm sure there's nothing to worry about then.'

Before Sharmila could say anything, a woman with a warm smile and hideous Christmas jumper, probably in her late forties, came out of the office.

'Welcome, welcome. I'm Jill, Jill Ford. My husband, Graham, and I own Pineford Inn. We've been looking forward to your arrival. It's a pity Graham isn't here to meet you. He's somewhere setting up for tonight but I'll introduce you soon. Anyway, what was I saying? Oh yes, we're pleased to have you both staying with us. I'm sorry there's been some confusion about your booking but we only have you staying here until Monday. But I knew your booking was arranged on behalf of Thomas Adams. He stayed at the inn when he visited last year, you know. Such a lovely man, may he rest in peace. Anyway, I had a moment of genius and checked against *his* name and I found a note that Mr Bell, our local attorney, wants to meet with you. I'm sure he'll be able to clear up everything. Of course, if there's been a mistake, we'll do everything we can to sort out a room for you. Although, we are booked up for the season. But you're probably going to worry until you know what's going on, so let's see what I can do.' She glanced at her watch. 'If you're not too tired, I can contact Mr Bell now and ask him to meet you here?

His office is in town, but it can be difficult to find if you don't know your way around. If he can't come here one of us can drive you in, I'm sure. In the meantime, here's a brochure for Pineford's WinterFest. We have hundreds of Christmas activities. You've come at the perfect time. We're having the tree-lighting ceremony tomorrow. That's our first big event.' She handed Sharmila the brochure and, with a broad smile, walked back into the office.

Sharmila blinked rapidly trying to absorb all the information. Warm-hearted, larger-than-life personalities weren't just a movie stereotype, at least not in Pineford anyway.

'It appears there's no room at the inn,' she observed to Penny as they went to sit on a couch by the fire.

'I'm sure they have a stable if you need it, though I suspect Jill Ford would give up her room if you don't have somewhere to stay,' Penny teased. 'I bet it won't come to that and Mr Bell will have all the answers.'

Sharmila nodded. To pass the time while she waited for Mr Bell to arrive, she read the lengthy list of activities for WinterFest. Pineford pulled out all the stops for the season. Some of the events were straight out of her dream Christmas.

Within an hour, she was sitting in a small private office at the inn opposite Thomas's attorney, waiting while he read through some files to remind himself of the details of Thomas's legacy. She folded and unfolded the hem of her sweater, knocked some imaginary dust off the knee of her trousers, then clasped her hands in her lap. Why was she so nervous? She'd faced lawyers and judges regularly in the past. And Mr Bell wasn't even adversarial.

But this would be the defining moment – when she found out whether Thomas's gift was real. When she had first heard the news, she was convinced there'd been a mistake. Why would he leave this holiday in Pineford to her? And what did his family think about it? How much did they know about her?

She still couldn't believe Thomas was making her fantastical dream come true. She'd turned her back on many more realistic dreams – mainly plans and hopes for the future – especially in the last few years. It was surreal that it was this whimsical wish to experience a true small-town American Christmas that was being granted.

Mr Bell cleared his throat, bringing her attention back to him. As he went through the bequest, Sharmila leaned forward.

'All right, let me check I've got this right,' she said. 'I'll be staying at Thomas's house while I'm here?'

'That's correct.'

'I thought his family was forced to sell Holly House years ago when he was a teenager.'

'That's also correct. Mr Adams repurchased it last Christmas. It's been vacant ever since. Don't worry, it's been cared for during that time. Lucas Healy, Mr Adams's nephew, has been taking care of upkeep since Mr Adams passed away. He's visiting Pineford for the holidays and, I believe, has just arrived in town, so you may want to meet him at some point. He's staying at this inn too.'

'Then shouldn't he stay at the house?'

'No. The terms of Mr Adams's will are clear. You are to stay at the property throughout December. Mr Healy knows about this and he doesn't have a problem, but he has asked for some maintenance to be carried out while you're there. It would be external work. It shouldn't interfere with your stay, though.'

'Well, of course, it's his property,' she replied, confused when he gave her a shifty look and cleared his throat.

'Finally, Mr Adams expressed a wish that you complete this list of activities while you're here.' He handed her an envelope. 'He called it your Christmas Wishlist.'

Sharmila chuckled. It sounded just like something Thomas would do. 'I can't believe he went to all this trouble.'

'Indeed. The terms of the gift state if you remain in Pineford until after Christmas Day and complete all the items on this list by the end of the year, then a sizeable donation will be made to a charity of your choosing.'

'Sizeable?' She paled when he told her the amount. She cleared her throat. 'OK. I guess that's an incentive.'

The matter of Thomas's wealth had never crossed her mind before; it was irrelevant. But thinking about it now, how else would he have been able to travel to the UK and also fly to India twice in the time she had known him. With the amazing holiday and hefty donation to charity, she realised there was more to Thomas than the slightly eccentric old American she knew.

'Miss Mitra, there are a few conditions I need to tell you about. You are free to talk about the wish list with other people. However, I'm afraid there's a provision that you must keep this potential donation a secret, otherwise you forfeit it.' There was the barest of movement on the attorney's lips.

'But why? That's strange. Why would Thomas want me to keep it a secret?'

Mr Bell was finding it harder to keep a straight face. 'My instructions are this condition has been included because that's what happens in the movies.'

Sharmila slumped back in the armchair and laughed. The first real laugh she'd had in ages. Who could have imagined Thomas mama would turn out to be Santa Claus and her fairy godfather wrapped up in one?

Mr Bell left a few minutes later. She could wait until she was in the privacy of her room to read the letter, but she was alone in the office now and too excited about Thomas's wish list for her.

She opened the envelope, pulling out a sheet of paper. She recognised his handwriting straight away. They'd kept in touch through letters in the post rather than email, which he'd considered a necessary evil for business purposes, and only then, when a phone call wasn't possible. Handwritten letters also appealed to Thomas's sense of whimsy and he'd always been proud of his penmanship.

She started reading the first page.

My dear Sharmila,
*   I've never been a man of many words so don't worry,*
this won't be a long letter.

Apart from the first day they met, she would never have described Thomas as a man of few words. Whenever he spent time with her family, particularly her dad, it was always a matter of trying to find a gap in the conversation if she or her mother wanted to speak. She carried on reading.

*   I never thought, in visiting England again after so long,*
that fate would have led me to your aunt's café, and it
would be the beginning of a whole new adventure for me.
Traveling to India for Durga Puja and Holi and learning
about your culture and traditions were highlights of my life
but getting to know you and your family was one of my
greatest blessings. You all opened your hearts and your
home to a lonely, slightly cranky old man and welcomed me
into your family as an honorary Mitra.
*   You have given me so much, I wanted to give you some-*
thing in return—a chance for you to spend Christmas in a
small town doing all the festive activities we talked about as
we watched your Christmas romance movies.
*   I wish I could be with you as you experience the American*
Christmas you have longed for. I wish I was there to share
my memories of Pineford with you. Even though I won't be
with you in matter, I'll always be with you in spirit. (See how I
used what your parents taught me about Hinduism!)

Sharmila half-laughed, half-sobbed as she read Thomas's words. It was so typical of him to inject humour into his poignant message.

*But I don't want this to make you sad; Christmas should
be a time for joy. So to help you get into the true spirit of
an American Christmas, I have ten wishes for you to fulfill.*

*I hope you have fun with these wishes. You, Sharmila
Mitra, are a very special person who deserves all the happiness
in the world.*

Much love,

Thomas mama

Sharmila took a couple of shaky breaths, determined not to be
sad since Thomas didn't want that. She turned over the sheet. It
was a list titled '*Ten wishes for Christmas in Pineford*'.

Wish 1 Enter and complete the Puzzle and Pie Contest
Wish 2 Build a snowman in the Snowdreams Competition
Wish 3 Enter the Festive Dessert Competition
Wish 4 Enter the Gingerbread House Competition

She snorted. She could guess why Thomas had chosen these
particular wishes. Most of them were quintessential seasonal
activities. And they should be easy enough to do – she'd seen
each of them on the brochure for Pineford WinterFest.

**Wish 5 Take part in the Pineford Christmas Spectacular
Parade**

She rubbed her chin. Did that mean she had to actually be
in the parade, like on one of the floats? How would she even go
about taking part in Pineford's parade? Perhaps Jill could point
her in the right direction.

Wish 6 Go ice skating on an open-air rink
Wish 7 Drink eggnog by an open fire

Eggnog? She grimaced. Thomas had laughed when she asked why anyone would want to drink cold custard. Now, she was going to find out.

Wish 8 Host a Christmas party

A party! Her stomach churned at the prospect of getting to know people well enough to ask them to a party. But it was Thomas's wish, so she would have to find a way.

Wish 9 Pick out and cut down your Christmas tree

She took a deep breath, holding back tears. Thomas knew how much fulfilling this wish meant to her.

Wish 10 Recreate the final scene from a Christmas movie

She rolled her eyes. Thomas was a crafty old man. He probably expected her to pick one of the romantic films – the kind they'd bonded over. He was such an old romantic at heart. But those films were about falling in love. Love and romance were the furthest things from her mind. The only difficulty in completing this wish would be finding a scene that only had one or, at most, two characters so she could do it with Penny. She was *not* going to embarrass herself by asking other people for help with this one. She made a mental note to check the ending of *Die Hard*.

She finished reading the letter and folded the sheet of paper, putting it back in the envelope and pressing it briefly to her heart before she wiped away her tears.

Ten wishes, three weeks, and a whole lot of Christmas spirit to look forward to.

Chapter 2

Zach drummed his fingers on the reception desk while he waited for his cousin, Lucas, to come down. He turned when a door opened behind him. A petite South Asian woman exited the room.

He narrowed his eyes. Could this be *the* Sharmila Mitra – the very reason he was in Pineford?

She looked up at him, glanced down at his clothes, and cleared her throat. Barely giving him a polite nod, she walked towards the elevator.

He watched closely as she bumped into Lucas as he was coming out of the elevator. To a casual observer, the action may have seemed accidental, but Zach had first-hand experience with the tricks women like her used to get attention. As expected, Lucas was laughing as he helped her regain her balance. And right on cue she placed a hand on his arm, offered an apology, followed by a stunning smile before moving away to meet her friend.

She was convincing. He would give her that.

His mouth twisted. It was no surprise she hadn't smiled at him the way she did at Lucas. He knew her type. She'd judged him based on what he was wearing – worn jeans, a workman's shirt, and a battered jacket – and showed no interest.

'Hey, Zach, you're here,' Lucas said as they greeted each other with a handshake and shoulder clasp before Lucas pulled him in for a hug. 'It's been too long.'

'Far too long,' he replied with an apologetic head tilt. 'I'm sorry. I've been meaning to visit Boston but work has been too busy.'

'I've missed hanging out with you, man. But you're here now,' Lucas said, beaming at him.

Zach returned his grin, then inclined his head in the direction the woman had disappeared. 'Do you think that was her?'

'Probably. There can't be that many Indian ladies staying here. We'll find out soon enough,' Lucas said. 'They're serving hot drinks on the patio later this evening. I asked the owner to introduce me. You should come so you can meet her too.'

'She's not what I expected.'

'Because she's a bit homely?'

Zach frowned. Homely? Admittedly he hadn't seen her up close, but her large dark eyes, prominent cheekbones, and delicate jawline gave her an arresting quality. Tight-fitting jeans encased slim legs that were surprisingly long for her height and the loose-knit sweater clung to her curves. Homely was the last word he would use to describe her – she was closer to his definition of beautiful.

They walked to a quiet area where they wouldn't be overheard.

'It's so good to see you, Zach. I know this isn't a good time, what with your company's international expansion, but it's great that you could come and we get to spend time together.'

'Of course. Anything for you and Izzy,' Zach replied. Anything for family. Growing up he and Lucas had been more like brothers than cousins. They may now live thousands of miles apart, but he would always be there if Lucas or Izzy needed him.

He recalled Izzy's phone call after Thomas's will-reading. She was upset and angry as she told him what Thomas had left Sharmila Mitra.

'What was Uncle Thomas thinking?' Izzy had said. 'This all-expenses-paid vacation to Pineford he's giving her is more than

14

generous. But to give her two voting class shares in our business. It doesn't make sense. You know what that means, don't you? If Lucas and I disagree on a proposal, Sharmila Mitra – a complete stranger – will get to make the final decision! Even *you* don't have voting class shares. If he left them to you at least that would make sense.'

Zach had listened without trying to say anything; he knew she needed to vent to someone.

'We can't even challenge the will,' Izzy had told him. 'Uncle Thomas was mentally competent, and the legacy stands. Can you imagine what it's like for Lucas and me? How would you feel if one of your business partners left their shares to some stranger rather than you? Or perhaps you don't care about the family business since you walked away.'

Zach stiffened as he recalled her words. He hadn't missed her emphasis on 'family'. He'd become used to the accusation he'd walked away from the company, but it still stung.

Zach's grandfather had started Endicott Enterprises. When Zach's father joined straight after university, Thomas was already working for the company and had even played Cupid by introducing his sister, Zach's mother, to him. When Zach's father had taken over as CEO, he made Thomas and Bill, Lucas and Izzy's father, his co-owners. Although Uncle Bill had left the business several years ago, Lucas and Izzy had taken over his role after they finished college. Zach had also joined the company in the beginning, and the expectation had always been that he would eventually take over from his father as the CEO. Instead, Zach had left to start his own tech-based company in California.

But despite what Izzy implied, even though he had left the business, Zach still cared about what happened to it. Which was why he was in Pineford when he should be working on an important deal back in San Francisco.

'It's a strange situation, isn't it?' Lucas said, breaking into his thoughts.

'What? Thomas's will?'

'Yeah, his condition that Sharmila has to stay in Pineford until Christmas and complete some tasks to get the full inheritance. It's a little bit exciting. I can't wait to meet her properly, to see what she's like.'

Zach grimaced. When the three of them had discussed how to deal with Thomas's will, Izzy had come up with their only option, so far, which was that one of them should go to Pineford to stop Sharmila completing the tasks. Izzy would have been the perfect choice – she was a force to be reckoned with when she set her mind on something. But she had a deal that was near to closing so she couldn't leave Boston. Lucas offered to go in her place, which was when Izzy privately asked Zach to join him. To look out for him. She knew Lucas was reluctant to go against what Thomas wanted, although neither she nor Zach fully understood Lucas's reasons.

It sounded like Izzy was right to worry that her brother's friendly nature would make him vulnerable to Sharmila, the way Thomas had been.

'Remember, you'll need to be on your guard,' Zach said. 'Uncle Thomas was no fool and Sharmila Mitra managed to trick him.'

'Don't worry about me, Zach. I'll be careful.' Lucas was quiet for a few minutes. 'Izzy mentioned that Sharmila and Uncle Thomas could have been in a relationship. You don't seriously think that's true, do you?'

'It does make sense to me.'

'I don't see it, though. Uncle Thomas never showed any interest in anyone in a romantic way, ever. At least not since Aunt Carla.'

'True. But what other explanation could there be for Thomas to leave her so much?'

'Maybe they really loved each other.'

'If that was the case, don't you think he would have told us about her?'

Lucas chewed his bottom lip. 'It still feels wrong, what we're planning to do.'

'Thomas was vulnerable when Sharmila met him. We're doing the right thing protecting him from his mistake.'

'Perhaps we should get to know her first, before we make any decisions. What if Uncle Thomas had his reasons?'

Zach had expected Lucas would think this – to want to believe in the best of people. Lucas had the biggest heart of anyone Zach knew. But he wasn't a fool. Neither was Thomas.

Sharmila Mitra must be smart and devious if she'd managed to manipulate Thomas. He knew Thomas – he wasn't someone who would have been easily taken in by a con artist. Had she pretended to care for him? Had Thomas been deceived by a pretty face?

'Uncle Thomas may have had reasons for leaving her an inheritance, but he was tricked into it,' Zach asserted.

'You really think so?' Lucas asked. He rubbed his chin, the doubt clear.

'That's the only reasonable explanation.'

'But she doesn't even know about the full terms of the gift.'

'No, she doesn't. But I'm sure she was hoping that Thomas would leave her something more than a vacation. She's probably already thinking about what else she can get out of the Adams family. Which is why I'm staying in the barn, so I can keep an eye on her and make sure she doesn't overstay her welcome,' Zach replied.

'Wouldn't it be easier and fairer if we just told Sharmila about the inheritance?' Lucas suggested.

The terms of the gift stated that if anyone informed her of the inheritance, she would automatically get it without needing to stay in Pineford or complete the tasks.

'And offer to buy her out, you mean?' Zach asked.

Lucas nodded.

'Izzy already brought this up. We don't have the finances. You won't be able to raise funds from the business until this inheritance condition is sorted out and I can't help out right now because my capital's tied up in my company's expansion. Besides, if we tried to buy Sharmila out, we don't know whether she would even sell or what price she would ask for. Let's be realistic. If Sharmila went after Thomas for his money, it wouldn't be cheap to buy her out.'

'Uncle Thomas has only left her 2 per cent of the shares. Izzy and I still have 49 per cent each. Would it be so bad if Sharmila kept them?'

Zach watched the conflict on Lucas's face as he wrestled with the idea of interfering with Thomas's wishes. 'It's not only the shares, remember,' he pointed out.

'I know. If only there was a way to separate the shares and the house.'

'But there isn't. And she doesn't deserve either.'

'We don't know that. Perhaps she's a genuinely nice person who cared about Thomas and deserves both.'

'Why do you think Thomas made the gifts conditional? He could have left them to her outright. I think subconsciously, Thomas wasn't sure about her.'

Lucas furrowed his brow. 'Maybe you're right. Plus, Izzy seems to think the same, and that's two against one.'

Zach hated seeing the indecision on his cousin's face. 'If you don't feel comfortable with what we're going to do, Lucas, then I don't want to force you. I can do this alone. Izzy won't mind if you go back to Boston.'

Lucas shook his head. 'No, the one good thing to come from this whole situation is the chance to spend more time with you.'

Lucas was right. If Zach had to be away from San Francisco to help his family, at least he would have a chance to reconnect with his cousin. He hadn't meant to let their relationship suffer because he'd moved out of state.

'I guess we're doing it then,' Lucas said. 'The first step will be finding out what tasks are on that list. That sounds simple enough. I heard one of Uncle Thomas's attorneys was here earlier so I'm sure Sharmila has the list. Let's try to find out this evening at drinks. I hope it's going to be easy to stop her from completing the tasks, otherwise we have to make her return to England before Christmas Day and I doubt she'll want to give up her vacation.'

'It shouldn't be too hard to find out what's on the list. I suspect once she learns you're Thomas's nephew, she'll assume you're wealthy and, chances are high, she'll want to get to know you. Once she does, I'm sure she'll tell you everything about the list.'

'Me? Why not you? You're not bad looking, and you're wealthier than I am.'

'Thanks for the compliment,' Zach said with a smirk. 'But she's not going to know who I am. I'm going by Zach Lawrence, remember? Nobody's going to know I'm an Endicott.'

'Do you really think that's necessary, Zach? She won't have heard your name.'

Zach murmured noncommittally. He didn't particularly want to keep his identity a secret – he'd been dubious when Izzy first came up with the suggestion that Zach pretend to be a handyman so he could stay near Holly House and keep an eye on the property.

Izzy had also pointed out Sharmila could become suspicious if both of Thomas's nephews were in Pineford at the same time she was. Lucas couldn't take on the handyman role because he knew nothing about electrics and carpentry. It always surprised Zach that someone who ran the family construction company would be unwilling to get his hands dirty. Zach had loved working at the company's building sites during his summer vacations. If he hadn't found a greater love in computers and the technical design side while at college, he would have stayed in the family business and pitched in on-site when he could.

He would enjoy doing handyman jobs while he was in town – it would be good to be hands-on again. And Zach Lawrence was his name, just not his full name. Besides, he liked people getting to know him without the expectations, assumptions, and interest that came with the Endicott family name.

He knew he was trying to justify the deceit. It didn't sit

comfortably on him. But family came first. If Zach's staying on the property would give Izzy some reassurance and his small deception ultimately would help his family keep the shares and the house, then he would do it. Hopefully, it wouldn't have to be for too long.

'Are you sure you want to stay in the barn?' Lucas asked. 'You haven't even seen it.'

'I'm sure it will be fine. As long as it has electricity, I can manage.'

'Have you considered there might not be any internet?'

'I have considered that. And I've come prepared.'

'I hope you're not going to work all the time, Zach.'

'I'm not. We'll have time to find out what's on the task list and stop her completing it.' He would make time. He'd always looked out for Lucas, even though they were the same age. Lucas was too friendly, too happy to see the best in people, too excited by all the possibilities. Zach knew from experience the glass was rarely half full.

'I think we should take part in WinterFest.' Lucas thrust a brochure into Zach's hands.

He clenched his jaw. 'Maybe. If I have time while I'm also trying to stop Sharmila, do my real job, and work as a handyman around the property. Which reminds me,' he said, reaching into his pocket, 'we should swap keys. Let me go unload my luggage.'

Lucas walked with him to his rental car, which Zach had picked up at the airport. He removed his bags then carried them to the company truck Lucas had driven from Boston. They wanted to make sure there was nothing to suggest Zach wasn't the handyman he was pretending to be. Izzy had thought of everything. If she ever wanted to change careers, she would make an excellent evil mastermind. He was glad they were both on the same side.

The side that was going to stop Sharmila, one way or another.

Chapter 3

Later that evening, Sharmila stood by the open French doors. So many heads turned in her direction, curiosity on their faces. But all welcoming expressions. She expelled a breath. Nothing obvious to worry about here.

'Miss Mitra,' Jill Ford called out, walking over to her. 'There you are. I've been waiting for you to join us. How about a mug of our delicious hot chocolate? It's the perfect drink for a night like this.'

'Please, call me Sharmila,' she replied, following Jill to a table with a large pot of hot chocolate.

Jill repeated the name, making a fair attempt to get the pronunciation right. 'This is my husband, Graham,' she said, introducing her to a tall, broad, bearded man who filled a mug for her. They chatted about Sharmila's plans during her holiday while she tried to choose a topping from the bowls filled with marshmallows, chocolate chips, coconut shavings, crushed peppermint candy canes, and what appeared to be some kind of chocolate cereal. Finally settling on whipped cream and crushed peppermint, she scanned the patio.

There were several lit braziers, each surrounded by three or four chairs, most of which were already occupied. Off the patio, further into the garden, there was a more secluded area with thick log benches around a large, circular stone fire-pit, illuminated by strings of fairy lights hung from the branches of nearby trees. An older couple were sitting there but the benches next to them were empty. The couple beckoned her over.

Sharmila did a quick assessment. Likely to be guests of the hotel. Probably unlikely to meet them again after this evening; definitely not going to see them again after the holiday. Minimal risk of a brief social interaction turning into something deeper.

She could do this.

She took a deep breath, then walked over to the fire pit. After she sat down, they introduced themselves. They were visitors from Canada who were driving down to visit their daughter for the holidays. They told her all about their plans for their vacation. She was happy to let them talk about themselves; she preferred it to them asking her questions. They chatted for around ten minutes before the couple stood and excused themselves, wanting to turn in for an early night.

Sharmila was about to take the first sip of her hot chocolate, when she was interrupted by Penny's voice calling out, 'Wait a minute, you can't drink that!'

Sharmila almost spilt the liquid as she quickly brought the mug down and stared into it. What was wrong with her hot chocolate?

Penny took the drink out of her hands. 'You're looking so pretty over here in the firelight,' Penny said, her eyes going from the fire pit to her and back again.

'Uh, thank you.' Why was her friend acting weird?

'Yes, by the *open fire.*'

Sharmila finally twigged what Penny was getting at. She couldn't believe she'd missed that she was sitting by an open fire. The only thing she needed now was some eggnog and she could cross off one of the wishes on Thomas's list.

As she was about to search for Jill or Graham to ask whether they knew where she could get eggnog, she spotted Jill heading her way holding a glass mug with what looked like a milky concoction inside.

'Penny said you wanted to drink eggnog tonight,' Jill said, handing Sharmila the mug.

Sharmila mouthed her thanks to Penny, not surprised her friend had arranged it already. Penny had loved the idea of Thomas's Wishlist when Sharmila told her about it and promised to help her.

'Not many people like eggnog nowadays so I don't bother making it,' Jill continued. 'But this is my special recipe. I've perfected it over the years. The secret is to use lots of spices. It's hot but I always say eggnog is best drunk warm. It tastes better and you don't have to worry about raw eggs. Do you like eggnog then?'

'I've never tried it before,' Sharmila said. She couldn't believe Jill had gone to all that trouble for her.

'Oh?' Jill gave her a curious look.

'Thomas Adams wanted me to try it, I think,' she admitted.

'Oh, Thomas. Yes, of course. I heard he left a list of activities he wanted you to do while you're here. Is this one of them?'

Sharmila's eyes widened, surprised to hear other people knew about her list of wishes. Just how much did the people in Pineford know about her?

'Yes, that's right,' she replied, forcing the corners of her mouth up.

Jill waited, clearly expecting Sharmila to give her more details, but Thomas's wish list wasn't something she felt comfortable sharing with someone she'd just met, no matter how friendly she was. She hadn't even shown Penny the letter, just given her a summary of what items were on the list.

'Oh, that reminds me,' Jill said when Sharmila stayed silent. 'I must introduce you to Thomas's nephew, Lucas. He arrived this morning. A late booking so we were lucky there was a room available for him. Anyway, he asked me to point you out. I'm hoping he'll join us this evening.' She placed a hand on Sharmila's shoulder before turning to go back inside.

'Hey, isn't that a coincidence, Lucas being in Pineford the same time as us,' Penny said.

'Oh yeah, I completely forgot to tell you – Mr Bell already told me Lucas was here.' Sharmila nibbled her bottom lip. Thomas had spoken a lot about his nephew. She got the impression, from little things Thomas said, that he sometimes found Lucas frustrating to work with but there was always great affection underlying any comments. He spoke so fondly about his nephews and niece, especially when he shared stories about them when they were children. 'It's not that much of a coincidence, if you think about it,' she continued. 'He probably knows I'm here for the holidays. Wouldn't you want to meet the person your uncle gave this amazing opportunity to, a person you've never met before?'

'I suppose,' Penny said. 'And to hear what Thomas got up to in India.' Penny's phone pinged. She glanced quickly at the message then put the phone away. 'Work, sorry.'

'Did your client meeting go well?' Sharmila asked.

'Yes, they were happy with the broad concept but want me to make a few adjustments. Shouldn't take me long and I promise it won't interfere with our plans.' As a freelance graphic artist, Penny could work on projects of her choosing from around the world. Even though Penny insisted it wasn't a big deal, Sharmila knew she'd turned down a large commission to accompany her on this holiday, instead deciding to work on a smaller project that was more manageable for their trip.

Penny reached over for her mug and took a loud gulp. 'This is the most decadent hot chocolate ever,' she said, smacking her lips. 'It's so rich, I'm already full and I haven't even drunk half of it yet. I imagine this is how Augustus Gloop felt when he drank from the chocolate river. I can't stop drinking it.'

Sharmila raised her eyebrow a fraction. 'I'm glad you're enjoying it.'

'I am. I don't think I've ever had hot chocolate made from scratch before. It's so good this way, like nothing I've ever tasted!' she replied, taking another gulp, moaning with pleasure.

Sharmila giggled despite herself. Penny was really laying it on thick.

'You know, you could join me and drink some of this eggnog. I'm sure it's very tasty.' She cautiously sniffed the mug. It smelled of spice and milk, or more like custard mixed with cream soda and cinnamon.

'Don't want to waste this deliciousness.'

'Maybe I should have some hot chocolate first. Line my stomach. You know, I don't ever remember drinking hot chocolate growing up. We've always been such big tea drinkers. A mug of freshly made hot chocolate would be a real treat for me too.'

'Oh no, Sharms. This stuff is so filling you'll have no room for the eggnog, and that's a waste of an opportunity to finish a wish.'

Penny was right. Drinking eggnog was on her wish list. Thomas wanted her to try it. Thousands of people drank eggnog every Christmas – it couldn't be that bad. And Jill had made it with her special recipe. Sharmila brought the mug up to her lips. She opened her mouth then quickly closed it again, lowering the mug.

'I think you should try some of this too, Penny. I don't want you to miss out.' She held the eggnog out to her.

Penny gave her a cheeky grin. 'I'm good, thanks.'

'What about joining me out of, you know, friendship and solidarity?'

Penny shrugged. 'Maybe we're not that close.'

She laughed. 'Apparently not! Don't think I'm going to forget this. OK then,' Sharmila said, taking a deep breath. 'It's time. I'm going to do this.'

Penny pulled out her phone ready to take the photo while Sharmila took her first sip. It wasn't as bad as she'd anticipated. Not the worst thing she'd drunk. Although it was like drinking a milky custard.

'First wish done,' Penny cheered. 'That was egg-citing.'

Sharmila groaned. 'Tell me you didn't just make an egg pun.'

'Egg-actly.'

'Please stop.'

'Oh, you're no fun. I could go on. There's no eggs-piration date on my puns.'

'No, I think that's en-oeuf,' she replied with a giggle. 'And I think that's enough of this eggnog too.'

'I'm sure Thomas wanted you to finish it.'

'Really? We've already taken the photo. He didn't ask for a video.'

'Sharmila! That's not getting into the spirit of Christmas now, is it?'

'Hmm.' She took another sip. Giving Penny a sideways glance, she took another one and let out a small moan of delight. 'You know this isn't bad at all.' She swallowed some more. 'You really should try it.'

'Hmm. I'll pass, thanks. I don't trust you.'

'Charming! But seriously, I think you'd like it.' She thrust the mug in Penny's face again.

'Nope. It doesn't smell good.'

'It tastes better than it smells. Really. I think I may prefer it to hot chocolate.'

Penny narrowed her eyes suspiciously but she slowly took the mug from Sharmila. She expected Penny to take a sip, but to her surprise Penny took a gulp instead. Her face turned sour. Sharmila watched as Penny glanced around, probably looking for somewhere to spit the eggnog out but when Penny saw Graham approaching, she had to quickly swallow the drink, clenching her mouth. Sharmila couldn't help laughing as Penny mouthed the words 'I hate you' as she handed the mug back.

'My wife makes great eggnog,' Graham said, in a conspiratorial whisper, 'but I have a secret ingredient that makes it taste even better.' He pulled a small flask from his breast pocket. 'Rum. Would you like some?'

'Please,' Sharmila replied, grinning back and holding her mug towards him.

'Cheers!' he said, after pouring her a generous measure.

'Ah, this is the stuff,' Sharmila said. The rum made the drink richer, creamier, smoother. 'Thank you.'

After Graham left, she turned to Penny. 'Do you want to try it now?'

'No! I will never trust you again, Sharmila Mitra.'

They both giggled.

Sharmila stretched her legs out. 'I can't believe I've completed my first wish. Thanks for arranging that, Pen.'

Penny waved her hand in a gesture of dismissal. 'One down, nine more to go. Which one do you want to do next?'

'I read the WinterFest brochure. The first competition is this Sunday, the puzzle one. Then there aren't any more competitions until the following weekend, Saturday evening I think, for the dessert competition. The snowman competition is a week on Monday, the gingerbread one is the Saturday after, and the parade's on the twenty-fourth.' She ignored Penny's snigger of amusement that she'd already memorised the schedule of events. 'Perhaps we should start ticking off the wishes that don't have a specific date, like ice skating and cutting down a Christmas tree.'

'Don't forget the last scene from a Christmas film.'

'Yes, of course. The last scene. How could it slip my mind? I don't fancy involving other people in this wish so I'll need to find a film that only has two people.'

'If you only want two people, perhaps you should choose one of your romantic movies,' Penny suggested. She nudged Sharmila in the ribs. 'You could ask mister tall, dark, and buttoned-up over there. Maybe he could help with your last wish.'

She followed Penny's gaze. The ridiculously good-looking man in the jeans and battered jacket who'd caught her eye as she was leaving the office earlier that day was standing by the table waiting to be served. And next to him was the man in the suit she'd bumped into while she'd been gawking at his friend.

Sharmila's throat went dry and heat began to radiate through her body. It had been such a long time since she'd experienced the remotest hint of attraction to another person, she was as stunned now as much as she was earlier.

'Well. What do you think?' Penny asked.

'About mister power suit? No, thanks. He looks like he puts work above everything else. He's still wearing his suit under his overcoat.'

'You're so judgemental! You haven't even met him.' Penny laughed.

'I don't need to. I recognise the type very well. Once bitten and all that.' But she didn't want to think about Hari right now.

'All right then, what about the man next to him?'

Yes. What about him? What was it about him that drew her attention?

It wasn't his perfect face with its perfect strong jawline, perfect straight nose, or perfect defined cheekbones. And it wasn't his perfect hairstyle – dark hair cropped at the back, lush and long, swept off his forehead at the front. Whatever it was, it was giving her the perfectly reasonable urge to throw her arms around the thick woollen sweater stretching across the perfect breadth of his chest and rub her cheek along the perfect amount of light beard growth.

Down, girl.

Was this what happened when you went too long without sex? She knew, more than anyone, good looks didn't mean a thing if there wasn't substance behind them. No, it wasn't simply the way he looked. There was something familiar about him. But if she'd met him before there's no doubt she would have remembered it.

She quickly averted her gaze when he looked in their direction. Had he caught her staring at him? If he was doing a quick scan of the room, there was no reason he'd know she'd been observing him for a while. She wasn't the only one on the patio who found the two men interesting.

She sneaked another glance, her heart starting to race when she saw Jill coming towards her with the two men in tow.

'Sharmila, this is Lucas Healy,' Jill said, indicating the man in the suit. 'Thomas's nephew.'

Sharmila stood and reached out to shake his hand.

'Fancy bumping into you here,' Lucas said, with a broad grin as he clasped her hand.

Sharmila gave a small giggle at his reference to their earlier meeting. Of course the person she'd walked into at reception was Thomas's nephew. There'd been so much to wrap her head around she hadn't put two and two together before. But now she was finally getting to meet the nephew she had already heard so much about.

'I'll leave you all to get to know each other better,' Jill said as she walked away to tend to her other guests.

Sharmila introduced Penny, deliberately keeping her attention off Lucas's companion. 'I'm sorry for your loss,' she said. 'Thomas was an incredibly special person.'

'Thank you. Do you mind if we join you?' Lucas asked, sitting opposite. 'This is Zach Lawrence. He's going to be doing some work around the house. I hope the attorney mentioned that he'd be staying in the barn on Holly House property.'

Sharmila gave a brief nod in Zach's direction. There was no way she was going to risk shaking his hand; she couldn't predict how her body would react if they touched. Her body was clearly going off on a frolic of its own.

'It so great to finally meet you,' Lucas said. 'I've been dying to ever since we found out my uncle was flying to India. You won't believe what a shock that was for my family because the only place he ever travelled to before was England. And I hadn't heard much about you before.'

Sharmila's smile faltered. It sounded like an accusation even

29

though there was nothing in his expression to suggest that. 'Oh, really? He talked about you all the time. And your sister, Izzy, and your cousin, Teddy, isn't it?'

She didn't miss Lucas and Zach exchange glances. Had she said something unexpected?

'That's right. We call him Teddy,' Lucas said. 'I'm surprised Uncle Thomas talked about us to you.'

'Oh, all the time. He told me all about his childhood and growing up in Pineford with his sisters. I guess that would be your mum so you probably already know the stories. I loved hearing about their adventures through the woods and looking for the best fishing spots for their biggest catch or most-fish-caught competitions. Thomas claimed he always won but I'm not sure that was the truth.'

Lucas was nodding, encouraging her to continue.

'He enjoyed working with you and Izzy in the family business.' Not strictly true, but an embellishment of the truth. 'He was disappointed when Teddy left the company to start his own firm. But he always followed Teddy's success. He regretted not telling Teddy how much he admired him and how he was proud of everything he'd accomplished so far.' She went quiet, embarrassed that she'd spoken so much about Teddy instead of sharing one of Thomas's stories about Lucas. 'He spoke about you a lot too. He adored you,' she finished weakly.

Zach leaned forward with a puzzled expression on his face.

'Did you know Thomas?' Sharmila asked him, after catching the look on his face.

'Yes.'

What a curt response. Zach hadn't said much or asked many questions since he and Lucas sat down, which wasn't surprising since they were talking about Lucas's uncle. But he seemed interested in the conversation. Was he the strong silent type or just rude?

'Are you here in Pineford until Christmas, Lucas?' Penny broke the growing silence.

'For the most part,' Lucas said. 'I have some business in the area and decided to spend the holidays here, but my company operates from Boston, which isn't too far away, so I'll be travelling back and forth. It felt like the perfect opportunity to get some work done on the house and to take a bit of a break.'

While Penny asked Lucas more about his work and plans, Sharmila made a Herculean effort to keep her attention on the conversation, but her eyes kept darting to Zach. Luckily, he was captivated by the wooden planks burning in the fire and hadn't noticed. The same couldn't be said for Penny if the way she was smirking at her was any indication. Sharmila deliberately shifted her focus to the trees.

When the conversation started to dwindle, Penny stood up and announced she was getting another hot chocolate. Sharmila instinctively rose to go with her, not only desperate to sample some after Penny had hyped it up, but to escape the awkwardness of the past few minutes. But Penny was pushing her back down to her seat, trying to communicate something with her eyes. Whatever it was, Sharmila couldn't interpret it. She shrugged and handed her mug with the remains of her eggnog to Penny to take back.

'Is that eggnog you were drinking?' Lucas asked. 'Where did you get it? I didn't see any on the table.'

Sharmila laughed. 'I'm afraid Jill made it specially for me. You see, your uncle left me a wish list of activities to complete while I'm in Pineford, and drinking eggnog was one of them.'

'A wish list?' Lucas said. He glanced at Zach. 'You mean like a list of tasks you have to do?'

'Sort of. Not really tasks though. They're more fun, festive things for me to try.'

Lucas's face lit up. 'I would love to know what sort of festive things my uncle planned for you.'

Sharmila was about to reply when a phone rang.

'Oh sorry, that's mine,' Lucas said as he pulled out his phone and checked the caller. 'I'm sorry, I have to take this. It's my sister. It's probably about work,' he said, heading back inside.

She was slightly relieved. Lucas may be related to Thomas but she didn't feel comfortable sharing all the contents of the wish list with him any more than she had with Jill. And Lucas would probably be more curious about why his uncle chose to give her a wish list, which would lead to personal questions. She didn't want that.

But it meant she was left alone with Zach. They sat in silence. Zach was still staring broodily into the fire, his fringe falling onto his forehead. She resisted the urge to stroke it back into place. This was ridiculous. At the age of 30, she was acting like a schoolgirl with a crush.

They couldn't continue on like this, not saying anything. They were both fully grown adults.

Boring, prosaic conversation was needed. If she was lucky, once they'd spoken for a few minutes she would get over this inexplicable, unexpected, and unwanted attraction.

She cleared her throat. 'Do you live locally or in Boston, Mr Lawrence?'

'It's Zach. And I live in San Francisco.'

'That's a long way to travel for maintenance work, isn't it?' she asked, trying to picture how far San Francisco was from Pineford.

'I'm here as a favour to Lucas.'

Again there was silence. What was his problem? Was it her or was he like this with everyone? She could understand if he was shy but she didn't get the impression that was it. She expelled a long breath. She wasn't going to force him into having a conversation with her. She was about to make her excuses …

'My family grew up in this area,' he said, surprising her that he'd volunteered information. 'I wanted to see it.'

'It's like a busman's holiday, then? You're going to explore the area while you're working here?'

He made an indecipherable sound.

She wasn't sure whether she'd used a British term he wasn't familiar with or whether he wasn't interested in a conversation with her. Losing patience, she looked round for Penny, who was speaking to some other guests round one of the braziers. Should she join her?

Did she really have the energy to carry on a one-sided conversation with Zach? Although, one good thing was, after a few more of his monosyllabic grunts, she would be over this inconvenient attraction.

As Zach expected, once Lucas left, Sharmila showed little interest in talking to him. She hadn't even given him the courtesy of a handshake when she met them – too busy focusing her attention on Lucas once she realised he was the wealthy nephew of a wealthy older man.

He clenched his jaw. They'd made an error in assuming, because they hadn't heard much about Sharmila, Thomas hadn't told her much about them. It was pure luck that his uncle had referred to Zach by his childhood nickname, Teddy, rather than use his real name to Sharmila.

They couldn't rely on luck going forward.

Was it true what Sharmila said? Had Thomas been proud of him and the company he'd built? His uncle had never given him that impression. After Zach left the family business, he always believed Thomas was disappointed and felt betrayed by his decision. Zach's father was the same. Whenever Zach spent time with the family, conversation would always turn to the increasing workload and additional stress his departure created. After a while it became easier to avoid family events altogether.

He turned his thoughts away from the memories of that time.

If Thomas spoke to Sharmila about his family and growing up in Pineford, then there was more to their relationship than they first thought. Or perhaps Sharmila asked the right questions about Thomas's family and business to determine whether he was a 'mark'. Zach was familiar with this type of behaviour. Zach's ex-fiancée, Annette, had also shown a lot of interest in him and his background. At the time, he loved that about her, believing she was genuinely interested in getting to know him better. It was only later he realised it was more to check on his financial status.

He and Lucas would have to be smarter going forward. Be careful what they shared with Sharmila and be on their guard. They needed to find out more about her and her relationship with Thomas.

It was interesting that Thomas had left her a wish list not a task list. That didn't sound like the Thomas he knew. His uncle was always a stern, almost unapproachable man. A wish list didn't sound as difficult to complete as a task list. What kind of *wishes* would be on it? His thoughts were interrupted by Sharmila's voice.

'You mentioned your family grew up here,' she said. 'Do any of them still live in the area?'

'No. My mother grew up here, but she left when she was young. She used to tell me stories about this town. When Lucas mentioned he needed help with some maintenance work, I volunteered.'

'How do you know Lucas?'

'I used to work on his company's construction sites when I was younger and we've kept in touch.' It was easier to stick to the truth whenever possible.

For the first time since he sat down, she turned to face him directly. Her dark brown eyes, reflecting the flickering firelight, were seductively compelling and it took an immense effort to shift his gaze away and to the fire. Had she used the same expression of wide-eyed innocence on Thomas?

'Did I hear you're living in a barn, Zach?' she asked.

He mentally rolled his eyes at her feeble attempt to make polite conversation. 'It's a converted barn on the property. Have you been to Holly House before?'

'Not yet. I only found out we'll be staying there a few hours ago. I've never seen it, but I feel like I know it already from the stories Thomas shared. It always sounded quite magical. I can't believe I'm really here, in Pineford, about to stay in the home Thomas grew up in.' She spoke quickly, her whole face lighting up, alive with anticipation. His breath caught at the radiance of her expression.

He had to be careful. If she could distract him with her eyes and smile, she would probably devour Lucas. Zach had been fooled by a pretty face before, so he would be able to spot any warning signs and look out for Lucas, who could easily fall in that trap.

Was her excitement about the house a warning sign? She may not know that inheriting Holly House was part of the inheritance, along with the shares, but she was interested in the property. That was clear.

When his uncle had bought back their family home last December, Zach's mother mentioned she couldn't wait to stay in the old place. It was the first thing she'd been excited about since his father's sudden death three years earlier. After losing her brother too, she'd become even more nostalgic about Holly House. There was no way Zach was letting some woman con his uncle into leaving it to her instead, breaking his mom's heart.

Izzy's suggestion that he stay on the property to keep an eye on Sharmila was even more necessary now. They needed to find out what tasks, or wishes apparently, were on her list as soon as possible.

'Do you have plans for your stay?' he asked.

'Uh, not much yet, we've only just arrived. But there's so much to do and I want to see everything in Pineford. I want the whole American experience.'

'Like?' he pressed, hoping she would reveal more about the list.

'Like food. I watch loads of American films and have seen the most amazing food. I want to try everything. Pancake stacks and waffles in syrup. And snacks. Like crisps with all the different flavours. There's one I saw with white cheddar. Doesn't that sound amazing? But also the sweets and chocolate and doughnuts.'

If he didn't stop her, she would probably name every food in the country. She was babbling. Was she nervous?

'When are you moving into Holly House?' he asked.

'Oh, Monday morning.'

To Zach's relief, Lucas and her friend Penny rejoined them. They must also have been talking about Holly House since Lucas said, 'We were all surprised when my uncle bought it back last year. He wasn't that sentimental.'

'Not sentimental? Really?' Sharmila sounded surprised. 'I thought he was sentimental, especially the way he spoke about Christmases in Pineford. Like when he and his sisters roasted chestnuts in the garden. And when you were younger, he would take you out to find someone who sold fire-roasted chestnuts.'

'You were talking about Christmas even though you met in the summer?' Zach narrowed his eyes.

Sharmila lowered her chin to her chest and bit her lip. 'There's a channel that runs "Christmas in July" films. I was watching one of them at the time.'

'Christmas in July,' Lucas repeated. 'What kind of movies are those?'

Sharmila scrunched her nose. 'They're kind of made for TV. It's not everyone's cup of tea. I was surprised your uncle liked them, to be honest. I usually had one of the films on in the background while I was working. Thomas noticed and asked why I was watching a Christmas movie in the summertime.'

She sounded slightly embarrassed about the movies. Or was she hiding something from them?

Lucas leaned forward. 'That sounds so fun. I'd love to hear more about it. And about your list. Look,' he said, holding up his mug, 'I managed to get some eggnog too. I love this stuff.'

'You do?' Sharmila asked. 'Even more than Thomas's Double Chocolate, Double Cream, Decadent Hot Chocolate Delight?'

Lucas's smile faltered. Zach didn't blame him. They hadn't

heard that name for years. Not since they were young boys and Thomas would sneak them into the kitchen late at night and make it for them. It was their little secret, and one of the few times Zach could remember his uncle being fun. He was normally so aloof.

'I haven't had that in years.' Lucas looked in Zach's direction but Zach gave a slight shake of his head. 'My uncle did make the best hot chocolate. What else is on your list besides eggnog?'

'Oh, I don't have it with me,' she replied.

Zach picked up on the brief hesitation before Sharmila answered. Was there a reason she didn't want to share the list with them? Maybe she was worried they'd find out there was more to it then completing a set of wishes.

'Oh, don't worry, Sharms,' Penny said. 'I remember. There are ten wishes altogether and most of them are competitions. The first one is the Puzzle and Pie competition on Sunday. Lucas, if you're not too busy, why don't you join our team?'

Zach noticed Sharmila stiffen, opening her mouth to speak, but Lucas was already accepting the invitation. It would be their first chance to block the inheritance.

Sharmila yawned suddenly. 'Excuse me,' she said, trying to cover her mouth. 'I think the time difference is finally catching up with me. It's after two in the morning my time. I think I'm going to call it a night. It was lovely to meet you, Lucas. I'll see you on Sunday at the puzzle competition, if not before.' She stood up and then turned towards him. 'Zach, it was nice to meet you too. I'm sure I'll see you around.'

Penny got up and excused herself too. They gave a small wave as they walked away.

Zach watched Sharmila chat with Jill briefly before going inside. Even from a distance he could see she was more relaxed than she'd been when she was talking to him and Lucas.

'What do you think about Sharmila then?' Lucas asked.

'I don't know. Hard to get much out of her.'

Lucas spread out across the bench. 'She seems friendly.'

'Do you think so?'

'Yeah, maybe a little shy at first. She opened up when we started talking about Thomas.'

Zach was right to worry about Lucas's tendency to see the best in people. If he didn't intervene, Lucas would probably let Sharmila have everything in the will and give her some of his own shares too. 'Hmm. You know she's probably after something,' he said.

'I don't know, Zach. I can't see her being some big schemer. Don't get me wrong, I don't know whether she should get the shares and Holly House, or even this Pineford vacation. But from what I can tell so far, I think she's nice.'

'Trust me on this, Lucas. She's an opportunist. She doesn't know about the inheritance yet, but maybe she was disappointed all Thomas left her was this all-expenses-paid trip. I bet she was expecting something more for her efforts. Now you're here, she could be setting her sights on you and is trying to pique your interest.'

Lucas laughed. 'Then I have to give it to her, she's subtle – letting her friend ask all the questions. Trying to get my interest by not showing any interest in me at all.' He cocked an eyebrow. 'Is that a classic move from the gold-digger's playbook?'

'Don't pretend women haven't done that to you before.'

Lucas shook his head. 'Never. Why? Is that what happened with Annette?'

Zach knew Lucas meant well, but he didn't need his sympathy. He was over Annette the moment he said goodbye.

His ex-fiancée had been charming. Infinitely interested in everything and engaging everyone around her, making them feel like the most important person in the room. He wouldn't exactly call Sharmila charming. She was a contradiction. Most of the time she was reserved, but then there were those few moments when she came to life over the smallest things. He couldn't work her out.

Maybe Sharmila hadn't specifically set out to target Thomas

for his wealth, the way Annette had targeted Zach. But at the very least Sharmila took advantage of a lonely older man. How else had she convinced someone who thought exciting international travel was going between the US to England to travel to India and join in various festivities.

Lucas was right – she was subtle. But that only made her more dangerous.

Zach was more determined than ever to keep an eye on Lucas – to make sure he wasn't taken in by Sharmila.

'Come on, let's forget about Sharmila and go enjoy ourselves. I could do with a beer and some loud music,' Lucas said. 'I passed a bar on the way into Pineford – let's try it out. We can't do anything more tonight anyway. Besides, I know with the three of us, we'll be able to stop Sharmila completing whatever's on that list.'

Zach rose from the bench. If only he had Lucas's confidence.

Chapter 4

The following day, for the entire journey from the inn at the outskirts of Pineford to the central shopping area, Sharmila kept her eyes firmly shut. Her internet search hadn't turned up any details or photos of the town – all she knew about it was what Thomas had told her. And at that time, he hadn't seen Pineford in over forty years although she knew he'd since visited the town the previous December.

The Pineford of her imagination was a mix of Disneyland's Main Street, Santa's Village, and a Winter Wonderland with quaint stores bathed in light, wide cobbled streets, and lampposts made from peppermint candy canes. Even the most optimistic person couldn't expect reality to live up to that.

'We're here,' Penny said, turning off the car engine. 'You can open your eyes.'

By infinitesimal degrees, Sharmila raised her eyelids. First, she saw grass, lots of grass. Not what she was expecting. Then a structure in the distance came into view. Opening her eyes fully, her face lit up with delight.

She rushed out of the car over to the gazebo. She couldn't resist doing a little twirl with her arms open wide while she waited for Penny to reach her.

'This is amazing! I honestly thought gazebos in the centre of town were a film stereotype. Thomas told me Pineford had one but I didn't imagine it would be exactly like the movies.'

Penny shrugged. 'Stereotypes usually start somewhere. And you always mention the beautiful gazebos when you go on about your films. When I saw this one while I was searching for parking, I knew we had to stop here.'

Sharmila surveyed the area. The gazebo was in the middle of a large grass square. On the other side of the adjacent roads, the white buildings were exactly what she imagined. Georgian? Victorian? She was never great at architectural history. From what she could make out on the placards in front, they were offices.

'I guess this is like Pineford's main town green or square maybe, but I don't see any shops,' she said.

'We drove past a row of shops on the way. I hope it doesn't spoil the surprise too much, but the road with the shops is called Main Street.'

Sharmila clapped her hands in delight. 'I knew it! It had to be. Shall we?'

She stuck her elbow out and Penny immediately linked arms. They crossed the road and walked towards a diner on the corner of the main shopping street.

Apart from a large Christmas tree in the middle of the green, which Sharmila presumed was for the tree-lighting ceremony that evening, some lights hanging across the gazebo, and a couple of small Christmas trees around it, the green hadn't evoked any seasonal charm. She began to get a sinking feeling Pineford wasn't the holiday town Thomas remembered.

She was wrong.

Taking in the expanse of Main Street was like looking at a still from one of her films. The road was divided by some kind of pedestrian area down the centre. This middle strip had old-fashioned lampposts with cast-iron bases and ladder bars, and what appeared to be glass panes in the lanterns; each had an ornately decorated foliage wreath hanging from it. Between the lampposts were small, illuminated Christmas trees.

From bakeries to bookstores, florists to bric-a-brac stores, every shop was ablaze with lights. Twinkly bulbs of all colours and sizes. Around doorways, hanging from gables, on blackboards, or highlighting animated tableaux in boutique windows.

They chose a store at random to enter. The interior was as decorative as the exterior. A basket of candy canes was shoved in front of her. Sharmila nodded politely at the store owner's effusive greeting. She stood patiently answering the owner's questions about who they were and why they were visiting Pineford. After a while, she excused herself and moved to one of the displays. She didn't want to be rude, but she also didn't want to answer personal questions from someone she didn't know. Perhaps the owner acted the same way to all tourists – part of the old-town charm – but it was too much for her.

It was a completely different experience in the next shop they entered. As soon as they walked in, the clerk glanced Sharmila's way and a look of concern passed over her face. Sharmila noticed the clerk discreetly tracking her movements around the shop, while Penny was able to wander around the displays without any problems. Sharmila cleared her throat and, when she got Penny's attention, she tilted her head in the direction of the clerk. Penny watched for a moment, then her mouth fell open as she grasped the situation and indicated they should leave. They made a quick exit.

Penny shook her head in disbelief. 'I can't believe how blatant she was. It's so wrong.'

'It's not the first time in my life that's happened and it won't be the last,' Sharmila replied in a matter-of-fact tone. 'I'm used to it.'

'But you shouldn't have to be.'

Sharmila gave her a rueful smile. 'No, I shouldn't. Come on, let's go back home. I'll brave the shops another day.'

They linked arms again and walked towards the town green

only stopping when they reached a large, old white building with a sign for Pineford's Historical Society.

'Do you mind if we go inside?' Penny asked. 'You know I'm a total history geek. I'm dying to find out more about this town. There could be a tourist centre in there as well.'

Sharmila nodded then chuckled when her stomach gave a loud rumble. 'I was too excited to eat breakfast. I think I'll risk grabbing something from the diner while you nerd out on history. Do you mind?'

'No, of course I don't. This way I won't need to worry about you getting bored. Besides, I know you're not interested in the history of a town, but the romance of it all.'

They hugged and parted ways.

Sharmila took off her scarf and overcoat as she stood by the door of the diner, trying to figure out whether she should find her own table or wait to be seated. In many ways, it was like her aunt's café with its cosy charm. Unfortunately, since it wasn't that busy, all eyes turned her way as soon as she entered, and they didn't stop following her when a waitress came over to show her to a table by the window. She concentrated on the menu, hoping the chatter would soon restart.

Barely five minutes after she ordered, a stack of pancakes, bacon, blueberries, and maple syrup appeared in front of her. She rubbed her hands with glee. Americans certainly knew how to do breakfast. She was about to dig in when a shadow crossed her table.

'Hello. I'm Jackie Lennard, the Mayor of Pineford. Welcome to our town. Are you Thomas's friend Sharmila?' She pronounced it *Shur-mile-er*.

'Hello. Yes, I'm Sharmila Mitra,' she replied, subtly making it clear her name was pronounced *Shar-mill-a*. 'I'm pleased to meet you.' She held out her hand.

The Mayor repeated her name but pronounced it exactly the way she did the first time.

'Please call me Millie if it's easier,' Sharmila said.

'Oh, that's sweet of you, but I would like to learn how to

pronounce your name correctly. Please, could you say it one more time? I will get it right, I promise.' After a couple of attempts, she managed to perfect the pronunciation. 'Oh Sharmila, I have so been looking forward to meeting you. Ever since Thomas was here last December and said he hoped you would come visit Pineford for a few weeks. Is it everything you were expecting it to be?'

'So far. I only got here yesterday so I haven't had the chance to explore yet. Everything looks so beautiful around here.'

'Well, you've arrived at the perfect time. We have the Christmas tree lighting in the garden square this evening – you must come.'

'Yes. I saw that in the brochure. I'm looking forward to it.' Sharmila had watched so many tree lightings in her films, she couldn't wait to experience it for real.

'And how are you finding your stay at the inn?'

'Very comfortable. The owners have been really kind.'

'I'm pleased to hear that,' Jackie said, her face lighting up. 'Jill's my sister.'

That explained a lot. They both had that quality of making you comfortable within moments of meeting them. If Pineford ran a Mrs Claus competition, she had no doubt Jill and Jackie would be strong contenders for it, although neither of them could be older than late forties.

'I know Thomas was planning to give you a list of Christmas activities to complete while you're here. Did he?'

'Yes, he did.' Sharmila knew she wasn't going to get away with such a brief answer. 'He called it my Christmas Wishlist.'

'Oh, that sounds like so much fun. We would love to help you with it in any way we can. Do you have it with you?'

Sharmila shook her head. 'I don't actually. It's at the hotel. My friend Penny and I only popped into town to have a quick look around. This is the first chance we've had to see Pineford. But some of the items are WinterFest competitions. The first one is the Puzzle and Pie Contest tomorrow evening.'

Jackie pursed her lips together. 'The puzzle competition has an online registration and the deadline to enter was weeks ago. Let me check whether there are any tables available.' She excused herself to make the call.

Sharmila waited, but her appetite for pancakes deserted her, replaced with a worry she was going to fail to complete one of Thomas's wishes – not to mention lose the charity donation.

'Right,' Jackie said, returning to her table after her call. 'The tables are all booked up.'

Sharmila's heart sank.

'But luckily Mr Bell registered you for one a few weeks ago.'

'He did?' Sharmila asked, her voice squeaking in surprise.

'Yes. He must have done it once you confirmed you were arriving. Thomas probably asked him to.'

Sharmila relaxed. She should have trusted Thomas would have made sure everything was taken care of. 'Thank you. Do I need to register for any of the other competitions?'

'Hold on, let me check.' Jackie started tapping on her tablet. 'Right, from what I can see there is a mixture of online registrations before the event and sign-ups on the day. But I don't organise the events, I'm afraid, although I help out on the day of course. There's a committee that oversees everything. Is there anything else I can help with you, my dear?'

Sharmila paused, debating whether to ask for more help. Thomas must have had reasons for choosing the activities on her list and, as much as she hated having to ask for help, she knew she couldn't complete some of the wishes on her own. 'Actually, there are two wishes on my list I'm not sure about. Maybe you can tell me who I need to speak to.'

'Of course, if I can. I've got a few minutes spare.' Jackie sat at the table while Sharmila talked about the wishes to take part in the parade and host a party.

Jackie opened her tablet again. 'Liz is running the parade this year. She'll be the best person to speak to. We tend to have the same set-up each year, but I'm sure we'll be able to fit you in.' Jackie paused to type something before she looked up and resumed speaking. 'I've sent her an email about you, so that should all be in hand. Now about your party, I'll need to think about that. We have a WinterFest activity planned every day up until Christmas, so it might be tricky to organise one before then. Does it have to be a big party?'

'I don't think so. A few people from Pineford, I suppose, although I haven't met many yet.'

'The day after Christmas could work. You're still here then, aren't you?'

'Yes, I'm here. A Boxing Day party would be good.'

Jackie gave her a confused look, and Sharmila remembered Americans didn't usually celebrate Boxing Day. Then Jackie clapped her hands together. 'Oh, I have an excellent idea. Are you free on Friday?' At Sharmila's nod, Jackie continued, 'Meet me at 7 p.m. Let me have your cell number, I'll text you the address.'

'It's a UK number so you'll probably need an international code. Will that be a problem for you?' When Jackie shook her head, Sharmila gave her the number. Friday was almost a whole week away, but if Jackie wasn't worried about leaving it that long before getting things organised, then she would have to trust her. It had been such a long time since Sharmila allowed herself to rely on someone other than herself.

'I will see *you* at the tree lighting later,' Jackie said as she left.

Sharmila didn't miss the wink Jackie gave her. She narrowed her eyes – something was up.

That evening, there were already crowds gathered in the square by the time Sharmila, Penny, and the other inn guests arrived for the tree lighting. Sharmila didn't think they could possibly get a good view until Jill told them to follow her as she pushed through the people, making her way to the front without any difficulty to where Graham was waiting. He'd been reserving their position for over an hour.

46

Murmurs of impatience were starting to gather noise in the crowd. It was only a minute after the scheduled start time of the event. Clearly Pineford residents expected punctuality.

As they waited, she could feel curious eyes drifting in their direction. She refused to look around to confirm her suspicions, focusing on the Christmas tree instead. She was in a group of tourists, out-of-towners. Naturally, the townspeople would be interested in *all* the new visitors, not her specifically. Just because the mayor and Jill happened to know about Thomas's list, didn't mean she was the main source of town gossip.

Penny nudged her repeatedly with her elbow. Sharmila tried to ignore her, recognising it as Penny's standard signal for pointing out attractive people. But the nudging continued until curiosity finally made her follow Penny's gaze.

Lucas and Zach. They were talking to a group of men, seemingly on friendly terms.

'Stop it,' she mouthed back at Penny.

What would it take to convince her best friend she didn't need a man? She wasn't after a holiday romance – which is all it could be when she lived across the ocean.

Sharmila glanced again in Zach's direction. She hadn't seen either of them since the previous night.

Lucas and Zach were physically similar in many ways. Both tall, broad-shouldered but with slim builds – Lucas a slightly washed-out blond version of Zach.

She bit her lip trying not to snort as groups of women of varying ages tried to casually position themselves near the two men. Were good-looking men such a rarity in Pineford?

OK, yes, they were more than good-looking. They were exceptionally handsome men. They'd stand out anywhere, small town or large city. Her attention went to Lucas again. Even though she felt she almost knew him from how often Thomas spoke about him, and he'd been friendly during their brief exchange the previous evening, there was something about Lucas she didn't trust yet. She couldn't explain why.

Zach caught her gaze and gave her a terse nod in greeting, then turned back to the other men. Sharmila pinched her lips together. Those other women were welcome to him. Was his face permanently fixed in a scowl or was it something about her that evoked that expression? It didn't matter. She didn't care what the rude, taciturn man thought of her.

She continued to watch as a woman, probably in her late sixties, walked over to Zach and tapped him on the shoulder. He turned around and his face transformed as he greeted the woman. Sharmila's breath caught. If he ever turned that kilowatt smile in her direction, she'd go weak at the knees.

She was pulled out of her thoughts when she heard her name being called by Mayor Jackie. Sharmila looked around, desperately trying to work out what she'd missed while she was focused on Zach.

'Please come up here and join me, Sharmila dear,' Mayor Jackie called, her expression hinting at impatience at having to repeat herself.

She was propelled forward by Jill and the other guests. She grabbed Penny's arm dragging her along too, but Penny managed to move to the side, leaving Sharmila standing centre stage with the mayor.

Jackie motioned for Sharmila to come closer and introduced her to the crowd. 'Now, for those of you who don't know, this is Sharmila Mitra and she will be staying in Pineford this Christmas as a gift from Thomas Adams, whose family, as you all know, was one of the founders of our town. Thomas has also given Sharmila some activities to do while she's here – wishes on a Christmas Wishlist.' She beamed at Sharmila, who instantly regretted sharing Thomas's name for his list. 'Some of these wishes include our very own Pineford WinterFest events. So why don't we give Sharmila and her friend a true Pineford welcome.'

The crowd cheered, seeming to forget only moments ago they were in a hurry for the tree-lighting event to start.

'I thought,' Mayor Jackie continued, 'rather than merely attend tonight's tree-lighting ceremony, wouldn't it be fantastic for Sharmila to press the button?'

Sharmila's eyes widened, excitement washing over her. Spending Christmas in Pineford was already a dream come true for her but being offered the chance to press the button that would herald the start of WinterFest – marking the beginning of the seasonal celebrations – was more than she ever expected. She didn't care that she was the centre of attention. She only cared that she was going to turn on the lights.

She followed Jackie to a podium with a large button, which her fingers itched to press. She couldn't wait to see what the town was like fully illuminated.

'Ready?' Mayor Jackie asked as the crowd quietened down.

Sharmila took her position next to the button.

At Jackie's instigation, the crowd began the countdown from ten. After they called out, 'ONE!', Sharmila pressed down hard on the button. She held her breath, silent along with the crowd, waiting for the first light to flicker.

For what seemed like an eternity, but was probably only a few seconds, nothing happened. She glanced in Jackie's direction, worrying she'd done something wrong. Jackie coughed at a man standing nearby. Sharmila realised the giant button was purely for show when the man flipped a switch and suddenly the bottom of the Christmas tree was filled with tiny lights. The rest of the tree began to follow, until finally the star at the top twinkled.

The sounds of more switches being pulled preceded the lighting of the gazebo, the trees in the square, the hanging lanterns dotted around, then finally, the buildings facing the square.

Sharmila joined the crowd in their festive cheers. Christmas in Pineford had officially begun.

Chapter 5

On Sunday evening, Zach walked into Pineford Exhibition Hall, the venue for the Puzzle and Pie Contest. This was the first of the competitions on Sharmila's list — and their first chance to stop the inheritance.

Finding a way to block Sharmila from completing a 500-piece puzzle in two hours wasn't going to be easy. Since no spectators or other teams were allowed to distract or approach the tables when the competition was in progress, their only chance to interfere was if they were a part of Sharmila's team. Lucas had made the right decision agreeing to join them.

Zach saw Sharmila sitting at a table next to Penny and Lucas. Although she appeared relaxed and comfortable, laughing at something Penny was saying, her body language was more reserved with Lucas.

Zach furrowed his brow. Was she genuinely wary of Lucas? Or was she playing hard to get? That must be it, because she didn't have any reason to be suspicious of Lucas. Maybe it was the same tactic she used to charm Thomas.

It was a good idea he was the one living on the property, not Lucas. Lucas could easily be misled at times. Sharmila would have wound him round her finger in moments.

Lucas waved as Zach approached the table. 'Great, you're here. Now we can discuss puzzle strategy,' Lucas said.

Sharmila blinked a couple of times. 'Sorry, did you say puzzle strategy?'

'That's right, Sharms,' Penny said. 'Do we have one?'

'Does anyone?' Sharmila replied. She cast a quick glance at Lucas, as if she was worried she'd upset him, and looked relieved when he chuckled at her question.

'How do you tackle puzzles?' Lucas asked.

'I've never thought about it. Side pieces first, I guess.' Sharmila's expression still showed confusion.

Zach cleared his throat. 'Lucas, why don't you take charge and tell us what we should do?'

'That's a really good idea,' Sharmila said. 'We'll follow your strategy, Lucas. It sounds like you know what you're doing.'

Lucas quickly outlined a plan for them to turn every piece picture-side up, sort them by colour and pattern, and then by number of tabs and blanks.

'Tabs and blanks,' Sharmila repeated.

'The knobby bits and the holes,' Lucas said. 'I wonder if we could use some plates or dishes to help categorise the pieces.' He went off to search for some.

The noise in the room fell to a dull murmur as the contest started and the contestants put their heads down to work on their puzzles.

Lucas started putting together the frame of the puzzle while Zach helped Sharmila and Penny sort the other pieces by colour and pattern, exactly the way Lucas instructed. Sharmila and Penny still appeared stunned as they executed Lucas's strategy. He didn't blame them. Lucas was taking this competition too seriously – which wasn't their plan.

Earlier that day, Lucas and Zach had discussed what to do this evening and agreed their best hope was to work through the puzzle as slowly as they could, meaning Sharmila wouldn't finish it in time. He hadn't bargained on Lucas's competitive nature taking over – he now seemed determined to win the contest instead. And, with the clock ticking, Lucas was proving good at ignoring Zach's pointed stares and subtle reminders of their original goal.

'A puzzle and pie competition is unusual for a winter festival, isn't it?' Penny commented.

'They're becoming more common. It's an easy one to do any time of year. You can always find a puzzle with a seasonal picture,' Lucas replied.

'Thomas told me one of his favourite childhood memories was his family's annual Christmas jigsaw puzzle,' Sharmila said, as she compared a piece against the box lid. 'They would start a new jigsaw on December first, then leave the puzzle out on the table and each time anyone walked past, they could add a little bit more. But the last piece couldn't be placed until Christmas Day.' She was smiling sweetly, as if she was lost in the memory herself. Then she blinked suddenly. She glanced across at Lucas. 'Oh, but I'm sure your mum already told you this story.'

Zach noticed her initial wariness around Lucas had disappeared.

'No, I don't remember hearing it before. Zach, have you—' Lucas broke off as Zach nudged him. Lucas cleared his throat then started to cough.

That was a close call. For a moment, Zach wondered whether the pretence was worth it. But even in the short time they'd been in Pineford, he was enjoying the anonymity of his disguise, the chance to get to know people without the adulation and expectation that came with being a relative of the Adams family and one of the main employers in the region. He noticed Lucas encounter it each time they bumped into someone from the town. And how would they explain the truth to Sharmila without giving away her inheritance? Besides, they'd committed to it as soon as Zach had been introduced to Sharmila.

'Yes, my family did complete a puzzle every Christmas when I was younger,' Zach offered, as if that was the question Lucas had been about to ask. 'My parents and I would all sit together to work on it, but we would finish it all in one evening.' He chuckled. 'Lucas's strategy sounds a lot like the one my parents used.' His family had carried on the tradition even after Zach left for college. He wondered whether his parents continued it after he left for California.

He grimaced. He wasn't supposed to be reminiscing about his Christmases growing up, and he certainly didn't want to revisit the past. He couldn't afford to be distracted and needed to focus on how he could stop Sharmila from completing the puzzle.

He stood up, offering to fetch pie and drinks for the others. While he poured their drinks, he looked over at their table. Even from a distance he could see the enthusiasm on Sharmila's face as she worked on the puzzle. The way her tongue peeked out as she concentrated was cute. Her eyes lit up when she managed to slot a piece correctly, the same way they had when she pressed the button at the tree lighting – the sheer happiness in her expression had taken his breath away. She couldn't fake that kind of joy.

For a moment, he understood why Lucas felt so torn at the idea of interfering with Thomas's gift to Sharmila. Maybe Thomas really was trying to give her a full Christmas experience. Their plans would get in the way of that.

Zach shook his head. He wouldn't let Sharmila make him doubt himself. Getting people to feel sympathy for her was probably how she exerted her influence over Thomas. Although the Thomas he knew would never have let compassion rule his head.

He wasn't going to spend any more time trying to reconcile the stern, occasionally unapproachable man he knew with the person Sharmila described – the man who told stories about Double Chocolate, Double Cream, Decadent Hot Chocolate Delight and who left a stranger a Christmas Wishlist. He knew his uncle. Thomas would have only acted out of character if he'd been manipulated. It all came back to that simple fact.

Zach wasn't going to be swayed by Sharmila, nor her desire to experience the spirit of an American Christmas – he wouldn't let anyone come between him and his family. Once he'd prevented her from inheriting the house and shares, there was nothing to stop her staying in Pineford and taking part in the other events.

From the corner of his eye, he spotted a person at another table weaving a pen through their fingers. Zach recognised the movement.

When Zach was a child, he'd spent months practising sleight-of-hand magic tricks to show his parents. An idea came to him. Putting his hand in his pocket, he weaved a coin through his fingers. Yes, he still had the technique. If he could perform sleight of hand, he could palm a few puzzle pieces. Then, with a few pieces missing, Sharmila wouldn't be able to complete the puzzle.

It wasn't the strongest plan, but it would have to do.

Back at the table, he gave Lucas a light tap hoping to indicate he'd come up with an idea but Lucas was too engrossed to pay attention.

Luck was on his side, as not soon after he returned to the table, Sharmila accidentally knocked over a dish of puzzle pieces, which scattered across the floor. As Zach bent down to help Penny gather them up, he managed to sneak a couple of pieces away. Hopefully that would stop Sharmila from completing her wish.

They continued working on the puzzle. Zach grinned, pleased that nobody had spotted his actions. It wouldn't be long before someone on their team noticed pieces were missing. Lucas huffed with annoyance when the first table finished. He became more determined to get second place, which was the last remaining prize. Unfortunately, that was claimed within minutes of the first.

There was less than fifteen minutes left in the contest and they were almost finished when Penny exclaimed, 'I think some pieces are missing.' She pointed to the table. 'See, there are ten spaces but only seven pieces.'

Lucas turned to look at Zach while Sharmila covered her mouth with her hand.

'Do you think they're on the floor from when I knocked over the dish?' she asked. 'Come on, we need to search for them. They must be here somewhere.'

Lucas and Penny followed as Sharmila shot to the floor. Zach joined them, pretending to help their search.

'Check your clothes in case they fell on them,' Lucas suggested.

Zach almost snickered – good thing he'd thrown the pieces in the trash with their cups and pie plates. He made a show of patting himself down.

'Hey, it's Sharmila, isn't it?' a lady called from a nearby table.

'Uh, yes, hi.' Sharmila gave a small wave.

'I thought so. I'm Julie. We were at the tree lighting yesterday. Is something up?'

'We're missing a couple of pieces. I think I dropped them. We won't be able to complete the puzzle without them.'

'Oh dear!' Julie exclaimed. 'Is this one of the activities on the wish list Mayor Jackie mentioned?'

Sharmila nodded.

'That's no good,' Julie said. 'Which pieces?'

'The ones for the house,' Penny replied.

Julie glanced round at the others on her table. They all nodded without saying anything. 'We have all those pieces. You can have them.'

'That's really kind of you,' Sharmila said. 'But, I don't want you to get disqualified, Julie.'

'The pieces must be here somewhere,' Zach said. 'We can keep looking.' He hadn't spent the last two hours here when he could have been catching up on his real work, only to have his efforts undone by someone else.

'That's fine. The top prizes have already gone, so it doesn't matter to us anyway,' someone next to Julie said.

'Do you think we could get disqualified if you give us your pieces?' Zach asked.

'Yes, then Sharmila won't complete Thomas's wish.' Lucas gave him an imperceptible wink. Of course, *now* he remembered their plan.

Sharmila tapped a finger against her chin. 'Actually,' she said slowly, 'the wish says I need to enter the competition and complete the puzzle. It doesn't say I have to complete the puzzle as part of the competition.'

'You're such a lawyer.' Penny laughed.

'Aren't you splitting hairs?' Zach said.

'It does sound as if you're trying to bend the rules a little,' Lucas said.

Sharmila pursed her lips.

'Don't worry,' Julie said. 'I have an idea.' She picked up the pieces from her puzzle and walked round to their table. Taking a few steps back, she dropped the pieces on the floor.

Sharmila and Penny exchanged surprised glances then, almost simultaneously, grinned.

'Hey, I found the missing pieces,' Penny called, as she walked over to collect them.

'Excellent. I guess we didn't see them when we looked before,' Sharmila added.

'At least we can finish the puzzle now,' Penny said.

'And stay within the rules of Thomas's wish,' Sharmila replied, with a pointed look at Lucas.

'That's great,' Lucas said with genuine enthusiasm.

'Yeah, great,' Zach responded drily while he watched Sharmila put the final pieces in her puzzle.

She cheered as Penny took a photo for the wish list.

'That's two wishes done,' Sharmila said. 'And we've only been here a couple of days. We're going to storm through these wishes.'

Sharmila and Penny high-fived each other and excused themselves to chat to Julie and her table.

'Well, we tried,' Lucas said with a rueful smile, though he didn't sound too disappointed by their failure. 'Penny said there were other competitions on the list. I'm sure we can stop one of those. We can find out what her other wishes are tomorrow.' He took out his phone, checking the time. 'It's not that late. Let's go find somewhere we can relax.'

Zach appreciated his cousin's attempt to reassure him. 'Sure. I'll follow you back to the inn then we can go in the truck so you don't have to drive.'

'You're the best!' Lucas said, giving him a fist bump.

Zach could have done with going straight home to the barn. He needed to focus on his real work, which was already starting to pile up. But he also wanted to spend time with Lucas. That was something he'd missed when he moved to California – the closeness they once shared. He was determined to get it back.

Chapter 6

Holly House was on the outskirts of Pineford on the other side from the inn. Luckily, there was relatively little traffic as Sharmila drove slowly, taking in the town's scenic views. After crossing a steel truss bridge, she took a narrow road through some woods. Even though it was morning, the light escaping through the leafy canopy was faint. Soon the trees cleared and the way opened straight into a large carriageway with a central grass area. On the right of the drive was a large barn converted into a three-car garage. She drove past and parked in front of the house.

Penny whistled. 'I can't believe they expect us to slum it in this place.'

'It'll be tough, but we can make it work,' Sharmila said, shaking her head in disbelief. Whatever she'd been expecting Thomas's childhood home to be, this large colonial-fronted building was not it.

She got out of the car and walked backwards until she was standing on the grassy area, tilting her head, trying to take in the whole building. 'This does not look the way Thomas described it.'

'How did he describe it?' Penny asked, coming to stand next to her.

'Something smaller, more quaint, I guess. I don't know. Like a lodge. Or something out of *Little House on the Prairie*. A couple of rooms and a barn.'

Penny laughed. 'Only you would complain the house is larger than you expected.'

'I'm not complaining.' How could she complain about getting to live there for the next three weeks?

'I know,' Penny replied, making a slow 360-degree turn. 'Well, there is a barn. In fact, you have three barns if you include the garage.'

'Three?'

Sharmila followed Penny's gaze. From where she stood, she could see the house sat in extensive grounds. There was no fence separating the front yard from the back and, barely visible, behind the house was a small building probably used for farming or housing horses in the past. She looked back at the garage. There wasn't any sign of a living accommodation above it. Zach wasn't living there – he must be living in a different barn. The left side of the driveway broke off into a large road, which curved back into the woods and ended at a single-storey timber-framed building. That was probably where he was staying.

Not that she was that concerned with where he lived. But it was better knowing he wouldn't be on their doorstep, particularly since over the last couple of nights he had an irritating habit of turning up in her dreams. But she could admit she felt some comfort knowing he wouldn't be too far away, as they were two women living alone in a secluded house in an unfamiliar place.

'What do you think Thomas's family intends to do with all this land?' Penny asked. 'You know, if we were in one of your films, Lucas would have plans to build a massive superstore here, against the wishes of all the Pineford residents. And you would come up with a master plan to stop him, saving the town and saving the day.'

Sharmila threw her head back and laughed. Penny would usually pretend she wasn't interested in any of her films, but she always suspected Penny was a secret fan.

'Let's hope that's not true,' she said. 'It would be a shame if they sell Holly House after Thomas went to all this effort to buy it back. I think he may have wanted to retire here.' She sighed wistfully. 'If I owned this house, I would never want to leave.'

'Maybe you should buy it off Lucas and emigrate.'

'If only!' She worried her top lip with her teeth. 'I feel so guilty making Lucas stay at the inn. Perhaps we could take one of the barns and let Lucas and Zach have the house.'

'You can't do that,' Penny protested. 'The house is part of your Christmas gift and Thomas wanted you to stay here.'

'You're right. We're only here for three weeks anyway. Lucas will have the rest of his life to enjoy this place.'

'My lady, would you care to join me for a stroll around the perimeter before we head inside?' Penny suggested, adopting an upper-class accent and dipping into a curtsey.

'I would be delighted.' Sharmila bowed.

They walked to the back of the house where there was a large patio with outdoor seating and a covered dining area with a built-in stone pizza oven. A large fire pit in matching stone was dug into the courtyard. Down some steps, the extensive lawns were broken by a small brook. Over a Japanese bridge, the gardens inclined gently towards the edge of a lake.

'Can you imagine what this place will look like when it's fully covered in snow?' Penny said. 'You could go sledging!'

'We'd probably end up crashing into the lake, knowing our co-ordination.' She lifted her hands, catching a few of the wet snowflakes, which melted on contact with her skin. 'I wonder if the snow will get heavier soon.'

'The snowman building competition is a week away. They must be expecting it by then.'

Sharmila shivered. 'Yes, I sense there's going to be a heavy fall soon.'

'Hate to break it to you, love, but you don't have a special snow sixth sense.'

Sharmila gave Penny a knowing look. 'You mark my words. By the middle of the week, everywhere will be blanketed in snow, and I can build my first snowman of the holiday.'

'What about the competition and the wish?'

'I don't think there's anything to say I can't make a snowman outside of the competition but point taken.'

'Come on,' Penny said. 'Let's go explore inside, have a cup of tea, and plan how we'll do all your other wishes.'

The magnificent grounds should have prepared Sharmila for the house's interior, but the modern, open-concept space still took her breath away. They walked round with silent reverence. The foyer was filled with boxes of decorations stacked against a large central staircase, with a formal dining area on the right and a formal living space on the left. A brick fireplace separated the living room from an eat-in kitchen. The whole place would be perfect for entertaining guests when they hosted their party.

A corridor off the living area led to the main bedroom with its floor-to-ceiling windows overlooking the gardens – the house's slight elevation allowing a view of the entire lake. Upstairs were three additional bedrooms and a small library overlooking the foyer. There was also a fully finished basement with a small cinema room and a wet bar.

After they finished their tour, they went into the kitchen, modernised with all expected appliances. Well, nearly all.

'No electric kettle,' Sharmila said, glancing round. 'Do you suppose this kettle on the hob is part of the décor or does it actually work? Not that it matters because we didn't buy any food or drinks.' She opened a few cupboards at random. Although they were filled with crockery and glassware, there wasn't a bag of coffee lurking.

Penny gave her a smug look, reaching into her rucksack. 'Thankfully, unlike you, I had the foresight to take some of the teabags from the inn.'

Of course she had. At least it wasn't only Sharmila's family that took complimentary drinks from hotels.

'I only have the fruit tea ones, though,' Penny continued. 'But that's good because we don't have milk or sugar either.'

'We really didn't think this through properly.'

'And that's so unlike you. But we should make a grocery list and go into town later. Why don't you bring Thomas's Wishlist out? We need to formulate a plan of action. Make sure we have time to get everything done.'

Sharmila went to get her handbag. She pulled out the Pineford WinterFest brochure and a piece of paper she'd written the list on. After Jackie mentioned her wish list at the tree-lighting ceremony, people had come up to Sharmila curious about what was on it. She suspected the interest wasn't going to fade anytime soon. Thomas's letter was too personal to share so she made a copy of the wishes. Most of them, anyway. She deliberately left out a few wishes – ones she didn't want everyone to know, such as the last item.

'Can you forward the photos of the eggnog and puzzle competition to me?' she asked Penny. 'I need to send them to Mr Bell.'

'Are you sending them as you go along?'

'Yeah. I think it makes the most sense – that way if there's a problem he can let me know and I can redo them if I can. OK then,' she said, flattening the sheets. 'We should decorate the house as soon as possible, empty those boxes in the hall, and get them out the way. Let's make "getting a Christmas tree" a priority.'

'Good plan. I don't suppose the WinterFest brochure has anything about where we can find trees locally?' At Sharmila's head shake, Penny said, 'I'll grab my laptop, and we can search. Hopefully, this huge house has internet.'

Sharmila shrugged. 'Hang on, let me grab the binder Mr Bell gave me from the car. He said it contains all the manuals and instructions for this place. I'll bring in our suitcases too.'

As she opened the front door she narrowly avoided Lucas's fist in her face as he was about to knock.

'Oh, Lucas, Zach. Hi.' She wasn't expecting to see them. Had Penny invited them?

'Hi, Sharmila,' Lucas said with a bright smile. 'I hope we didn't come at a bad time.'

'Not at all. I was about to grab something from the car.'

'Zach and I were picking up groceries for his stay. I didn't know whether you had time to get any, so we picked up some supplies for you. Bread, milk, that kind of thing.'

She noticed they were both holding brown paper bags.

'Thank you. That's very thoughtful of you. We were just saying we need to do a shop. Please go in. Penny's in the kitchen.' She stood aside to let them pass, then went to the car. She grabbed her bag with the binder, deciding to leave the suitcases in the car until after Zach and Lucas left.

When she joined them in the kitchen, Lucas was standing over Penny's shoulder trying to see what she was reading.

'Can I offer you something to drink?' she asked, relieved she'd made that copy of the list. She couldn't explain why she was reluctant to share the full wish list with Lucas when he was Thomas's nephew, but her gut told her to be cautious with him. That wasn't a surprise. Her gut told her to be cautious with everyone. 'We have fruit tea or water.' She grabbed the kettle and walked over to the sink.

Zach joined her. 'You don't need a kettle. This is a four-way faucet,' he said, showing her how it dispensed the different streams of water.

Penny widened her eyes and smirked. 'Boiling water straight from a tap. Fancy schmancy! I guess the kettle was only for show.'

'Tea then?' Sharmila offered again.

'There's some coffee in one of the bags,' Zach said.

She turned to get a cafetiere she'd seen in one of the cupboards.

After she prepped the coffee, she took the groceries out of the bags. She beamed when she pulled out a bag of white cheddar crisps.

'I hope you like those,' Lucas said. 'Zach said you would. He added some other chips and snacks he thought you'd like to try too.'

Catching Zach's gaze, she inclined her head in a gesture of thanks. Why had her heart fluttered a little at the idea of Zach remembering her throwaway comment the first evening they met? Perhaps because it was unexpected. He hadn't exactly been approachable or friendly then – not the way he was with some people at the tree lighting. Perhaps he was just being neighbourly. They would be living near each other, after all.

She began putting away the groceries. Moments later Zach started to help by putting away the items for the fridge. Occasionally they would pass each other. His close proximity made her nervous, causing her to drop items. Zach picked them up. As he handed them to her, their fingers touched and she let out a pathetic giggle at the unexpected tingle.

Bending to put the tins in the pantry, she took a few moments to pull herself together. She was behaving like a silly schoolgirl who'd never been in the presence of a handsome man before. Again.

As she rose and turned, she bumped into a hard chest. Strong hands held her shoulders to steady her. She lifted her head to apologise, but the words failed as she connected with magnetic forest-coloured eyes.

'This is a lovely house.'

At the sound of Lucas's voice, they broke their connection.

Sharmila hurried over to the table, her cheeks warm. She didn't dare look Penny's way. 'Haven't you been here before?' she asked Lucas.

'No, but I've seen photos. The house was sold long before I was born.'

'Well, please feel free to wander around,' Sharmila offered.

'That would be great. If it's OK with you, we could do a quick survey – check whether any work needs to be done inside.'

'Of course, it's your house.'

She caught the look Lucas exchanged with Zach. Her eyes narrowed. She waited until they moved out of earshot. 'What do you think is going on?' she asked Penny.

'What do you mean?'

'They're both acting strange today. Being super friendly. Bringing us groceries. Something doesn't add up.'

Penny shook her head, rising to throw her teabag away. 'Being friendly is strange to you? You, my dear, are far too suspicious. It's small-town hospitality, that's all.'

'Sure, that would make sense. Only they don't come from Pineford. They have no reason to be friendly to me. In fact, it would make more sense if Lucas was annoyed he has to stay at the hotel instead of his family home.'

'Maybe he hopes if you get to know him better, you'll invite him to stay here with us.'

'Never going to happen.'

'Maybe he fancies you.'

'Even more far-fetched.'

'I don't know. I'm picking up the vibe he's trying to flirt with you. Shame, he has no chance.'

'Exactly right.'

'Because you're more interested in Zach.'

'What?' Her voice rose an octave. 'That's absurd. I'm not interested in Zach. I'm not interested in anyone that way. You know that.'

'It's OK if you are. Hari wouldn't expect you to remain alone for the rest of your life.'

'It hasn't even been two years, Penny,' she replied quietly.

Penny placed her hand on Sharmila's shoulder, bending slightly to meet her eyes. 'No one says you have to fall in love again. But you can have a little fun, a little holiday romance. And there are two perfectly fine specimens right here waiting for you.'

Sharmila was prevented from giving a response by the perfectly fine specimens' return.

Zach positioned himself far away from her near the door, leaning against the counter. There was no risk of their making contact again. Lucas grabbed his mug then moved to stand by Penny, reading over her shoulder.

'Is this the famous wish list then?' he asked.

'Yup,' Penny said, handing it to him. 'You can take a look if you want.'

Sharmila narrowed her eyes as she noticed Lucas counting the wishes. They'd already told him she had ten wishes to complete. She wanted to avoid any questions about why some wishes were missing so she walked up to him and held out her hand.

'I need to check something, do you mind?' she asked.

He shrugged and handed the paper to her.

'Do you know of any Christmas tree farms nearby?' Penny asked. 'We need to cut one down.'

'Actually, I do know of one,' Lucas said. 'It's about an hour away, though. But I can take you there. Maybe the day after tomorrow. Can we use your truck, Zach?'

'Sure,' Zach replied. 'I can drive you.'

'No room for all of us,' Lucas said.

'Oh, that's OK,' Sharmila protested. 'We don't want to put you to any trouble. I'm sure we can find our way if you tell us the address.'

'I insist,' Lucas said.

'But …'

'I have a meeting on Wednesday morning, but we can head out after lunch.'

'Really that's not necessary.'

'Please,' Lucas said, with the look of a young puppy dog wanting a treat. 'I'd like to help you complete my uncle's wishes. It'll make me feel like he's still near.'

Sharmila relented. Lucas was Thomas's nephew – it would give her a chance to hear more stories of Thomas. And at least Zach wouldn't be in the car.

Chapter 7

Zach stretched, flexing his fingers ready for a couple of hours at his computer. This situation with Sharmila couldn't have come at a worse time. Although his partners were understanding, even encouraging him to take a much-needed vacation, the important deal he was working on was at a critical stage and he had several other projects that he needed to keep an eye on. It wasn't a great time to be away from San Francisco.

He had hoped it would be a quick trip – that they would easily be able to keep Sharmila from the inheritance – and he would be back in his office within a week. But he hadn't expected Lucas to fall under Sharmila's charm so quickly. Lucas had already offered to take her tree hunting – not the actions of someone trying to sabotage the list. Izzy had reason to be worried about her brother. If Zach's presence was putting Izzy's mind at rest, that alone was a good enough reason to stay in Pineford.

The only problem was his handyman role. There wasn't much maintenance to do around Holly House since the previous owners and Thomas had made sure it was kept to a high standard. He couldn't justify staying around much longer unless he took jobs around the town.

Although they'd been here only a few days, he and Lucas had

got to know some of the locals from hanging out at Pineford's one bar on the outskirts of town. One of the men mentioned he'd been helping out an older woman with jobs around her house since her husband passed away, but he was real busy with his main job and wasn't a handyman. Zach immediately volunteered to help. When the woman, CeCe, found out he was staying at the Adams's place, she couldn't wait to share stories about the times she played with Thomas and his sisters as a young girl.

But he couldn't afford to be distracted now, as the work from his real job was piling up. He put his head down and powered through as much as he could.

A couple of hours later, he was in the middle of a tricky report when there was a knocking at his door. Opening it, he came face to face with a large artificial silver Christmas tree. A muffled voice came from behind the tree as it started to topple forward. In self-preservation he lifted the tree, bringing it inside and leaning it against a wall.

'Oh, this is nice, isn't it?' Sharmila was standing in the doorway, surveying the barn.

He closed his eyes. He didn't want visitors.

'Can I help you?' he asked, making no effort to invite her in.

She raised her eyebrows. 'I'm sorry to disturb you. I didn't know whether you had a tree yet and thought you might like that one to decorate the place.'

'What?'

'A Christmas tree. Do you want it? I bought it when we went out to today.'

'Then why don't you want it for the main house?'

She bit her lip. 'You remember Thomas's wishes? It says I have to choose the tree and have it cut down. The place we went to wouldn't allow us to cut down any of the trees. And anyway, by the time we got there, it was closing and they had hardly any real trees left.'

Zach cocked his head. It sounded like he had misjudged Lucas. Perhaps Lucas had been trying to help after all.

'Anyway,' Sharmila continued, 'I didn't want to waste our journey and Lucas was feeling so bad about it, so I bought this artificial tree. It was either this or the most pitiful, bare tiny real tree. I was thinking the house is big enough and I could put it somewhere, but, I don't know, I think one large real tree will look more magnificent.' She shrugged. 'Anyway, this is spare and it's yours if you want it.'

Zach looked back at the tree, then at the distance to the main house. 'So you dragged it all the way over here? You could have asked me if I wanted it and brought the tree over if I did.'

Sharmila laughed. 'Well, that does sound more sensible. But Penny already started bringing it over here and I went along with it.'

'Penny?'

'Yes. Penny. After she knocked on your door she suddenly found somewhere she needed to be,' she said with an amused shake of her head.

His lips twitched. Was it possible Penny was trying to set them up? Unfortunately, she'd picked the wrong man.

'Do you like it?' she asked, looking at him expectantly, making no effort to leave. With a sigh of resignation he indicated for her to enter.

'I don't decorate for Christmas,' he said gruffly.

'Really? Why not?' She was removing her scarf and jacket as she walked around the living area.

Great, she was making herself comfortable. He didn't want her here. This barn was his sanctuary. His Sharmila-free zone. Where he could forget about beautiful women with warm smiles that took his breath away.

When she directed one of those smiles towards him, Zach quickly turned away to gather his thoughts.

She sat down on the sofa as he took the armchair perpendicular to her.

'I've not decorated for years, not since I moved to San Fran,' he said. 'I used to spend Christmas with my family but now I'm on my own. It's not worth the hassle to decorate when I'm constantly working and hardly at home.'

'You work in the evenings too? I always thought construction was a daytime thing.'

Zach grimaced. He needed to watch what he said about his real life. Being dishonest didn't come naturally to him. As much as he was enjoying the anonymity, he wasn't used to having to remember which lies he'd told. He rubbed his forehead. Being vague and keeping as close to the truth were his best options. 'We do what it takes to get the job done.'

She nodded with understanding. 'Are you staying in Pineford for the holidays or do you have to return to work soon?'

'I'm one of the owners of the company. I can delegate.' Which was the truth. 'Well, thank you for the offer of the tree but as I said—'

'You're not working all hours while you're here. Why don't you decorate this year? Thomas left us so many boxes in the house; we can spare some tinsel and baubles. I can help if you want. I'm sure Lucas won't mind but I can ask him if you're worried.'

He choked back a laugh at the idea of his asking Lucas for permission for anything.

She rose then walked over to the tree, reaching out to touch a branch. 'I hope you don't mind that it's artificial.'

He shrugged. 'Artificial is fine.' What was he saying? He didn't want or need any kind of tree.

'Did you have real or artificial trees when you were younger?' she asked.

'Real. Always real.' And he always went with his mom and dad to pick out the tree. It was their tradition to herald the start of the festive period.

'Oh, I bet that was glorious. Can there be anything more Christmassy than the smell of fresh pine? I've never had a real tree before. I've never had any tree.' A flush crept across her cheeks, as if she was embarrassed by her admission.

'What?' She loved Christmas. Out of all the people he knew, only his mother loved Christmas more. Why would someone who loved Christmas that much never have had a real tree? Even though he had no interest in getting involved – all he wanted was for her to leave – he found himself asking, 'Why not?'

'My family are Hindu so we didn't celebrate Christmas. I guess it would be more accurate to say we didn't do anything for the season. A lot of Hindu families do the whole tree and trimmings. Mine didn't. In fairness to my parents, my sister is ten years older than me and she didn't care that much about it so they didn't bother. When I was young, I understood Christmas was a religious thing and it wasn't my religion so it wasn't a big deal. As I got older, and I started watching all these Christmas films, they always showed something magical about the season. Like a real spirit of Christmas, particularly in America.' She was silent for a moment then shook herself as if coming out of a trance. 'Sorry, didn't mean to go on,' she said with an embarrassed laugh.

'Didn't you want to decorate your apartment?'

'My flat isn't that big and I'd have to drag a tree up three flights of stairs. Anyway, it seemed a little indulgent to start decorating just for me.' She stopped abruptly. 'Sorry, I'm talking about myself a lot.'

'Did Thomas know you never had a real tree? Is that why it's on your wish list?' She'd given him the opportunity to end the conversation and instead he'd asked more questions. What was wrong with him?

But it was helpful to gather as much information as he could if they were going to have any chance of sabotaging the wishes.

She nodded. 'Yes. All these Christmas movies have these amazing trees, beautifully decorated, with piles of presents in front of them on Christmas Day.'

Zach nodded. That sounded exactly like Christmas mornings

with his family before he stopped going to them. 'And you didn't have that?'

'No tree, no presents under the tree. Not for Christmas anyway. My sister and I were given presents for birthdays and other festivals, of course. Although by the time I was around ten, my parents didn't bother buying presents. They told us how much we could spend and we told them what we wanted them to buy. It was great.'

He couldn't imagine growing up without presents under a tree and being surrounded by giftwrap on Christmas morning. But there was so much affection in her tone, it was obvious she had a happy childhood.

'I can see why the idea of a real tree would be special to you but why the need to cut it down?' he said.

'Oh, well, that's all Thomas. He told me he always went with his sisters to a nearby farm and they would choose a tree together, then his father would cut it down. That's what he missed most when they had to sell Holly House. I think he wanted me to experience what he had.' She sniffed while blinking rapidly. 'I'm so sorry I'm boring you with all of this. If you don't want the tree perhaps you could find somewhere to donate it? Or find somewhere else on the property we could put it.'

'No, I'll keep it. Thank you.'

'You will?' Her broad smile was infectious.

For a few moments they stared at each other, until she tore her gaze away, her smile faltering.

'I'm so pleased you decided to keep it.'

'Where do you think I should put it?' he asked when it seemed she was about to leave.

As she looked about the place, he had this desperate urge to know what she thought of the barn. He loved it – it was more to his taste than his modern apartment in San Francisco. The conversion done by the previous owners was high quality. Only the beams in the ceiling and thick stone walls indicated it used to be a barn.

The front door led directly into the main living area, which was minimally furnished with a rustic coffee table, sofa, and armchair near an open fireplace. The kitchen was simple, set against the back wall with a country-style kitchen table dividing it from the living space.

His bedroom was in a similar minimal rustic style with a bed, closet, and dresser. He'd added a desk to set up a makeshift office. His high-tech equipment would raise a lot of questions if she ever saw it. Luckily she would never go in his bedroom, although his imagination immediately saw her on his bed.

'Oh anywhere,' she replied, dragging his thoughts back to décor and away from his bed, thankfully.

'This is such a gorgeous barn,' she continued. 'I love the house, but this would be a wonderful place to spend Christmas too. To be honest, I imagined Holly House to be more like this. Anyway, I've taken up enough of your time. I'll bring round some decorations later.'

After the way his mind wandered to the bedroom moments earlier, he made no effort to detain her this time.

She was a confusing woman.

He couldn't wrap his head around Sharmila's relationship with his uncle. Although she spoke fondly about Thomas, nothing she said suggested there was a romantic attachment between them. The Thomas she described to him, the man who went to the trouble of arranging a whole vacation so he could make Sharmila's wishes could come true, wasn't the man he knew. His uncle had never done anything like that for him or his cousins, and they were family.

But then, he, Lucas, and Izzy already had wonderful Christmases growing up.

There was no reason to deny Sharmila the simple pleasure of picking out a tree to cut down. She'd only completed two wishes. There would be other activities they could interfere with.

He flicked through the contacts on his cellphone then made a few calls.

Chapter 8

'This really is very kind of you, Zach,' Sharmila said for the third or fourth time that day.

The last thing she'd expected that morning was Zach standing on her doorstep, offering to take her to a nearby farm where she could cut down a Christmas tree. He hadn't exactly been welcoming when she went round to his barn the previous evening. When he'd opened the door in his green shirt unbuttoned at the neck, the colour matching his eyes perfectly, his strong forearms displayed by the sleeves rolled up to his elbows, it was all she could do to stop drooling. She'd thought she'd irritated him when she started babbling to cover her nerves.

'I hope I'm not taking you away from your work.'

'Lucas won't mind.'

They'd been on the road for over an hour, driving through mostly empty fields and farmland, the occasional tree, the occasional animal – nothing that held her interest for long. Zach had been looking straight ahead pretty much their entire journey. Which was good – he needed to concentrate on the road. But when he didn't even spare a glance in her direction when she tried starting a conversation, she couldn't help feeling this was a huge imposition on him.

But he was the one who had offered to take her to this farm. Why? Was it as a thank you for giving him the Christmas tree? Had her gift meant that much to him?

His mixed signals were confusing. One minute he was hardly speaking to her, the next he was going out of his way to help her.

She stared out the window.

These days she usually didn't encourage people to engage in conversation with her. Exchanging polite greetings was more than enough interaction. But she was acutely aware of his presence and fighting the urge to move closer to his warmth. She needed a distraction. Fast.

She tried again. 'How did you find out about this farm?'

'I heard about it from someone.'

'Oh.' When he didn't offer further clarification, she said, 'This is a lovely area. Really peaceful. I love how small Pineford is and how it isn't filled with the hustle and bustle of larger towns and cities.'

Zach snorted.

'What?' she asked. 'You wouldn't live somewhere like Pineford?'

'I'm sure small-town life seems appealing in all those movies you love to watch but when you've spent your life in a big city with everything you could want close by, it's hard to give that up.'

'Oh, I don't know about that. I work in Birmingham, which is the second biggest city in England. But I lived in a small village for a while and I loved the slower pace of life there.'

'How long did you live there?'

'In the village? I was there for over a year. I moved back to Birmingham a few months ago. It was really hard to go back.'

'Why did you move back then?'

'For work.' She bit her lip. Why was she telling all this to Zach? She didn't usually open up to people about her life, not since Hari's death. The last person she spoke with this way, the only other person, was Thomas. She looked over at Zach. There was something about him that reminded her of Thomas. A quiet gentleness maybe. She shook her head. She was being silly. She missed Thomas, that was all.

'I thought you worked in a café,' Zach said, throwing her a puzzled glance.

'That was only temporary. I needed to get out of Birmingham for a while and my aunt offered me a job in her teashop to help me out.'

'Where did you work before then?'

'In a law firm.' She needed to move away from the direction the conversation was going. 'Hey, can I put some music on? Does this truck have Bluetooth?'

'No Bluetooth and the radio doesn't work.'

Great. But silence could invite more questions about her personal life. She couldn't have that. 'So, er, what were your Christmases like growing up?'

To her surprise he described some of his family's traditions, telling her one of his favourites had been the stockings that his mother prepared and hung over their fireplace. They were always full to the brim with the usual items like chocolates, candy, and stationery but his mother also included 'coupons' for fun activities they could do together. He had loved collecting the coupons over the course of the year.

It sounded like an idyllic childhood.

'And you don't spend Christmas with your family anymore?'

He glanced at her. 'No. Not for years.'

'What do you do instead?'

'I'm either working or I go on vacation with friends.'

'And don't your parents mind?' Even though her family didn't celebrate the season, it had still been a time for them to get together. It would be strange not to be with her sister's family this year, but Sarita insisted she couldn't turn down Thomas's gift.

'My father passed away a few years ago,' he said quietly.

'I'm so sorry for your loss.'

'Thank you.'

Sharmila widened her eyes and covered her mouth with her hands. 'Is that why you don't celebrate Christmas?' she asked, mortified at the thought she'd been pushing him about Christmas when it could be a sensitive time since his father died.

His mouth quirked. 'No. That's not the reason. I haven't spent Christmas with my family since I moved to California. It used to be one of my favourite times of the year. My mom loved pulling out all the stops. Celebrating the season became less important as my work grew more demanding.'

'I can't imagine growing up with your kind of Christmas and not wanting to experience that every year.'

He shrugged. 'I got older.'

'Too old for the magic of Christmas?' Sharmila scoffed.

No response. There was silence in the truck again. This time she had no desire to break it.

She glanced across at Zach, trying to work out why she wanted him to keep talking with her when she actively avoided touching on personal topics with others. What was it about him that was putting her at ease, back to her former self somehow?

She hurriedly looked away when she caught his gaze. She pulled out her phone and put her earphones in. Zach wouldn't care if she was being rude – he'd probably even welcome it knowing she wouldn't be pestering him anymore.

The farm was deep in the countryside, lying off the main road up a single lane path. They passed large pastures of crops and grazing animals. It wasn't until they came closer to the farmhouse that she saw the land behind the building was hillier. And full of evergreens.

She craned her neck desperate to get to the trees.

'Are you sure we're allowed to cut down our own trees at this place? Is it even a working Christmas tree farm?' she asked, worried she'd come on another wasted journey.

'It's not a Christmas tree farm.'

'Then—'

'The owners are my friends,' Zach admitted, reluctantly. 'They happen to grow evergreens on their property, which they sometimes supply to retailers. They don't sell directly to the public, but I asked if they could help with your wish and they told me it would be fine for you to come over and choose one to cut down.'

'So, your friends are doing this as a favour to you?'

He inclined his head in acknowledgement.

She took a moment to digest what he'd done. Why had he gone to so much trouble? When Lucas offered to take them to the farm the first time, she'd noticed the look Zach had given him. He hadn't been pleased. He hadn't exactly made much effort to get to know her or Penny better; in fact he sometimes acted as if they were an irritation to him. But not only had he taken time from his work to drive her to this farm but he'd arranged the visit as a special favour.

Zach Lawrence was one confusing man.

'You didn't have to go to so much trouble,' she said.

'It was a phone call. It's nothing.'

'It's not nothing to me. Thank you.'

He looked over at her and their eyes held for a moment. The air grew thick and heavy. She cleared her throat.

They both got out of the truck. Sharmila waited next to it while Zach went to meet his friend.

She returned their wave when they looked in her direction but Zach made no effort to introduce her. She shrugged. If he didn't want her to meet his friends, she wouldn't force him to.

The amount of snow on the ground had increased as they drove north. Here, where the trees stood in neat rows like sentinels, the hills were covered in almost a foot of snow.

She clapped her hands and danced a little jig in delight. Somewhere out there was her tree. Her first ever real Christmas tree.

*

'Why are you standing there?' Zach asked. They'd walked up the hill path and from their vantage point they could see the evergreens stretching in front of them.

'I'm paralysed by choice.'

Zach cleared his throat to cover his laugh. 'They're all the same. I'm sure any tree will do.'

She turned her head to look up at him, widening her eyes and rounding her mouth in fake shock. 'How can you say that? The perfect tree is out there and I have to find it.'

'There are a lot of trees out there. How will you know when you find the perfect one?'

She shrugged and looked back over the trees. 'Don't know. I didn't realise there would be so many varieties of pine tree.'

He grimaced. 'They're not all pine trees. Technically they're all evergreens, but there's a mix of pine, spruce, and fir here.'

'Well look at you, Mr Tree Expert.'

He folded his arms. 'I'll have you know, I worked at a Christmas tree lot for a couple of years while I was at school.'

'No way!'

'Why does that surprise you?'

'Well, you're such a …' She broke off.

'Such a what?'

'Such a person who doesn't decorate for the holidays.' She gave a lopsided grin.

He couldn't help grinning in response. 'Do you know what kind of tree you're after?'

She shook her head. 'Not a clue. Maybe it will call out to me?'

'I think you may be giving trees magical properties they don't have.'

She rested her hand on her hip. 'I see the Spirit of Christmas has completely left you in your old age.'

'I'm not a Grinch. But a tree is a tree.'

'We'll agree to disagree. Thomas said he always knew which tree to cut, that you would know if it's the perfect fit for you. It's important I get the right one.' She walked off without looking to see if he was following.

He caught up to her when she'd wandered down a row of firs with smooth silver bark and dark, dense green leaves in a conical crown.

'I think this is the kind I want.' She breathed in. 'Ah, smell that. Isn't that exactly what Christmas should smell like?'

He stood waiting for Sharmila to pick out one of the trees. She hadn't moved but was looking at him expectantly. 'What?' Had she really expected him to sniff the air?

She shrugged. 'Nothing.' She turned back. 'Definitely this kind of tree. But which one?' She walked up and down the rows, between the trees, standing in front of one or two for a couple of minutes, moving away, coming back, touching some of the leaves, holding up branches to her nose.

She would be the worst person to go furniture shopping with.

He glanced at his watch. He would give her another thirty minutes, after that he was choosing the tree for her.

Suddenly she let out a yell.

He rushed over to her. 'Are you OK? What's wrong?'

'This is it. I've found it. I've found my tree.'

He released a breath. She was hopping from one leg to another oblivious to the panic he'd experienced. He was immediately captivated by the expression of pure joy on her face. He cleared his throat. 'Are you sure? Did it call out to you?'

'Yes,' she nodded emphatically, 'but it was more a gentle murmur of my name. That's probably why you didn't hear it.'

His lips twitched at her comment. She was becoming more and more of a contradiction. Most of the time she seemed reserved when she was around people other than Penny, including himself. But then she also had this playful side. She was what Thomas would call 'a delight'. His smile fell. This playful side was probably an act.

Despite Zach's limited responses during the journey to the

farm, her openness with him unexpectedly led him to reciprocate. She was amusing. Interesting. Intriguing.

Was that how she got past Thomas's defences? His uncle wasn't someone he thought would be susceptible to feminine wiles but he also wasn't the kind of person who made magnanimous gestures. It didn't make sense for Thomas to include Sharmila in his will without some manipulation on her part.

He couldn't let himself get distracted. He had to remember he was here because she had tricked Thomas into leaving her an inheritance. There was a lot at stake if he wasn't successful with the plan.

'Oh no,' Sharmila exclaimed, breaking into his thoughts.

'What's wrong?'

'We didn't bring an axe or a chainsaw. How am I going to cut down the tree?'

He snorted. 'Do you think anyone's going to trust you with an axe?'

'Hey! I'm not that clumsy!'

'May I remind you the first time we met, you bumped into Lucas. Then you knocked over the dish at the puzzle contest. Then you dropped things *and* bumped into me when you were putting away the groceries. You're not going to cut down the tree.'

She opened her mouth as if to argue, then closed it with a slight huff. 'Fine. Fair point.'

She was cute when she was irritated. He shook his head. He wasn't doing a great job at not letting Sharmila distract him.

'I'll give Ben a call. He can send someone up here.' He arranged for his friend to meet them, then disconnected quickly when he saw Sharmila trying to wrap her arms around the tree and burying her head in the branches.

'What are you doing?' he asked.

'Um, just checking the tree's girth?'

'Its girth? I see.' He tried hard not to laugh. 'Worried it will be too wide for your foyer?'

She nodded slowly, avoiding his eyes. It was clear she'd been hugging the tree and was too embarrassed to admit it.

'Does the girth feel the right size?' he asked.

'I'm not sure. Why don't you come over here and help me check? You've got a wider wingspan than me.'

'I'm not hugging the tree,' Zach replied.

'I'm not hugging it!' Sharmila protested. 'I'm measuring! It has to fit on your truck, doesn't it?'

'It will fit.'

He was about to tell her the tree would be secured in netting for the drive back when he noticed her shoulders shaking as she buried her face back in the branches. The sudden change from their playful exchange had him automatically taking a step forward with concern. 'Sharmila?'

She said something but the words were muffled in the tree.

For a moment he tried to imagine what she could be feeling, choosing her first real Christmas tree. It must be overwhelming for her.

Without thinking he put his hand on her shoulder, taken aback slightly when she turned round and threw herself at him, wrapping her arms round his waist, burying her head against his chest. Gingerly, he put his arms around her.

She was a tiny thing but she fit perfectly against him. Uncomfortable awareness heated his body. He grabbed her shoulders and gently pushed her away.

'Someone will be here any minute.'

She nodded, still a little shaken. 'I need to take a photo next to the tree. Will you do that for me, please?'

He took care not to touch her hand when she passed him her phone. After snapping a few photos, he looked them over. In all of them she looked beautiful standing in the white snow framed against a giant tree – she was small, delicate, and had a slight glint of tears in the first couple of photos, but gradually a breathtaking smile emerged as she glanced at the tree next to her.

She did a little dance when they saw Ben and a couple of men arrive with a chainsaw. She couldn't be faking her joy at finding her tree. There was no need for her to put on an act with him – she didn't know who he really was.

But was she genuine? Or was he being taken in by a beautiful woman, again. In an ideal world, until he worked her out, he would have limited his interactions with her. But that wasn't an option until he stopped her getting the inheritance. The sooner he did that, the better. She was too enticing for his peace of mind.

Chapter 9

'A little bit to your left, a little bit more. A bit more. Oh no, too far.' Sharmila laughed when Zach shut his eyes and moved his lips soundlessly. Probably praying for patience.

After the brief awkwardness of their unexpected hug earlier, they ended up having a great time as they joined his friends for coffee and cake while they waited for their tree. In familiar company, Zach had been charming and funny. More approachable. More human.

There were no awkward silences this time on their journey back to Pineford. They discussed their favourites – movies, books, foods, music. Of course, they had barely anything in common, but their tastes complemented rather than contradicted each other.

In a different lifetime, she might have enjoyed getting to know him even better, finding out whether the attraction was mutual. But despite what Penny said, she wasn't interested in romance, not even a brief holiday fling.

'Is this to your satisfaction, my lady?' he asked with a small bow, finally positioning her tree where she indicated.

She held her hands up, framing the tree – paying more attention to the man supporting it than the tree itself.

In a different lifetime, she reminded herself.

'Sharmila, is this where you want the tree?'

Sharmila shook her head to clear her thoughts. 'Yes, that's the spot. That's perfect. I'll bring the stand over.'

Within minutes Zach had installed the tree, ready for the first decorations. They stepped a few paces away to get a better view.

'There's a ladder in the garage. We'll need it for the higher branches. I can get it for you,' Zach offered.

She nodded, not really paying attention. She stood with one arm folded, her chin in the other hand.

She had no idea how she was supposed to start decorating. What should she put on first – lights, tinsel? Presumably, she should work from top to bottom, but didn't the tree topper go on last? Did people follow a specific method? Was there a rule about the position of baubles? And after the tree was done, there was the rest of the house to decorate.

'What's up?' Zach asked. 'You look miles away.'

She scrunched her nose and gave an embarrassed shrug. 'I don't know how to decorate a tree. I was thinking I could watch some video tutorials to get some ideas.'

Zach smiled down at her. 'Why do I get the feeling you're an overthinker.'

She held her palms up. 'I just want everything to be perfect. You know it's my first proper tree. I have to get it right.'

'It doesn't matter how you decorate, as long as you like it.'

She glanced up at him. 'It has to be perfect. I don't want people to look at it and think it's hideous.'

'Who's going to see it?'

Sharmila reached out to fluff some of the branches. 'All the people who come to the party.'

'Party?'

'It's one of Thomas's wishes for me. I have to host a party here. I don't know when it is yet. I'm meeting Mayor Jackie soon to decide the best date so that it doesn't clash with any of the other Pineford events.' She shuddered. 'I don't know what Thomas was thinking, asking me to host.'

'You don't like parties?'

'Do I look like the kind of person who loves parties?'

Zach lifted a shoulder. 'I'm guessing no.'

'Don't get me wrong. It's not like I hate the people here or anything. But I don't really know them, and I'll have to entertain them. They'll probably have all these expectations about how a party should be organised. I'm worried I'll let them down. Frankly, it scares me a little.'

'I'm sure nobody coming to your party will care what the place looks like.' He put a hand on her shoulder. She was sure it was meant to be reassuring but instead warmth flooded through her at its comforting weight. She took a deep breath and moved a step away.

'Haven't you seen how the town is decorated? Even the inn. It's a wonderland! No, I'm certain they're going to have high expectations.' She tapped a finger across her mouth. 'I wonder if there's a town decorator I could hire to help me. Maybe I'll ask Jackie.'

'Isn't decorating the place on your list?'

She shook her head. 'No, it's not. We found a note Thomas left for me taped to one of the boxes of decorations. He wrote he hoped I'd have fun fixing up the tree and house, and he wanted to make sure I had loads of decorations to choose from. He really went above and beyond to arrange all of this for me.' She stared down at her hands briefly but composed herself before Zach could ask her what was wrong again. 'That reminds me, I need to sort out some of these decorations for you. They'll help to get into the festive spirit.'

'Are you suggesting I'm in need of festive spirit?' he asked.

He bit his lip while giving her a small smile. It was one of the sexiest things she'd ever seen. Enough of this. She had to get it together, or she'd end up launching herself at him.

'If the Grinch-sized shoes fit,' she said.

'I already told you I'm not a Grinch. Do I look like I have a pot belly and a snub nose?'

Her eyes were drawn to his chest. No, he definitely did not

look like he had a pot belly. She could imagine a firm six pack under his shirt. But she didn't want to be thinking about that.

To distract herself, she moved towards the tree and began fluffing some branches. Suddenly she felt a sharp prick on her finger. She quickly withdrew her hand and sucked her finger to stop the bleeding.

'Here, let me look.' He took her hand and brought it to the light, turning her finger around to get a better view.

Her mouth went dry and her breathing started to accelerate. If even the simplest, most innocent touch of his hand caused flames to rush through her, then Zach Lawrence was a bigger danger to her equilibrium than she thought. She needed to stay away from him.

'I think you should be all right without a Band-Aid, but I can get one if you want,' he said.

She shook her head, not trusting her voice to come out steady. She went over to one of the boxes, hoping he wouldn't see that her cheeks were still warm.

'Do you have a knife or box cutter?' she asked, regretting it immediately when he reached into his pocket, drawing her attention to the front of his jeans. She bent her head quickly, closing her eyes.

It had been years. Why was her body reacting now? Perhaps because it had been such a long time since she'd been held tenderly. Their brief hug among the firs left her yearning, actually yearning, for more.

Penny would encourage her to just go for it. But what was the point? Even if Zach was interested, and that wasn't a given – he was the epitome of blowing hot and cold – he was American, she was British. An ocean divided them. She wasn't one of those people who could have a fling, even a brief holiday romance would develop into feelings, and she wasn't ready to open her heart even a crack.

Zach opened the rest of the boxes and started to go through

them. He'd been so generous it would be rude to send him away when he was only trying to help. She could keep herself under control. But afterwards, she was going to avoid him at all costs.

They arranged the decorations into piles. Sharmila was organising the baubles when Zach lifted out a small white box wrapped with a bright red bow.

'This box has your name on it,' he said, handing it to her.

She carefully unwrapped the bow and lifted the lid. Under Zach's curious gaze, she read the note out loud.

Sharmila,

   For your first real Christmas tree I had this ornament commissioned especially for us as a way of mixing our two cultures. I hope this can be the start of a new tradition for you, and your tree is filled with a new ornament every year. Merry Christmas, my dear.

   Thomas mama

With tears in her eyes, she lifted out a turquoise bauble – Thomas's favourite colour – shaped like an Indian elephant, decorated in Indian floral patterns. It was the perfect combination.

She took a couple of centring breaths as her eyes started to water again. She sensed Zach move closer to her. They turned towards each other. She was about to walk into his arms when a noise alerted her to someone's presence.

'Sorry to interrupt,' Lucas said. 'I was looking for Zach. Can I have a word?' He indicated towards the door and Zach followed him out.

'What's going on?' Lucas asked as soon as they stepped outside. 'What were you doing?'

'Not here. Let's go to my barn.' Zach led the way, taking the time to gather his thoughts. Lucas had a right to know what had happened but he wasn't sure he had a good explanation.

'So, what's going on?' Lucas asked again once they were inside. 'Have you changed your mind about Sharmila? Do you think we should let her have the inheritance?'

Zach pinched his lips together. 'Why would you think that, Lucas?'

'I saw you. You were about to hug her. I thought maybe you changed your mind and wanted to help her complete her list instead. I wish you'd told me before I went out of my way with the tree. But no matter, we can both help her now.'

'I haven't changed my mind,' he said, going to the fridge to grab them beers.

'Wait, what?' Lucas looked at him with confusion as they sat down. When Zach didn't offer any further explanation, Lucas added, 'I still think we're making a mistake interfering with Uncle Thomas's wishes. He wouldn't have made all this happen without good reason. Maybe we should give Izzy a call and rethink the plan.'

Zach pressed his lips together as they waited for Izzy to answer Lucas's call. There was no chance Izzy would change her mind. The phone call would only convince her she was right to ask Zach to look out for Lucas, although he wasn't looking forward to hearing her reaction when she found out about the tree.

'What were you thinking, Zach?' she shouted. 'How's that helping us?'

Zach remained silent.

'After I offered to drive Sharmila to a farm, I asked Izzy for help with ideas,' Lucas said. 'She went to a lot of effort finding a farm that doesn't let you cut down your tree. If you hadn't taken her to your friend's place, the nearest farm she could cut her own tree is over two hours away. As well as trying to interfere with the wishes directly, Izzy thinks we should also try to delay her as much as possible so she runs out of time to complete all of them.'

Zach sighed again. 'Why didn't you tell me what you were planning?'

'We didn't think you'd try to mess with it,' Izzy snapped.

Zach grimaced. He had no explanation for why he went out of his way to help Sharmila. He looked over at the tree she brought round. 'She said she never had a real tree before. If you'd seen her today, looking for the perfect tree …' He trailed off.

'Oh, I get it now. Typical Zach being Zach. You can't help yourself.'

He narrowed his eyes at the contempt in Izzy's tone. 'What's that supposed to mean?'

'Always wanting to play the knight in shining armour. Falling for every sob story. This is exactly how Annette managed to fool you.'

'I'm not trying to be anyone's knight.' He wasn't. He didn't do that anymore. He learnt that hard lesson with Annette.

Izzy was right. He shouldn't have got involved. He'd come to Pineford to help Lucas stop Sharmila from getting the inheritance, and instead he'd helped Sharmila complete one of the more challenging items on her list. Perhaps he was the one needing someone to look out for him.

'I'm sorry I interfered with your plan. I didn't know. But, Lucas, did you find out anything new during your drive yesterday?'

'Not much, I'm afraid. I made a list on my phone.' He reached into his pocket looking for it, then laughed when Zach pointed out he'd used it to phone Izzy. 'I remember she has to be in the parade on Christmas Eve. I'm not sure how you think we can stop that one, Izzy. Other than that, I didn't get much out of her. Sharmila doesn't say much.' He leaned back, putting an arm behind his head and crossing his legs.

Zach's eyes widened. Not say much? Sharmila never ran out of things to say when they were together.

'What did you two talk about on your drive, Zach?' Izzy asked.

Once they got over the awkwardness of their hug at the farm, they'd covered a surprising range of subjects that had nothing to do with Christmas. He couldn't exactly share that with his cousins. 'Christmas, her list, nothing much,' he replied.

Lucas sat forward and took a slow swig of his beer. He drew his hand across his face. 'Izzy, maybe we should ask our accountants to look into buying out her share of the business.'

'And what about Holly House?' Izzy asked.

Zach rubbed his chin. 'I didn't know you cared about the house.'

'Mom is always talking about how wonderful it was growing up in Pineford,' Izzy replied.

Zach raised his eyebrows. He'd never heard Aunt Carol mention the town, unlike his mother who often recounted stories of her childhood, particularly about the magical Christmases at Holly House. After she lost Thomas, she had told Zach she wanted to go back to her childhood family home to feel closer to her brother.

'Why shouldn't Mom get a chance to spend her Christmases there?' Izzy asked. 'Why shouldn't we all?'

Zach agreed with her on that point. He felt the same. He wanted to be able to tell his mother they had Holly House, make her dream come true. He was silent as he contemplated Lucas's suggestion to buy Sharmila's inheritance from her. Would Sharmila even sell?

'Lucas, we discussed buying Sharmila out already.' Izzy's voice interrupted his thoughts. 'Even without the complication of the business, we aren't in a position to pay her the full amount it would take to buy her out.' The line went silent for a minute. 'Although I suppose she wouldn't know if we didn't pay her the full amount.'

Lucas and Zach exchanged looks. Buying Sharmila out of the inheritance was their easiest option, but it wouldn't feel right not offering her a fair price.

Why was he looking out for Sharmila's interest? If Sharmila was the opportunist they thought she was, she would find out the full value of the shares and Holly House before agreeing to a sale anyway.

He couldn't admit it to Izzy but there was a part of him that was starting to believe they'd got it wrong and Thomas left the gift to Sharmila without any manipulation on her part. He snorted. Perhaps Lucas's positive outlook was rubbing off on him. Or was he being made a fool of again?

'Didn't you say that you thought she doesn't deserve any money?' he said to Izzy, reminding her of the reason he came to Pineford in the first place – to stop Sharmila from inheriting.

'I don't,' she confirmed. 'But if we can get her to accept a low offer, it would be the easiest way for us all to get what we want. Look at it this way, you could go back to San Francisco.'

He couldn't deny that his life would be much simpler if he was back home, where he could pour himself into work and be far away from one pint-sized distraction. 'Do you want to get back to Boston, Lucas?'

'I'm happy working from here and driving back when I need to. Izzy, you're managing fine without me, aren't you?' His sister agreed. 'Besides, WinterFest sounds like it could be a lot of fun and we get to spend more time together.'

'Then you should run the numbers, Izzy,' Zach said. 'See whether you can make it work financially. My money is tied up at the moment, otherwise I would have gladly helped you out. That's even assuming Sharmila wants to sell. In the meantime, we'll stay in Pineford and concentrate on the list. But I think we should get our lawyers to look over the will again – check whether there's anything we've missed.'

Lucas nodded slowly. 'I guess it wouldn't hurt to get a fresh pair of legal eyes on it. Izzy can you handle that, please?'

'Sure, I'll get right on that. I'll be in touch as soon as I find anything. I've got to get back but good luck, guys,' Izzy said before hanging up.

'Even if I was convinced we're doing the right thing,' Lucas said, 'we still don't know the full list yet.'

'You're right. She's been a little cagey about her wishes, don't you think?' When Lucas didn't reply he continued, 'We know she has two weeks left and she's done at least two of the wishes already.'

'Three with your help, Zach,' Lucas pointed out.

Zach bit his lip and tipped his head in acknowledgement. 'I'm sorry. I've made it harder for us. But we do know there are ten wishes in total and she's completed three. You found out she's got to enter the dessert competition and the gingerbread one.'

'Don't forget the snowman competition.'

'Yeah, well, unless we can control the weather so it doesn't snow or buy up every single baking ingredient, I don't really know how we're going to stop Sharmila. And even I don't think we should sabotage the town parade.' He scratched the back of his neck. This wasn't going to be easy. 'I did find out Sharmila has to host a party but I have no idea how we could stop that.'

'You know, Zach, it sounds to me like Uncle Thomas wanted Sharmila to enjoy herself and have an authentic Christmas experience. I really don't feel right trying to ruin that.'

'I understand, Luc. I do. But does it feel right that Sharmila will get to cast the deciding vote on Endicott Enterprises whenever you and Izzy can't agree on a proposal?'

Lucas's shoulders slumped. 'OK, I'll help but I don't like it. I'll send Izzy the list of tasks we know so far, maybe she can come up with some ideas.'

'The dessert competition's the day after tomorrow,' Zach said, reading from the WinterFest brochure. 'Entries by 6 p.m. We don't have long to come up with something. And there are still two wishes we don't know about yet.'

'OK, I'll try to find out what they are,' Lucas said. 'I know there's something she's hiding, but I don't think Sharmila is a bad person. I'm not convinced there was anything romantic between her and Uncle Thomas.'

On that, he could agree with Lucas. Whatever the relationship was between Thomas and Sharmila, it was clear his uncle held a lot of affection for her, if the elephant ornament was anything to go by. Did Sharmila reciprocate his feelings? The jury was still out on that. The more he was around her, the more he wanted to believe she was genuine – which was why he had to be careful. He couldn't risk being fooled again. The stakes were much higher this time around.

Chapter 10

That Friday evening, there were several cars outside the address Jackie had given Sharmila. This didn't look like it was going to be a quiet, casual conversation about her party. Why had Jackie chosen the local bakery for their meeting?

'Come in, come in, Sharmila,' Jackie greeted her at the shop entrance. 'The other ladies are already here. Perfect timing. We're about to start.'

Nine voices went silent when Sharmila preceded Jackie into the kitchen. She stretched her mouth into an approximation of a friendly smile. Why did she feel like she was about to be interrogated?

She took a couple of centring breaths. *You can do this, Sharmila. You're only here for another two and a half weeks then you'll never see these people again. You're not going to get too close. You can do this.*

'Ladies, you remember Sharmila. I introduced her to you on Saturday. Sharmila, you know Jill of course.'

Sharmila nodded. She also recognised a few faces from the tree lighting. She concentrated as the women introduced themselves. She made sure to note Angie, the lady who'd followed her round the pottery shop the other day. Unsurprisingly, Angie's greeting was notably less welcoming than some of the others'. They were all part of Pineford Women's Club, which organised and helped with town functions and held fundraising events themselves.

'What would you like to drink?' Jill asked. 'I have cocoa, apple cider, or wine.'

Sharmila looked at the counters while waiting for Jill to pour her an apple cider. There were mixing bowls, baking trays, bags of flour, sugar, butter, milk, different chocolates, and sweets out.

Sharmila walked over to Jackie. 'I thought we were going to discuss ideas about the parade and party,' she mentioned quietly.

'Yes, yes. We can do that while we bake,' Jackie replied in her loud voice. 'We're making cookies for the Children's Christmas Carnival on Sunday. Now which one would you like to make?' She handed her a couple of recipe cards. 'Do you have a favourite cookie? I'm sure Gayle can find whatever ingredients you need,' she said, nodding to the bakery owner.

'Or I can pop down and pick something up. I own the general store. Have you been in yet?' the woman who had introduced herself as Patty asked.

'Not yet,' Sharmila replied. 'We've mostly been eating at Cinnamon's. But we will need to visit soon as we're running out of supplies.'

'Well, if I'm not there when you do come in, remember to tell the clerk to put your groceries on the tab.'

Sharmila jerked her head, taken aback by what Patty said. 'I'm sorry. What tab?'

'Mr Bell set up accounts for you on Thomas's behalf at my store, the inn, and the diner. Didn't you know?'

Sharmila gulped. He'd done what? 'No, I didn't. Are you sure? We've been paying for our meals at the diner. No one mentioned it.'

'I'll have to have a word with Becky. She shouldn't have been charging you,' Jackie joined in. 'I helped Mr Bell set everything up, so I know you have an account with them.'

Sharmila was overwhelmed by what she'd just learnt about

Thomas's generosity. She wished Penny had come with her – she'd know how to handle this. Instead, Penny had gone with Debby, the Historical Society lady, to a bar in a nearby town. To gather herself, Sharmila turned her attention to the cookies. 'I don't have a favourite recipe,' she said.

Gayle handed her a card. 'Not to worry. You can be in charge of measuring the ingredients then.'

Sharmila got to work as the rest of the ladies were given their instructions.

One of them came to stand next to her as she was pouring out some flour. 'I've been relegated to measuring dry ingredients as well.'

'I probably shouldn't be trusted with anything more complicated, anyway,' Sharmila confessed.

The lady laughed. 'In case you don't remember, or you didn't hear over the chatter, I'm Liz Jenkins. I teach at the high school. Everyone has been curious about you. We heard about Thomas Adams's gift and of course about your Christmas list.' Noticing Sharmila's expression, she continued, 'It's a small town. Your news was the most exciting thing to happen here since Mr Adams bought Holly House last year.'

Jill must have been listening in on their conversation as she called out, 'Come on, Sharmila. Don't be shy. We all want to hear more about Thomas and this list he's made for you.'

'Did you know Thomas well?' Sharmila asked the group, to deflect the topic from her.

'Not all of us,' a woman Sharmila couldn't remember the name of said. 'CeCe over there knew him when they were children, but I met him when he visited Pineford last year, when he decided to buy Holly House. I was friends with the previous owners. It caused quite the stir when Mr Adams told them they could name their price.'

'Susan's right,' CeCe replied. 'The Adams family certainly came full circle from having to sell the house to pay off their debts to their current financial position.'

Sharmila's mouth twisted – it felt wrong to listen to gossip about Thomas, especially about a part of his life he hadn't chosen to share with her.

She tried to change the conversation, but they wouldn't drop the subject. Instead their focus returned to Sharmila, particularly interested in knowing the details around how she first met Thomas.

'When we heard about Thomas's gift we thought maybe you were his girlfriend. But then we weren't too sure because he was a lot older than you,' Susan said.

Sharmila laughed. Why had the possibility never even occurred to her before?

'I never thought about our age difference. It never mattered since there was nothing like that between us. We were just friends. He became like family really and was practically adopted by my family. Our friendship started out of a shared love for Christmas but then we talked about what I celebrated instead. He was really interested and had so many questions about my culture and traditions, which I didn't know all the answers to. My dad loves nothing better than lecturing about India and Hinduism to anyone who will listen, so I asked him if he would video chat with Thomas the next time he came into the café. And the next thing I knew my parents invited Thomas to stay with them in India during our harvest celebration, and then they were making plans again for our spring celebration. I went over to Kolkata at the same time and it was so heart-warming to see Thomas with my family. They got on like a house on fire. And Thomas loved my mum's cooking, said it was the best he'd ever tasted. He was a very special man – I cherish our friendship.'

'Your parents live in India?' asked Liz.

Sharmila nodded. 'Now they do. They moved there after they retired.'

'You're Indian then,' Angie said.

'Yes.'

'But Thomas made a Christmas activity list for you. Christmas is Christian, not Indian.'

Sharmila looked around at the other women in the room. Most of them avoided her gaze, but Lydia exchanged a sympathetic glance with her. She was the only other person of colour there, and Sharmila suspected Lydia had heard Angie speak that way before.

'Actually, it's more a winter list, I would say,' Sharmila said to Angie, hoping her answer would be the end of that conversation. She busied herself with measuring out the ingredients.

Curiosity about her presence in Pineford and Thomas's list was understandable, but Sharmila wasn't in the mood to spend the entire evening answering questions. Luckily one of her strengths at work was interviewing people without their realising she was eliciting the information she needed, a skill she could use to avoid having to speak any more about herself. By the end of the evening, she knew about Susan's problem with her plumbing, Lydia's frustrations about her in-laws visiting for Christmas, Karen not getting all her presents in time, and most of the problems the WinterFest committee was having with the Pineford Christmas activities.

They then shared stories about some of the people in town, people Sharmila didn't know. It was mostly harmless gossip, apart from when Angie brought up one couple. When Angie described how the husband was working late or at weekends and was making phone calls in secret, it made Sharmila's divorce-lawyer antenna twitch. She tried to tamp down her worries about a woman she'd never met and probably never would meet. Instead, she concentrated on her mixing bowl.

Soon the scent of ginger and sugar filled the air as the first batch of cookies was ready to leave the oven. Sharmila wasn't much of a baker – that was something she was happy to leave to the professionals – but it would be good practice for the next day's dessert competition. And there was something restful about working with a group to make something for charity. It took her a moment to figure out she was being invited into a friendship group that had developed over many years, generations even, and that was something no wish list could have offered her.

The chatter soon turned to Pineford's WinterFest since most of the ladies were helping on the committee. By the time they were ready to decorate the final batch of cookies, it had been arranged for Sharmila to help Liz with the parade preparations, that way they could decide the best float for her to be a part of. They also agreed on the date for her party, 26 December, and many of the ladies volunteered to help her organise it. In return, Sharmila agreed to volunteer with the group at the Children's Christmas Carnival that Sunday.

With a factory line of women preparing the batter, decorating the cookies, and cleaning up, it wasn't long before there were trays of chocolate chip, oatmeal raisin, peanut butter, mint, s'mores, and snickerdoodle cookies ready to be packaged.

Sharmila started making tea shortly after arriving back at Holly House.

'Penny,' she called out. 'Are you home? Do you fancy a cuppa?'

Penny came to join her at the breakfast bar. 'How was the meeting?'

'It was actually a cookie bake. But it was good. There's a thing for kids the day after tomorrow. I snagged a few cookies for you to try,' she said, pushing the plate towards Penny and taking one for herself.

'Mm, these are delicious,' Penny moaned, with her mouth full.

'They should be, there's so much butter in them. Have another one,' she said, passing the plate again.

Penny's eyes narrowed even though she took another cookie. 'Why do I get the feeling there are strings attached to these biscuits?'

'I don't know what you mean.'

'Hmm, really?'

'Really.' She ignored Penny's disbelieving expression, turning away to make the tea and taking both mugs to the table. 'By the way, that kids' event I mentioned. Well, I've volunteered to help and I volunteered you too. Another cookie?'

'Sharmila! We were supposed to have a quiet day at home on Sunday. We have events nearly every other day.'

'I know. But I couldn't say no. You don't really mind, do you?'

Penny shook her head. 'Of course not, but I think I deserve the whole plate,' she said, pulling it towards her.

Sharmila brought her mug to her lips but didn't drink, chewing her inner cheek as her thoughts went back to the bakery.

'What's up?' Penny asked.

'Hmm, nothing,'

'Come on. I can tell something's on your mind.'

She shook her head. 'It's nothing. How was your evening?'

'It was great. But don't change the subject. What is it?'

'OK, well, everyone there was lovely but there was some gossiping and they were talking about this one lady,' Sharmila replied.

'What about her?'

'She's having some problems with her husband. It sounds like he's hiding things from her. And some of the things they described he's done, well, it got me thinking—'

'No.' Penny's interruption was emphatic.

'No what?'

'No, don't go looking for trouble where there isn't any.'

'I'm not suggesting anything—'

'Yes, you are.'

'Maybe. But in my experience—' She broke off when Penny laughed.

'You know what they say. You can take the girl out of the law but you can't take the law out of the girl.'

Sharmila grinned and shook her head. 'I don't think anyone says that.'

'You know what I mean. You're a typical divorce lawyer. You don't trust anyone.'

'Of course I trust people.'

'Really?' Penny quirked an eyebrow.

Sharmila held her hands up in a gesture of surrender. 'OK, I admit that being a divorce lawyer for high-net-worth clients has made me a little suspicious, particularly when they can start out being so agreeable and charming but then the knives come out.'

'Ah, I see. So it's wealthy, charming men you don't trust,' Penny teased.

'People, not just men. I don't trust wealthy, charming people,' Sharmila joked in return. 'But seriously, I know that I don't trust easily. People have to earn my trust. But it's hard to give. Not just because of my job. Even Hari lied.' One of the people she'd trusted most in the world had lied to her. 'His was a silly lie for a silly reason. If he hadn't lied to me—'

'No, Sharmila. There was nothing you could have done.' Sharmila opened her mouth but Penny repeated, 'No.'

'Fine, but he didn't need to lie.'

They were both silent for a few minutes until Penny spoke again. 'What about Lucas then?'

'What do you mean?' she asked, genuinely curious.

'He's so friendly but I've watched you and you're really reserved with him. He's Thomas's nephew. I thought you'd want to get to know him. He genuinely wants to get to know you.'

'Hmm.' How could Sharmila explain why she was ambivalent towards Lucas when she didn't know the reason herself? 'Lucas is friendly and charming but I can't help remembering that Thomas told me he wanted to retire from the family business but never felt he could because he didn't trust Lucas and Izzy to be able to work together.'

'OK,' Penny said, 'but I don't get what that has to do with your not being friendlier to Lucas.'

'If Thomas didn't trust Lucas enough to retire, then maybe there's something untrustworthy about him.'

'That's probably not what Thomas meant, and anyway that's work. Sharmila, you know I love you, but the way you are with Lucas, I honestly think you're developing an irrational distrust of people. Give people a chance. They're not that bad. At least give Lucas a chance. He's your link to Thomas after all.'

Sharmila briefly squeezed her eyes shut then nodded. Lucas was Thomas's much-loved nephew so on that basis alone she would make an effort to open up to him.

But it wasn't true that she'd developed an irrational distrust. She'd instinctively trusted Thomas, which was unusual for her at the time. And Thomas wasn't the only one.

'I trust Zach,' Sharmila said.

'Zach's not friendly or charming.'

Sharmila laughed. Maybe Zach had been a little gruff and aloof when they first met. But he was kind, going out of his way to help fulfil her wish, and she'd enjoyed spending time with him. She felt she could trust him. Open up to him.

Penny was right. She needed to move on, and she couldn't do that if she distanced herself from every new person she met. She'd become so accustomed to acting that way since Hari passed that it was affecting her life and had almost got in the way of her career.

From the moment she decided to train as a solicitor, working in family law was her goal. Getting a training contract, then a job with one of Birmingham's best family law firms had been a dream come true. And she was good at her job. Singled out early for promotion opportunities.

When Hari died her emotional state was fragile; she couldn't bear having to walk by his desk every day. She also found it harder and harder to deal with divorce matters. Seeing couples arguing over money, or children being used as pawns, was unbearable. She was close to losing her professional objectivity. She was fortunate her boss noticed before it reached the point of no return. The firm offered her a sabbatical, which she spent hiding in a small village and helping her aunt. When she returned to work, she moved to a knowledge-support role rather than a client-facing one.

It had been a difficult time. But she was due to have some fun after the last couple of years; to break out of her shell and live again. And maybe that's what Thomas had in mind too when he drew up the wishes.

Three wishes down, seven more to go, including Thomas's last wish: recreating the final scene of a Christmas movie. She groaned when an image of Zach under the mistletoe popped in her head.

Chapter 11

The next day, Sharmila stood in the kitchen scrolling through dessert recipes as she ate her lunch. The competition entries didn't have to be in until 6 p.m., which gave her six hours to create something worthy of entering.

It was going to be tight.

She already bought the ingredients for a sticky toffee pudding that morning when she stocked up on groceries for the week. But after she got back from the shops, Penny pointed out it wasn't a particularly Christmassy dessert. Rather than choose a different one, Sharmila hoped her internet search would throw up a festive take on the toffee pudding.

There were a couple of possibilities but they all involved getting additional ingredients. She worried her bottom lip. Perhaps she should change her search to look for desserts she could make with the ingredients she already had.

Her heart leapt when she heard the doorbell chime. Penny called out she would answer it, giving Sharmila a few moments to compose herself.

'Hi,' Lucas called as he came into the kitchen and sat on a stool next to the counter.

Sharmila smiled weakly, feeling a little deflated it wasn't Zach.

She hadn't seen him since they'd decorated her tree together, and he never returned to the house after he'd left to speak with Lucas. She'd been looking forward to seeing him again.

Moments later, Penny came into the kitchen followed by Zach. Her heart rate picked back up again.

He looked severe. Something had changed. Was he regretting his kindness with the tree, with offering her a comforting hug? Had Lucas said something to him?

She gave herself a mental shake. What could Lucas have said that would cause Zach to act in such an aloof manner?

'Oh hi, Zach!' Her voice came out in a high-pitched squeak. *Complete fail on the casual greeting there, Sharmila.*

'Zach was helping me out,' Penny said. 'I've had some spotty internet today.'

'There's been some disruption with the infrastructure over the last few days. The weather has probably caused it,' Zach said. 'Hopefully this place is up-to-date but be prepared for power outages. I've already checked outside the house for any problems.'

'As long as it's not today,' Sharmila replied. 'That's the last thing I need.'

Good, they were back to being casual acquaintances, pretending there had been no moment between them after the tree decorating. Perhaps she had read too much into it and it had all been a product of her overactive imagination. She looked at him from the corner of her eyes but he was chatting to Penny as he helped her make coffee for all of them.

'What are you going to make for this dessert competition?' Lucas asked.

'I thought a sticky toffee pudding. It's my … What's the phrase where you're known for cooking something?' Her mind went blank.

'Signature dish,' Zach said.

'That's it,' she replied with a smile, slightly brighter than necessary at the realisation Zach was paying attention to her even though appearances suggested otherwise.

'I need to get back to work. I'll see you guys later,' Penny said, taking her coffee out the room.

'Is sticky toffee pudding an Indian dessert? I've never heard of it before,' Lucas said.

'If you mean is it something people eat in India, then yes. It's not an everyday dessert but it's definitely available.' Not that there were Indian desserts as such, but some common regional dishes. 'If you're asking whether it was invented in India, then it depends on whom you ask. If you ask my dad, it probably was.'

Zach made a sound like he was clearing his throat to cover a laugh while Lucas only looked confused.

'Sorry, it's a running joke in my family,' she explained. 'My dad likes to claim some typically British things were invented by Indians. Don't get him started on how tea was "invented".' She used air quotes.

'Oh, I see,' Lucas said. 'I thought perhaps you were going to make an Indian dessert. I did some research and the closest Asian store is a couple of towns over.'

'Why were you researching that?' Sharmila asked, her eyes wide with surprise, even as she filed away the idea of her needing a specific Asian store for ingredients that were readily available in every food shop where she lived back home near Birmingham.

'I looked it up in case you wanted to eat some Indian food while you were here. The nearest Indian restaurant is there too. I'd be happy to take you if you need to buy ingredients.'

'That's very kind of you, Lucas. But I've never cooked … um … Indian desserts before and this is probably not the occasion to get too experimental.'

'What time does the competition start?' Lucas asked, looking at his phone.

'Entries have to be in by 6 p.m.'

'Then you have plenty of time.'

'I'm going to need every second. I'm not great at baking. Sticky toffee pudding is pretty much my entire repertoire. But I have a trifle in reserve.'

'Trifle. That's very British, isn't it? Can I see?'

'It's in the fridge. I used a cranberry brandy on the sponge to make it more Christmassy.' She licked her lips as she remembered her taste tests. 'The jelly needs a few hours to set before I put the custard layer on top and I think I may put a touch of cinnamon in it to amp up the festiveness.'

'Jelly?' Lucas looked both confused and horrified.

'I mean Jell-O.'

'I want to check the electrics. Is it OK to go down to the basement?' Zach asked, before Lucas could reply.

'Sure.'

'Do you want me to show you where everything is in case there are any problems later?'

She hesitated. 'That's OK. I better get moving with this batter.' Making the sticky toffee pudding was a higher priority than finding ways to make it festive.

Zach nodded, threw Lucas a glance, then went to the basement. He came back just as she was finishing the batter.

'I can't see any problems, but the weather can make it temperamental,' he said. 'You could lose power suddenly.'

'OK. Thanks for checking.'

She looked at the time. She desperately needed to go to the bathroom. Perhaps she should put the batter into the bowls and get them in the oven first. No, that would take too long. She excused herself and left quickly.

When she came back, she found Lucas sitting at the counter but Zach was nowhere to be seen. To hide her disappointment at the thought of Zach leaving without saying goodbye, she concentrated on pouring out her batter then putting the tray of pudding bowls into the oven. She wasn't used to cooking with gas so she crossed her fingers it would work.

While they waited for the pudding to cook, Lucas told her what it had been like working with Thomas. It was strange to hear this version of Thomas – he sounded different from the man she had got to know. Aloof, less open. It was as if they were talking about two people.

Penny came into the kitchen moments before the timer went off, with Zach closely behind. Sharmila didn't like the way her heart leapt at his return. She needed to stop obsessing over him.

'The moment of truth,' Sharmila said as she opened the oven door. Her mouth fell open. The dessert had risen and spread over the whole tray and onto the oven floor. That was not right. How had that happened?

'I take it it's not supposed to look that way,' Lucas said.

She narrowed her eyes. Lucas and Zach were trying really hard not to laugh.

'No, it's not,' she replied in frustration. 'I don't know what went wrong. I followed the recipe perfectly.'

'Perhaps you bought the wrong ingredients,' Penny suggested. 'You said you weren't sure what self-raising flour and bicarb of soda were here.'

'Maybe. But I double-checked. I'm sure I bought the right things.' She pulled her tablet closer to triple-check the ingredients. 'It's not the ingredients. Perhaps I used the wrong quantities.'

'Maybe if you can clean it up a bit more, you can still enter it anyway,' Lucas suggested.

Sharmila put a small spoonful into her mouth then spat it into some kitchen paper. 'This is absolutely disgusting. I can't enter this.'

'You could enter it, Sharms,' Penny said. 'Remember Thomas's wish only said you had to enter the contest. You can do that.'

'There is no way I'm entering this! That would be so embarrassing.' She laughed. 'And I don't want to poison the judges. At least I still have my trifle.' She walked over to the fridge.

The contents of the bowl wobbled wildly as she removed it

109

from the fridge. There was no way the jelly would set in time. If possible, it looked like there was even more liquid than before.

This was going from bad to worse. She was going to have to make another batch of puddings. She glanced at her watch. She still had enough time. But she didn't have enough dates. 'If I'm quick, I can pop to the shops and be back in time to make another batch before the deadline.'

'I'll go shopping with you,' Lucas offered.

'That's kind of you. But it's Saturday. I don't want to make you go food shopping on your weekend.'

Lucas shook his head. 'That's not a problem. I enjoy spending time with you.'

'If you're sure. Let me quickly clean the oven, then we can go.'

'I can clean out the oven for you before I leave,' Zach said.

She looked at him. 'Really?' What a kind offer. 'No, that's too much to ask.'

'You didn't ask. I offered.'

Zach really was the sweetest person – helping her and looking out for her.

'Thank you, then,' she replied. 'I'll just grab my coat and scarf.'

When she came back, she overheard Lucas say, 'You don't need to worry, I'll be fine.'

What a strange thing to say. What did Zach think she was going to do to Lucas? He was being a little overprotective. But she didn't have time to dwell on his behaviour – she needed to concentrate on making her entry.

It was much later than she expected by the time they got back from the shops. Lucas kept showing her American foods he thought she might like. He'd been so friendly and excited about her experiencing 'real America', she didn't have the heart to hurry him along. He dropped her back at Holly House then headed off.

She preheated the oven while she mixed up another batch of sticky toffee pudding. Zach had left the kitchen immaculate, even clearing up her earlier disaster and washing the mini pudding bowls.

She went to her room while she waited for the dessert to bake. There was a romantic comedy she wanted to watch. She still needed to find a Christmas movie to recreate for her last wish – perhaps she should be watching festive films instead. But she had over two weeks until the deadline. In fact, she had until New Year's Day to complete Thomas's Wishlist, so that was one item she could always do back home in England.

After a while, the timer went off. Even as she bent to open the oven door, she knew something was wrong. It was cold.

'Penny,' she called. 'Did something happen to the oven?' She pulled out the partially cooked puddings.

Penny joined her in the kitchen. 'Not that I know of.'

'There's no gas.'

'That's strange.'

'There was when I got back.' Sharmila paused. 'Oh, wait. Zach mentioned there could be some power issues because of the weather.' She tried the taps. Nothing came out. 'Yep. It looks like we've got a problem.' She ran her hand over her face, massaging her temples. The day had been one disaster after another.

'I'll run down to the barn,' Penny said. 'See if there's anything Zach can do.'

She was back a few minutes later. 'Zach's not there. Do you have his mobile number?'

'No, I have Lucas's.'

'Try Lucas. Maybe he knows where Zach is.'

No answer. She left a message. 'I really don't know what to do.' One thing was certain – she couldn't fix this on her own. 'We still have an hour until the entry deadline. That's probably enough time to make another batch of the dessert, but there's still the problem of the oven not working. Perhaps I'll ask Gayle for some advice so I don't muck it up again. And maybe Jackie or someone else from the Women's Club will let me use their oven, if they're not entering this evening.'

She looked up to see Penny staring at her with a huge smile.

111

'What?' Sharmila asked.

'It's nice to see you like this.'

'Like what?'

'Voluntarily reaching out to people, asking for help.'

Sharmila shrugged. 'Everyone here has been so kind to me, helping me out with the party and the parade. Not to mention Julie helping with the Puzzle and Pie Contest last week.' She paused, tilting her head. 'I've really had some bad luck with my wishes so far, haven't I?' She giggled. 'Thank goodness the town, and Zach came to my rescue. And—'

'And what?'

Sharmila shrugged. 'And I don't mind asking for help – it's not like I'm going to see them again after two weeks.'

Penny groaned. 'For a moment I thought you were opening up again.' She shook her head. 'Anyway, no time to spare. Let's go find Gayle and see if she can rescue this dessert disaster.'

Later that evening, Zach and Lucas were playing pool at the local bar and grill again. Pineford didn't offer many options for entertainment venues – the price of living in a small town.

Their efforts to ruin Sharmila's dessert-making had gone better than expected. At one stage he thought they really would end up buying all the flour in Pineford but Izzy proved to be a mastermind in coming up with ideas. Mentioning problems with the utilities due to weather was the perfect excuse to mess with the water, gas, and electricity. While Sharmila was in the washroom, he added extra baking powder to the sticky toffee batter while Lucas added water to the Jell-O in the trifle. Later on, Zach was easily able to stop the gas and water supply from outside the house. And Lucas's natural friendliness made Sharmila's trip to the shops longer than needed, although he suspected Lucas was oblivious to what he was doing.

They were back on track.

After Lucas potted the black ball he gave Zach a broad grin.

'It's almost like old times. If everything goes to plan this evening, are you going to return to San Fran or can you stick around?' Lucas asked, his expression hopeful.

Zach knew Lucas was still conflicted about whether they were doing the right thing by Thomas. Even though there was a part of Lucas that enjoyed making and executing their plans to stop Sharmila, for the most part, Lucas seemed to like the fact they were getting to spend more time together.

Zach missed his cousin and their old easy-going friendship. Being in Pineford was giving them a chance to reconnect. He wasn't ready to give that up yet.

'I think I'll stick around for a while. So far it hasn't been too bad keeping up with work,' he said.

'I wish we could have gone on a proper vacation. Gone away for skiing like we used to.'

'You have to come visit me in London once I'm settled there. We can take trips to Europe.'

'Yes! That would be so much fun,' Lucas agreed enthusiastically. 'You're so lucky your company's expansion is giving you the chance to live in England for a few years. I wish I could travel more. It's been great getting away from Boston and the office for a little while. I wish you'd come back. It hasn't been the same since you left.'

Zach looked down at his hands. He knew Lucas wasn't trying to make him feel guilty about leaving the family business, but he did anyway. 'It hasn't been that bad, has it?' he asked.

'Are you kidding?' Lucas replied. 'Izzy's been impossible.'

Zach listened as Lucas opened up about the problems he was having with the business, how he and Izzy could never agree on the changes they wanted to implement. The situation had become more fraught after Thomas's death because he'd been the majority shareholder and therefore decision-maker. Now Lucas and Izzy had an equal amount of shares.

For a moment, Zach was relieved Thomas hadn't left the

controlling shares to him. He would hate to get in between his cousins.

'You should have said something before. I may have left the business but I'm still part of the family. I'm always here for you. You know that, Luc.' He squeezed his cousin's shoulder.

'I do know. Thanks. Hey, it's almost six. Do you want to go to the dessert contest? See if we're successful?'

They drove back into town where the crowds were already gathering in the town hall. A long table had been set up at the front and entrants were placing their dishes next to a numbered card. The judges were looking at their watches, waiting for the moment the competition would close. There was no sign of Sharmila.

Zach turned to Lucas and gave a brief nod. It looked like their plan worked.

Mayor Jackie cleared her throat at the same time Sharmila came rushing in, holding a dish in oven mittens.

'I'm here. I have my dessert. I'm not too late to enter, am I?' she said in a breathless tumble.

Lucas and Zach exchanged glances. How had she managed to make a dessert? There was no way she could have restarted the gas and water, was there? He wouldn't put it beyond her abilities. She was clearly intelligent and resourceful.

And funny, and witty and pretty. And … He wasn't going to keep thinking about her positive traits.

After Sharmila had completed the entry formalities she came to stand next to them.

'You managed to make your dessert in the end. That's great,' Lucas said. They'd picked up, and ignored, her voicemails earlier.

'Oh yeah. I couldn't believe it when the oven wouldn't work. Luckily I met Gayle yesterday – she runs the local bakery. I asked for help and she offered me the use of her high-speed oven. It's not really meant for noncommercial use, but she was so generous. Just when everything seemed hopeless.'

'That was kind of her,' Lucas agreed.

Sharmila left them to stand among the other entrants.

Zach rubbed his eyes. That was it. Another one of their attempts had been unsuccessful. They were running out of options to stop Sharmila.

Was there even any point? Twice it looked like they'd stopped her, only for the town to step in and help.

How had she managed to get so many people to go out of their way for her in such a short time? She'd only been in Pineford for over a week. Perhaps it was the idea of helping Sharmila experience her first real Christmas and Thomas's Wishlist – whatever the reason, it was going to prove more difficult for them when the town was on her side.

'I guess that's that then. Four wishes done. Maybe it's a sign that we shouldn't be doing this,' Lucas said.

'I don't believe in those kinds of signs.'

They were silent for a moment, watching Sharmila smile at everyone congratulating her, as if she'd won first prize. There was this energy around her this evening he couldn't help being drawn to.

'I was wrong about one thing though,' Lucas said, his focus also on Sharmila.

'What's that?'

'Sharmila's not homely at all. She's beautiful.'

Zach looked sharply at his cousin. It shouldn't come as a surprise Lucas would think that; Zach always thought she was beautiful. But he couldn't explain why his stomach clenched at hearing Lucas's statement. It must be concern that Sharmila was weaving her spell on his cousin. That was the only possible explanation there could be.

Chapter 12

Set-up for the Children's Christmas Carnival was already in full swing by the time Sharmila and Penny arrived at the community hall. The ladies from Pineford Women's Club were all there, with a few others she'd seen in the town but hadn't officially met yet.

Sharmila looked around for Jackie. Unable to find her, she walked to the cookie table while Penny went to join Debby, who was creating an arts-and-crafts area.

'Sharmila, are you free?' Jill called over to her. Before Sharmila had a chance to respond, she continued, 'Perfect. We desperately need some help sorting out Santa's Grotto. We're already behind. Can you help out, please? I'll find other helpers and send them over.'

Jill directed her to Santa's Grotto, which was an office off a corridor at the back of the hall. She'd expected there to be someone to give her instructions but the room was empty apart from a small box of decorations. It didn't seem like it would be enough to create a magical North Pole. Although she could use her initiative to hang the baubles, she didn't want to risk setting it up the wrong way. Pineford, and its Women's Club, had its traditions – they were bound to have specific directions to arrange every decoration.

She walked towards the main hall to find someone who could give her instructions when she noticed Zach approaching her. She smiled tentatively at him.

'Jackie asked me to help with the grotto,' he said, his face expressionless.

Her smile fell at his coldness. Had she upset him somehow? Perhaps something had happened that had put him in a bad mood. Not everything was about her.

'I was about to look for someone to tell me what needs to be done.' She grimaced. 'There are only a few decorations in there. There must be more coming.'

He nodded. 'Apparently the props are on the way. The driver's delayed but he should be here any moment.'

They walked back to the office.

'I guess now we wait,' she said. She looked around at the chairs and tables stacked against the sides of the room. It was difficult to imagine the space as anything other than an office. 'I don't see how a few pieces of scenery are going to be able to disguise this room and make it look like the North Pole. I presume we'll need a chair or stool for Santa.' She tilted her head. 'Do children still sit on his knee, or is that not allowed anymore?'

He shrugged. 'Not sure. It's been a year or two since I paid a visit to Santa.'

She looked up from the decorations. His tone was serious, but a ghost of a smile played on his lips. She smiled back, relieved the tension had eased. 'I bet you loved telling Santa your secret wishes when you were younger.'

'That sounds unlikely for someone you think is a Grinch.' He gave her a pointed glance.

She gave a small nod of acknowledgement. 'Fair point. But it sounds to me like your Grinchification only happened as you got older.'

He frowned but didn't reply. The silence was broken by a knocking on the back door. Zach went to answer it, returning a few moments later followed by a man Sharmila hadn't met previously. Both were carrying boxes of wrapped presents.

'Sorry, sorry,' the man said. 'I was supposed to be here an hour ago, but there was an emergency at home. False labour alarm.'

'That's fine. You're here now. We can get everything set up in no time,' Sharmila replied.

'Here. All the details you need are inside,' he said, handing Sharmila a binder. 'Zach, can you help me bring in a few more things? I've got the walls and the throne in my truck.'

Sharmila moved out of the way as Zach and the man brought more boxes in. She momentarily debated offering to help them but instead read through the pages of instructions. Everything they needed to do was meticulously detailed – it wouldn't take long to construct the area.

As soon as the man put down the final box, he left, apologising that he couldn't stay to help because he had to hurry back to the farm. And she was left alone with Zach again.

'I think I should find Jackie to get more helpers,' she suggested. More people in the room would help dispel this new tension she started to feel in his company. Perhaps not so much tension – more a heightened awareness that was unwelcome rather than uncomfortable.

He held out his hand, so she passed him the binder, careful that their hands didn't touch.

'It doesn't look that complicated,' he said, flipping through. 'The two of us should be able to handle it. I'm sure Jackie will send people down if they're not busy.'

Whether intentionally on his part, definitely on hers, they avoided physical contact with each other as they worked quickly and in harmony – transforming the room from a drab office to a red-and-green Christmas grotto. With the walls and curtains up, all that was left were the tree, lights, and fairy bunting.

They made a good team, although there was no way Sharmila was voicing that thought.

As a finishing touch, she draped a throw across the back of the throne. She looked down at it and gave a quick glance at Zach. He wasn't looking in her direction. Unable to resist the urge, she sat down. The throne swallowed her. She felt tiny – less like Santa and more like one of his helpers. She pushed out her stomach, pulled her chin to her chest, and in her deepest voice, boomed, 'Ho, ho, ho.'

Zach turned from where he was attaching some lights. He laughed. 'I hope you're not going to suggest I sit on your knee.'

Sharmila choked as the image formed in her mind. 'Probably not a good idea. I'm not sure I make a convincing Santa.' She held up her hand. 'No comments about my elf-like qualities, please.' She rose and walked over to put the finishing touches to the tree.

'I bet you also loved visiting Santa when you were young,' Zach said.

'I never did that,' she replied.

He jerked his head back. 'You never visited Santa?'

She shrugged. 'No. I told you, my family didn't celebrate Christmas. I'm not even convinced going to see Santa was a big thing in my town. Maybe nowadays it is but back when I was a little girl, there were a couple of shopping malls that had a Santa, maybe a garden centre, but I never went. It never looked worth the hassle, waiting in line. Then there's the disappointment when you tell Santa your wish and it doesn't come true because your parents don't know what you asked for.'

'I suppose it must be that way for some children. My parents always encouraged me to send a letter to Santa, following my visit to see him, which they would post, of course.'

'Oh, that's clever of them. It sounds like you had loads of lovely Christmas traditions,' she said, a little wistfully.

'I guess.' He was quiet, a small frown forming. 'It was a long time ago. I'm surprised Thomas didn't put a visit to Santa on your wish list.'

She burst out laughing. 'Can you imagine! Thankfully, Thomas had the good sense to realise I would never sit on the knee of some strange man just because he's wearing a Santa suit! That would end the challenge immediately.'

'Challenge?'

Sharmila pressed her lips together. That was too close. She couldn't risk letting someone know about the charity donation, even if she trusted Zach not to tell the lawyer or anyone else. She was going to stick to the strict terms Thomas had set. She shook her head. 'I meant the challenge of finishing the items on my list.'

He stood watching her for a few moments. She'd piqued his curiosity, she could tell. She'd have to be more careful in future.

Why was she so comfortable talking to Zach when she tried to avoid opening up to others? It couldn't only be because of his handsome face – she wasn't that shallow. Was she?

She took a step back to survey the room. 'Well, I think we're almost done.' She frowned, looking in boxes and bags. 'Where are the presents?'

Zach pointed to the fake gift-wrapped boxes by the throne.

'No, I mean the real presents. Don't the children who visit Santa get presents from him?'

Zach grabbed the binder and turned the pages. 'They get a sweet and a token, which they take to a stall.' He shut the binder. 'That's a good plan, prevents long lines. This whole enterprise is meticulous.'

'It is,' she agreed. 'Although with the Women's Club in charge, I'm not at all surprised. I was blown away when I saw all the events they have planned for the Pineford WinterFest. Thomas told me about various activities he used to take part in when he was younger, but he never said it was part of an annual festival.'

'My mother never mentioned it either. I guess the festival idea is fairly recent.'

'Oh, I forgot your mother grew up here. Have you been able to check out places she used to visit? What's that been like? Has she been back to visit recently?'

'That's a lot of questions.' He stiffened, then walked over to put his jacket on.

Sharmila's lips turned down. And apparently, he wasn't going to answer any of them. She was getting whiplash from all his abrupt mood changes. 'Oh sorry.' She looked round. 'Everything in here looks good. I'm going to make sure the presents have been set up and everything is sorted.'

'I'm sure Jackie has it under control.'

'I know. I just want to make sure. Don't want to ruin any kid's enjoyment.' She laughed. 'I read somewhere Christmas isn't Christmas without any presents. That there's something special about presents on Christmas Day.' She was quiet for a moment. 'Is that true?'

'What?'

'Is opening presents on Christmas Day different from opening presents on your birthday?'

He looked at her intently for a few moments. In a kind voice he replied, 'I don't think there's a difference. And people around the world open their Christmas presents on different dates. Not everyone opens them on December 25.'

She gave him a sweet smile, touched by his attempt to reassure her she hadn't missed out by not having Christmas presents. It was very kind, but unnecessary.

'I'm going to leave before Jackie ropes me into being one of Santa's helpers,' he said abruptly.

'You're not staying around for the fair?'

'It's for families, not me. I only came this morning because someone asked if I was free to help with set-up. But I've now promised Karl, the man who delivered the stuff, I would help him over at his farm with things for the parade when I was finished.'

She nodded. She wasn't going to spend any more time thinking about Zach and his hot-cold personality or his musky cologne or his broad shoulders or his deep green eyes.

Stifling a small internal scream, she went back into the hall to check the presents table was set up. She wouldn't stay around once the event started. Even in the short time she'd been in the main hall, people kept coming to her asking questions, especially about Thomas's Wishlist, and she didn't want to spend her afternoon fielding even more.

After Jackie released her from any further duties, Sharmila went looking for Penny. Her jaw clenched when she saw her talking to Zach. Had he left and returned or was his comment about helping Karl an excuse to avoid talking to her?

She debated waiting until Zach moved away from Penny, but the crowds were already starting to come through the doors and she wanted to leave as soon as possible. Taking a deep breath, she went over to ask for the car keys.

'Oh, Zach, you said you were leaving. Why don't you take Sharmila?' Penny suggested with no attempt at subtlety.

'I was heading to Branley Farm,' he replied. He paused a few moments – Sharmila waited for his refusal. 'Holly House is on the way. I can drop you off if you're ready to leave now.'

She nodded and followed him out, turning quickly to cast dark looks at Penny, who only grinned and gave her a cheeky wave in return. Penny would make a great wing-woman. Only, Sharmila had no need of one.

'Are you cold?' Zach asked, glancing over at Sharmila as she wrapped her arms round herself. 'I can turn the heating up.' He reached out to fiddle with the buttons on the truck's dashboard.

'I'm fine, thanks.' Her smile was quick and forced.

He frowned. She was withdrawn. Something had happened between the time they set up the grotto and leaving the fair for her to close in on herself. Or maybe he was reading too much into her actions. He didn't know her well enough to interpret them.

'You didn't want to stay at the fair?'

'No.'

'It wasn't on Thomas's list?'

'No. Like you said, it's for kids.'

'I guess you have Christmas fairs in England?'

He couldn't explain why he was trying to engage her in conversation. Usually driving in silence would be perfect. He was trying to find out what was on the list, he told himself. That was the reason for all the questions. They still didn't know any more items.

'We have fairs,' she replied. He caught her glance before she turned back to stare out the side window. 'Nothing like the Pineford one, I don't think. To be honest, I've only been to the fairs at my nieces' school. They're not on the same scale.'

'Did you have a chance to check out any of the stalls before we left?'

She shook her head.

He concentrated on the road but sensed her looking at him. Even though they didn't know each other that well, he could guarantee she was weighing up whether to tell him something. Why he was so sure wasn't something he wanted to explore.

'I don't really like having all that attention on me,' she said in a haltering way. 'It gets a bit much.'

'What?' He laughed in disbelief. 'I constantly see you with groups of people.'

She inclined her head. 'I know. After the tree lighting, when Jackie told Pineford about my list, lots of people became really interested in me. I think Thomas deliberately chose activities where I would have to engage with the town.'

'Why would he do that?' The Thomas he knew wasn't a cruel man, and the list so far was full of light-hearted activities Sharmila could easily do. Too easily. It was proving to be difficult for them to obstruct her.

'I guess he really loves Pineford,' she replied with a shrug.

There was more to it than that. He waited for her to continue, but she remained silent. There was no point pushing it. He was right, though. Sharmila Mitra did have secrets.

He pulled into the driveway of Holly House and turned off

his engine. 'I'm heading over to Karl's farm now. I offered to help him look over and repair some of the props for the parade while he's working on the farm. If you don't have anything planned you could come with.'

'Really? I can?' Her smile pierced through him, filling him with warmth.

'Of course. Karl will be grateful for the extra pair of hands.'

'OK. What's the farm like? Is it like lots of arable fields with vegetables and crops, or does it have cows? Is it like a ranch with horses or is that only in Texas?'

'Whoa, so many questions,' he said, putting his hands up. 'You're going to see it all in a few minutes.'

Sharmila's smile fell, and the winter sunshine was a little less bright. He bit his lip. He was developing a habit of stamping on her joy. 'Why don't we keep it as a surprise.'

She gave him a tight smile. 'Is it OK if I get changed quickly?'

He shrugged. Her tight jeans and figure-hugging sweater looked perfect to him. 'If you're quick.'

'I'll be back in a flash,' she replied, opening the door to jump out of the truck as she spoke.

He was unnecessarily checking his tools when she returned less than ten minutes later. She was wearing a large winter coat and rain boots, both of which would be more suitable for outdoor work than what she'd had on previously. She threw a large bag into the back of the truck.

He raised an eyebrow. 'Are you planning to move in?' he asked as he started the engine.

She snorted then gave an embarrassed shrug. 'I didn't know if we would be working outside, so I brought some waterproofs with me. I don't like my jeans getting too wet and if we're lucky it might start to snow. Also, I didn't know if we would be going into their house, so I brought a change of shoes.'

He cocked his head. When he offered to take her to the farm, he hadn't expected her to help him out physically but to stay indoors

124

with Karl's wife, Chloe. But by the looks of things, Sharmila was planning to work with him.

If Annette had been in this situation, she would have no doubt reluctantly agreed to come with him to the farm, but expect to spend the whole time indoors with Karl and Chloe waiting on her. He mentally cursed himself for comparing the two. Sharmila wasn't Annette. Of course, she wasn't going to act in the same way.

That didn't mean she hadn't taken advantage of Thomas – a sick, dying man.

Annette had never been able to fool Thomas. Thomas had even warned Zach about her on several occasions, warnings Zach had ignored at the time. Yet somehow Sharmila had managed to convince Thomas to give her not only an all-expenses-paid holiday but also potentially leave her a considerable legacy.

If, as they suspected, Sharmila had developed a friendship with Thomas to benefit from his wealth, wouldn't there be some signs? So far, Sharmila had done nothing to suggest she was expecting anything other than the holiday. Apart from her mention of a challenge. He didn't get the feeling she was planning to stay in the house after Christmas – Izzy was wrong about that.

But it was still good that he was the one spending time with Sharmila rather than Lucas. Sharmila would have wound Lucas round her finger in moments. Even Zach had to remind himself she wasn't merely a beautiful woman he happened to meet on holiday. He was here for a reason. Instead, he was helping her out, giving her the benefit of the doubt, falling for her sob stories. At the fair, he'd even thought of ways he could arrange for her to visit Santa.

It didn't take long to arrive at the farm. Karl had already told him which barn the parade props would be in, but Zach took Sharmila to the farm shop first where he knew Chloe was working.

After brief introductions, he offered Sharmila a chance to stay with Chloe, hoping she would take Chloe up on it and it would create some well-needed distance between them.

Sharmila offered to help Chloe, who was closing up the shop, carry things into her home before joining Zach. Zach hoped once she got inside, she'd find an excuse to stay in the warmth rather than help him in a dusty, cold barn.

In the barn, he removed the covers from the floats and pieces of scenery. Most things were in good shape – it wouldn't take him long to make the repairs. Then he would clean everything, so it was ready for the parade. He made a mental note of the order he would tackle things as he opened his toolbox.

'Oh wow,' a reverential voice behind him spoke.

He turned then watched as Sharmila walked slowly into the barn, moving between the scenery, running her hand along the pieces.

'This is wonderful,' she said, turning to him, her eyes wide and glowing. 'I should have known Pineford's parade would be spectacular. We had parades in my town – but not like this.' She scrunched her nose. 'I feel like I say that a lot. Not like back home. Not when I was growing up. Not in my family. It's hard not to compare though.'

'What were your town's parades like?' he asked.

'Pretty much a Santa on a lorry.' She giggled. 'I'm exaggerating, there was a little more to it than that. It was organised by a small charity rather than the town itself. They didn't spend money getting floats like these. It was mostly local Brownie and Scout groups with Santa.'

He realised he enjoyed listening to her stories and wanted to encourage her to continue. But he couldn't risk falling deeper under her spell.

'Are you sure you don't want to go back inside with Chloe?' he asked, turning away from her, scrambling to think of a good reason for her to leave. 'It could get messy and I don't want you to ruin your clothes.'

'No, I'm OK. And it doesn't matter if these clothes get dirty.'

He shrugged. She would probably only last twenty minutes

max anyway, before making her excuses. 'There's a bucket by the side. If you start on washing down the undamaged pieces, that would be a help.'

'Sure,' she said.

She carried the bucket to a float with scenery designed to look like a snow parade with an ice palace. She grimaced then looked around the barn.

'What's wrong?' he asked.

'Loads of cobwebs.'

'Is that a problem?'

She gave him a puzzled look. 'No. I was looking for a stick or even better a large duster. If I wash these down without getting rid of the cobwebs first, the cloth will be useless quickly.'

'You could ask Chloe for a duster, or there are some sticks outside one of the barns. I can get them.'

'That's OK,' she said. 'I'll be back in a sec.'

After a few minutes, Zach paused to watch Sharmila as she wiped away cobwebs and washed down the props. She was happy in her own world, humming and whistling to herself. Even though she was in constant motion, there was something restful about her. He could watch her all day.

After she finished, she helped him with the repairs. He had to concede Sharmila made an excellent helper, carrying out his instructions without complaint and showing genuine interest in learning what he was doing. He placed the final repaired piece on the floor, then straightened, stretching out his back. He may have chosen a career in front of computers, but his first love was using his hands – building, constructing, repairing.

'Are we done then?' Sharmila asked as they left the barn.

Locks of hair had escaped her ponytail early on in their work. Strands now strayed across her cheeks, red from the cold and exertion, but there was no hiding the light of joy in her eyes. The total picture of her slight figure framed against the darkening winter sky and the mountains behind her took his breath away.

He cleared his throat and purposefully turned away from her. 'We're done here. You did a good job.'

She laughed. 'Thank you. Perhaps you should hire me on your crew.'

'Let's see how you do with our next job first.'

'OK,' she replied, rubbing her hands with eagerness. 'What is it?'

'We have to muck out the stalls in the barn. Where the cows are.' He watched with a small smile as her mouth formed a perfect O. 'Is something wrong?'

She shook her head. 'No, I was thinking I should probably change into my waterproofs if we're going to be mucking out.'

He wasn't expecting that response. 'We don't really have to clean out the barn,' he said.

She gave him a puzzled look. 'You made a joke?' She sounded stunned. Did he give her the impression he was humourless?

He shrugged. 'Yes, we're finished here. We can head back.' They started walking back to the farmhouse to return the keys.

Seeing this side of her made it harder to shake the idea if things had been different, they would have got on well together, and perhaps he would have explored the attraction simmering between them.

He needed to speak to Lucas. Fast. They had to make more effort to stop her from completing Thomas's list, not only for his family's sake but for his own sake too.

Chapter 13

'What do you mean there was a sign-up sheet?'

Penny's incredulity would have made Sharmila laugh but the disappointment from realising she'd already failed and was going to lose the charity donation was too overwhelming.

'Exactly what I said. We were supposed to sign up on this list if we wanted to enter the competition. I thought it was one Mr Bell had pre-registered for us online. I didn't know it was first come first served. I should have checked the instructions properly.'

She'd been looking forward to this ever since the snow started falling in earnest the evening before. All week, there had been small flurries but nothing heavy enough to settle. Despite reassurances from the Women's Club, she began to doubt there would be enough snow to hold the competition.

When she woke up that morning, the light coming through her bedroom window was brighter, sharper than usual. She guessed immediately it had snowed during the night. Looking out her window, the garden was blanketed in pristine white, stretching out as far as the frozen lake. Like a scene from one of her Christmas movies. Only this was real.

She rushed to pull on some warm clothes, then ran into the garden. The snow reached almost to her knees. Without thinking about it, she fell forward, certain the snow was soft enough to protect her but firm enough to support her. Then she ran, or dragged her legs, from the patio to the Japanese bridge and back for no reason other than to feel the snow move. The temptation to build a snowman had been strong – she'd resisted because of the competition. Now, it looked like she wasn't going to be able to enter it.

Even though it was still early on a Monday morning, the garden square was full of spectators. Spread out round the gazebo were fifteen stakes in the snow marking out the competitors' areas. Each stake had a couple standing next to it.

Penny looked around at the participants. 'Perhaps Lucas or Zach will step out and let us take their place.'

'No, that's OK,' Sharmila said, waving her hands. 'I don't want to bother them.'

'I'm sure they won't mind,' Penny replied, starting to move towards them.

'No!' Sharmila reached out to grab Penny's arm and bring her back.

'Sharmila, what's going on? Why won't you ask Lucas? I thought you were warming up to him after he helped you with the shopping on Saturday.'

Sharmila looked across to where Lucas and Zach were standing. She'd seen from the entry sheet that Lucas had taken the last slot. He'd signed himself and Zach up even though he knew this activity was on Thomas's Wishlist. Lucas could have asked her to be his partner if he really wanted to be in the competition – Zach didn't strike her as the type to want to build a snowman. There had to be a reason for them both to enter. But she couldn't make sense of it and until she could, it was better to keep her distance.

She looked at the other competitors. She didn't recognise any of them. Besides, she wouldn't have felt right asking them to give up their spot for her.

'Maybe it doesn't have to be Pineford's competition,' she said.

'Let me check. If it can be any snowman contest, then there's sure to be one somewhere nearby and I'll camp out overnight to take part if needed.'

Penny nodded, hopefully convinced by the optimism in her voice. She read her list. Unless there was another competition called 'Snowdreams' somewhere else, Thomas wanted her to take part in the Pineford one. She would probably have to bite the bullet and speak to Lucas.

'Good morning, Sharmila, Penny,' Mayor Jackie greeted them. 'Why are you standing over here? Shouldn't you be taking part today?'

'Unfortunately, I was too late to enter.' Sharmila grimaced.

'Is this one of Thomas's wishes?'

She nodded. 'But there's nothing I can do. I should have got here earlier.'

'Oh, we can't have this! You have to take part. Don't worry. I'm going to take care of this.' Jackie strode to the gazebo and spoke to the judges. She grabbed the clipboard holding the entry sheet and wrote something down on it. While one of the judges walked out of the gazebo, Jackie clapped her hands.

'Attention, everyone. Welcome to Pineford's thirtieth annual Snowdreams competition. Usually, fifteen pairs take part, but we have more than enough space and more than enough snow so I'm extending the participant list to twenty pairs. Sharmila and Penny have already signed up so if there is anyone else who wants to join, now's your chance.'

Sharmila turned to Penny, stunned at how quickly and efficiently Jackie arranged things. 'That woman is a force to be reckoned with. She's wasted in small-town politics.'

'Thank goodness she's on your side. I would hate to get on the wrong side of her.'

Sharmila smiled in agreement as they moved to one of the hastily added extra stakes.

She listened to the judges as they went through the rules. So many rules around building a snowman. Luckily they only had to enter, not win.

'OK,' Penny said, getting her tablet and digital pencil out of her bag, 'I'll draw up our design for the tableau. Do you have any ideas for a theme?'

'What are you talking about Penny?'

'Debby sent me some photos of previous winners.'

Sharmila looked over Penny's arm as she flipped through some of the photos. There was a snowman doing a headstand, one sitting cross-legged on a bench reading a paper, snow animals, snow superheroes, and snow Easter Island statues.

Her mouth fell open. 'Oh my goodness, they take this so seriously. I was thinking we'd make a basic snowman with a hat, scarf, and carrot nose. Maybe some sticks for arms.'

'Come on, Sharms! We need to put some effort into it.'

Sharmila was torn. She didn't want to dilute her friend's excitement, but unlike Penny, artistic work was not a strength. After the disappointment this morning she was relieved they were in the competition at all. Two piles of snow plonked on top of each other was enough for her. For Penny, she would compromise, a little.

'Can we keep it somewhat simple please?' Sharmila begged. 'I'm not going to be much help with the detail. I can roll lumps of snow into a ball, but that's about it.'

'We'll never win with that attitude!'

'I was going for a participation certificate.'

Penny huffed and walked away. Sharmila tried to see where she was going but lost track quickly as she went behind the crowds. Now, what was she supposed to do? She couldn't be in the competition without a partner.

Moments later Jackie came up to her with Zach close behind.

'What's going on?' Sharmila asked, looking from Zach to Jackie.

'I overheard Penny begging Lucas to let her be part of his team,' Jackie said. 'She said she didn't think you'd make it through the day alive if she had to be your partner.'

'Apparently, Penny thinks Lucas has a competitive spirit, which neither of us have,' Zach added with a shrug.

'Doesn't it make much more sense for you to swap teams?' Jackie patted her shoulder then walked off.

Sharmila looked over to where Lucas was standing. Penny was next to him with a smug look on her face. Penny gave her a thumbs-up before turning back to Lucas, drawing his attention to her tablet.

'I guess we're partners,' she said, looking up at Zach.

'Seems that way.'

'Well, don't sound too thrilled.'

'I wasn't planning on spending my day making a snowman.'

Then why had he and Lucas entered in the first place?

'If we just keep to the basics, then it's not going to take us long,' Sharmila said. 'I bet we could be done in under an hour. I'll make the head and you can start on the body. I'll help you when I'm done.'

'Shouldn't we start with the base?'

'What base?' she asked, her brow furrowing.

'The bottom of the snowman. Even if we're making a basic snowman, it should have a head, body, and legs or base. Three balls.'

'No, snowmen have heads and bodies. Two balls. That's all.'

He made a choking sound. 'I can't tell if you're joking.'

'I can't tell if you are! I know I haven't made many snowmen in my life but they only have a head and body.' She folded her arms when he pulled out his mobile.

'That's interesting,' he said, after doing a search. 'Did you know there's a difference between British and American snowmen?' He handed her his phone to read the article he'd found. 'On this occasion, I think we should go with your version. Takes less time.'

'I like the way you think, Zach Lawrence.' She reached out to return his phone and their fingers brushed, tingles shooting up her arm. She pulled on her gloves. There was no way that could happen again now.

While Zach was patting the body into a stable shape, he asked, 'What's the story behind the snowman?'

'Pardon?'

'Why did Thomas choose it as a wish? Didn't your family make snowmen when you were younger?'

Sharmila looked up from forming the head. 'No, unfortunately, my family were too poor to have snow.'

He opened his mouth but didn't say anything, as if he didn't know how to respond to that. Sharmila tried hard to keep a serious face but a giggle escaped her. Zach laughed along with her, which warmed Sharmila more than the cup of cocoa all participants were given at the start of the competition.

'No particular reason then?' he asked.

'No. Not every activity Thomas gave me has a deeper meaning to it. A lot of them were things that came up in the movies. I mean, don't get me wrong, we never entered any snowman competitions like this,' she said, gesturing around at the other entries. 'But I don't know whether that's because my family weren't interested or because England doesn't bother with it as much as America does. I will say, though, that you have a different kind of snow here.'

He smiled slowly. 'A different kind? This time I know you're joking. Snow is snow.'

'I'm not joking. Don't you think there are different kinds of snow?'

'I think there are different stages of snow – any skier knows that.'

'And you don't have much snow in San Francisco.' She knelt back ignoring the damp seeping through her jeans. 'My dad told me one winter there was chaos on the railways and the excuse given was it was the wrong kind of snow. Now I don't know what the right kind of snow is for railways but there is definitely the right kind of snow for building snowmen, and Pineford has the right kind.'

'The snow here is the same as the snow where I grew up.'

She smirked. 'If you say so. But you mentioned skiing. My mum went to school in Shimla. She skied a lot there and she was always complaining about the snow in England not being good enough.'

'Where's Shimla?'

'North India.'

'Is that where your parents come from?'

'Nope. My parents come from West Bengal. My mother went to boarding school in Shimla.' She concentrated on forming her part of the snowman, her cheeks warmed knowing he was staring at her. She finished the head and was about to help him finish the body when she took a step back. She didn't want to risk unwanted hand contact even with gloves for protection.

'We should probably get some carrots and buttons or something.' She shook her head in disbelief as she surveyed the intense concentration and determination of the other competitors. 'I don't think anyone here is going to help us out. Maybe I'll ask in the diner. I'll collect some twigs as well if I find any.'

'No hurry,' Zach said, giving a few final pats to the body. 'We've still got a few hours before the competition ends. But I think we're almost done.' He stood up to position the head.

Sharmila laughed. 'This is the most pathetic snowman I've ever seen.'

Zach stood back. 'It really is. It doesn't look right with only two parts. I think we need to create the third.'

'Are you serious?'

He lifted his shoulders. 'Even I'm embarrassed by this effort. Come on, we've got plenty of time.' He held out his hand to her. With a furrowed forehead she cautiously put her hand in his, realising immediately the gloves offered no protection at all from the heat of his touch.

'OK. I guess,' she said slowly.

'Great. I'll make the middle while you reform the base to be legs.' He grinned, displaying all his teeth, his eyes crinkling. Her heart performed a little flip-flop.

Was he actually enjoying the activity?

While working on the base, she couldn't help stealing looks at Zach as he bent to roll the snowball. His jeans were doing an excellent job of emphasising his pert behind. No matter what her brain said, her body was reacting to Zach. There wasn't anything she could do about it so instead of fighting it, she would accept her reaction to him. It's not as if she had any intention of acting on a physical attraction.

She chewed the inside of her cheek. The problem was, she didn't think the attraction was only physical.

Zach turned off the engine outside Holly House waiting for Sharmila to gather her things.

'I can't believe she forgot me,' she said.

He let out a snort, which he hurriedly tried to cover with a cough when he saw the same stunned expression Sharmila had on her face ever since she realised Penny had driven off after the competition.

He got down and walked round to help her off his truck, regretting that impulse almost instantly. To lift her down, his hands spanned her waist, fitting perfectly. He removed his hands as soon as her feet touched the ground, keeping the contact so brief he would only get the lightest imprint of how good she felt in them.

Shaking his head to clear the unwelcome thoughts, he said, 'They were too busy arguing to remember they didn't drive down together.'

She held up her hands in a gesture of helplessness. 'It's, it's unbelievable. She forgot me!' Her voice rose from the incredulity.

He tried to maintain a straight face, but her wide eyes and fish-out-of-water mouth was so comical he couldn't control his burst of laughter. She stared at him for a few seconds, her eyes growing bigger. She swatted him harmlessly, then her face creased and she threw her head back, joining him in the laughter.

He managed to gasp out, 'You'd better hide your prize before they get here.'

'They're never going to forgive us for that.'

'It's not our fault. We weren't trying to win the prize for the most unusual tableau.'

'To be honest, I don't even think that's a real prize. I think the judges made it up because they felt sorry for us.'

'Sorry for you, you mean,' he said.

'No, I'm pretty sure they felt sorry for you too.'

She looked up from fiddling with her gloves, their gazes locked, and he lost track of time. She gave a nervous giggle and moved away.

'Thank goodness you drove Lucas down,' she said. 'Otherwise I'd be trekking on foot and who knows how long it would have taken me to get back.'

'I'm sure someone in Pineford would have driven you back. They all seem to like you. You're a hit with this place.'

'How would you know?' she asked, a challenge in her tone.

He closed his eyes briefly. He didn't want her to know he'd been observing her the whole time.

Although participating in a snowman competition was one of the last things Zach wanted to do that day, Izzy's suggestion they sign up and take the last remaining spot sounded simple enough. They didn't think the Mayor would decide she was going to bend the rules for Sharmila.

He and Sharmila had finished making their first snowman before any of the other competitors. He had the chance to walk away there and then. Instead, he suggested they make another smaller snowman, then another, then another, and finally a tiny one that resembled a bowling pin, until they ended up with a set of Matryoshka snowmen. They decided not to dress their creations, which gave them some free time until the end of the competition.

With less than an hour left to go, he went to speak with some of the men from the bar rather than drive home. But he was always aware of where she was, noticing how she would keep a safe distance from the others, never spending too long with the same people. Almost as if she was putting up a barrier.

She cleared her throat, bringing his attention back to her, and looked at him expectantly.

'The Mayor changed the competition rules for you,' he said.

'Oh that. Jackie is probably more excited about Thomas's list than I am.' She started walking to the door.

'You're not excited about your list?'

'No, of course I am. It's just …'

'It's just what?'

She shook her head. 'Nothing. It's nothing.'

He opened his mouth, about to ask her to explain, when Penny's car pulled onto the driveway.

'Thanks for forgetting me,' Sharmila called out as Penny and Lucas got out of the car.

'It's your fault,' Penny replied.

'My fault? How is it my fault?'

'Pretending you weren't interested in the competition but secretly plotting how you were going to win.'

'Hey, maybe if you and Lucas had spent less time talking about design and more time in construction you would have had a better chance—'

Sharmila stopped in her tracks as a snowball slid down her clothes. Zach snorted. Had Lucas thrown that? He turned to his cousin, who was laughing.

'It was the only way to stop these two bickering,' Lucas said, with his hands raised in defence.

Sharmila was already gathering snow into a ball, which she then threw in Penny's direction. She covered her mouth when her aim failed, hitting Lucas firmly in the back.

'Oh, it's war, Miss Mitra,' Penny called out. Her retaliatory throw struck Zach as Sharmila ran behind him using him as a shield.

What were they playing at? They were all adults. He was thirty-five. He was not getting involved in a snowball fight.

As he turned to see what she was doing, more snowballs hit him in quick succession. 'What the—' he said, catching Lucas laughing at him. He narrowed his eyes.

'Hey, make your own,' Sharmila protested when he picked up some of the ammunition she'd been forming.

'Oh no, you're not going to use me as your defensive wall. It's time to attack.' He flung a small ball in Lucas's direction. 'Direct hit.'

If his business partners could see him now – doing a victory dance to celebrate a snowball hit, having a snowball fight in the first place – they would never believe it. But he was letting loose and having fun for the first time in years.

Maybe it was being around Sharmila. Maybe it was simply that he was on vacation in the snow, bringing back fond memories of his childhood, which he no longer wanted to push away.

He shivered when snow trickled down his neck. His fault for not paying attention. He turned around and took a closer look at Sharmila, who was biting her lip while trying to act innocent. He grabbed a lump of snow but instead of throwing it, he ran towards her.

She yelped and ran to the back patio, hiding behind the pizza oven.

'Don't think you're safe there. I will get you back for that.' A few balls were lobbed in his direction, but he sidestepped them neatly, while slowly gathering more snow and advancing towards her.

He could tell she was sizing up the distance between her location and the protection of the oaks. As she set off, he ran, catching her easily. She twisted to avoid the snowball, bringing them both toppling to the ground. They both laughed as the wind was knocked out of them.

Raising himself slightly, he looked down at her. Still laughing, her fresh face was ruddy, her warm brown eyes huge. He carefully brushed a snowflake off her cheek. Her breathing went shallow. His gaze focused in on her mouth. She swallowed then licked her lips.

He slowly bent towards her.

Chapter 14

Strong smells of meat and spices filled the air as the contestants bustled around putting the final touches to their entries for the Chilli Cook-Off that Tuesday evening. Sharmila caught the hopeful glances some of the contestants threw in her direction. Thank goodness she would be making her decision blind – the one good thing about being roped in as a guest judge.

Mayor Jackie was determined to involve her in all of the Pineford WinterFest events. She'd clearly appointed herself Thomas's helper in giving Sharmila a Christmas to remember. Although Sharmila had resisted on several occasions, she finally agreed to judge one of the WinterFest contests.

Her tolerance of alcohol was at the bottom of the staying-sober scale, which automatically excluded her from judging the hot toddy drinks competition. Judging the ice sculpting competition would have been safer on her taste buds and digestive system, but unfortunately for her, that was left to professionals. She would have gladly judged the Gingerbread House Competition, but since it was on Thomas's Wishlist, that wasn't an option. Which left her with the Chilli Cook-Off.

Penny nudged her. 'Your fellow judge has arrived.'

Sharmila furrowed her brow as Lucas walked towards them.

Penny told her he'd volunteered to be an additional judge after discovering she was also on the panel. She still didn't understand why Lucas had entered the snowman competition but, Penny was right, she had to stop seeing shenanigans where there weren't any.

At least Zach wasn't with him. She hadn't seen Zach since he ran from her after the snowball fight. She'd relived that moment often though – both of them falling over, the way he gently rubbed his thumb across her face, her pounding heart that had nothing to do with their recent run, all her attention focused in on his lips as they moved closer to hers. Then he had leapt away.

Was he about to kiss her or had that only been in her imagination? Had she invited a kiss? She wasn't ready to face those questions yet.

'Hi, Lucas,' she greeted warmly, determined not to think about Zach for the rest of the evening.

'Evening, ladies,' he said, rubbing his hands together. 'This is going to be fun. I've barely eaten all day waiting for this.'

'That was probably a good idea,' Sharmila replied. 'I wish I'd done that. I'm worried I'll like one dish so much I'll keep eating it and then I'll be so full I won't be able to judge the rest.'

Lucas threw his head back and laughed. A complete overreaction to her feeble joke. He was trying too hard. Or was she being unnecessarily critical? He was Thomas's nephew and Thomas spoke about him affectionately despite his frustration about not feeling able to retire.

As they walked together towards the judging area she overheard, 'It's not right that she's judging. We don't even know if she eats this kind of food. They eat curry, not chilli, where she comes from.'

Sharmila's shoulders sank as she recognised Angie's voice. It didn't come as a surprise she had some grievances about a certain guest judge.

Penny's eyes widened. She stepped forward, about to say

something. Sharmila put a restraining hand out, giving Penny a slight shake of the head.

'Good evening, Angie,' Sharmila said. 'Are you entering the contest today?'

'Oh, Sharmila,' Angie said. 'I'm glad I caught you before it starts. Don't you worry. I'm going to let Jackie know you won't be able to judge the chilli contest. I know how hard it is to say no to Jackie but don't worry, she'll listen to me.'

'Sorry, what?'

'Poor thing,' Angie said with false sincerity. 'Chilli is made from meat here and I know that will be a problem for you.'

Sharmila narrowed her eyes. 'Why?'

'I know your people don't eat meat and most of the chillies here will be made from beef. We shouldn't have put you in this situation, but I can sort it out.'

Sharmila took a couple of calming breaths. 'Thanks for your concern, but I'll be fine.'

'Now, you don't have to feel embarrassed. Everyone will understand that you can't be a judge because of your religion.'

'Well, that's very kind of you, Angie. And you're right, there are many Hindus who are vegetarian either for religious or personal reasons. And the cow is a sacred symbol. If you're interested in finding out more, I would be happy to tell you about it another time. But like any other religion or group, we don't all share the same customs and traditions. My family have always eaten meat, and we've always eaten beef. Believe me, I've had many excellent chilli con carnes in my life. It was a staple when I was at university. I pretty much lived on that and spaghetti bolognese.' She gave Angie the biggest smile. 'And on that note, it looks like they're ready for me. I'd better take my spot.' She reached out and patted Angie's arm.

'That woman!' Penny exclaimed as they moved away. 'Who does she think she is? I can't believe you handled it so calmly.'

'She was a bit rude,' was the only observation Lucas made.

Sharmila shrugged. 'Most people don't mean any harm when they make assumptions about different cultures.' She glanced back at Angie. 'I'm not convinced there wasn't any malice behind her comments though.'

The movies she loved always depicted small towns as having welcoming communities. For the most part, Sharmila had experienced nothing but warmth and kindness from the people she'd met in Pineford – but there were some who treated her with suspicion or kept her at a distance. It didn't bother Sharmila – it was something she'd experienced many times before and she would experience it again in the future.

But it was people like Angie who were the most draining to deal with, the ones who sounded so friendly and helpful but who were really making a point of highlighting differences.

'It's a shame the competition is judged blindly and you won't know if Angie's entered – I wouldn't put it past her to add some bodily fluids to the dish.'

'Ew, Penny. Now I'm not going to get that image out of my mind. Right before I'm about to sample anonymous bowls of food. Thank you!'

Penny grinned in response. 'You're welcome, pet. I'll catch up with you after you've crowned the winner.'

Sharmila and Lucas joined Jackie and their fellow judge, who owned a restaurant at the edge of town. Jackie handed them each a clipboard with a marking sheet. Sharmila gave it a quick glance – marks for presentation, aroma, consistency, taste, and aftertaste. With bonus points for inventiveness.

Inventiveness? What had she let herself in for?

The entries were laid out on a long table, each one with three small portions. There wasn't any rice or tortilla wraps. It was going to be mouthfuls of pure chilli. At least there were jugs of milk and water available.

When she noticed Zach had joined the milling crowd, her body automatically reacted to his physical presence – she was working

144

hard to get that under control. *Remember you are not going to spend any more time thinking about the contradictory man.*

She'd seen him on the property a couple of times earlier that day, but he barely acknowledged her. He was making it very clear he had no interest in discussing what happened between them during their snowball fight the day before. She must have imagined there was a mutual attraction. Hallucinated their almost kiss.

It was for the best. Thomas may have given her a Christmas experience straight out of a film, but she still had no wish to add a holiday romance.

Jackie called her and Lucas over to take their seats. As she approached, realisation dawned that she was expected to sample the food in full view of the town. Everyone staring at her, observing every little expression she made.

Lucas leaned over to comment on their situation, his self-deprecating joke about his appalling table manners making her laugh. She relaxed. There was nothing to worry about here. She could remain looking impassive. Time to put on her 'court' face.

She looked into the crowd. To her annoyance, her gaze kept zoning in on Zach, who was standing near the front ignoring everyone around him. He was frowning, of course.

She mentally rolled her eyes. Why did he even come if he wasn't happy to be there? It clearly wasn't because of her. Unless he was looking out for his friend; that comment he made only on Saturday was still fresh in her mind. As if Lucas was in any danger from her.

It was so hard to believe Zach was the same man who had held her in his arms among the pine trees only a few days after they'd met. Every time they got a little closer, he would distance himself afterwards.

Enough, she wasn't going to keep doing this. Going round and round in her head trying to decipher the enigmatic Zach. It didn't matter whether she'd misread the situation or whether they really were about to kiss. She was going to make sure nothing like this would ever happen again.

With a small sigh, she turned back to Lucas and the competition. As they sampled the dishes, she mentioned she'd been confused about why a chilli contest was part of the Pineford events – she couldn't recall watching a Christmas film with one in it. The restaurant owner pointed out it was a winter festival and there was nothing more warming than a bowl of hot chilli. But he added that Pineford's competition started out from an argument between two men, both boasting that their mothers made the best chilli in town. They held a contest to settle the dispute and it had grown ever since.

It felt like hours before they'd tried all the entries, then made their decision.

After the results were announced, the contestants came over to talk to her and Lucas. Naturally they wanted to know more about Thomas's Wishlist. But there was also a lot of curiosity about her personal life. She managed to deflect many of the questions about Thomas to Lucas, encouraging him to share stories about his family since they had left Pineford. As he chatted to them, she took a few subtle steps back until she was removed from the centre of attention. She went to collect her belongings, ready to find Penny and leave.

'They're starting to serve chilli to everyone if you want a proper meal now,' Lucas said, coming over to her. 'Someone's brought out cornbread and all the trimmings. And of course, there's some dessert too.'

Sharmila looked at the tables that were now fully covered in dishes. 'I'm not sure I fancy any more chilli. I think I've had more than enough. You go ahead, though.'

'Everything OK here?' Zach's low voice reverberated through her.

She took a few breaths to steady herself, still unable to control her physical reaction to his closeness.

146

'We're fine,' Lucas replied, a bright smile on his face. 'Aren't we, Sharmila?' He put his hand on her shoulder.

'Are you getting something to eat?' Zach asked.

'No, we had enough from the judging,' Lucas replied.

She was sensing a strange vibe between Lucas and Zach. It was similar to Saturday when Zach acted like Lucas's overprotective older brother. She moved away slightly so Lucas would have to drop his hand.

'If you're ready to go back to Holly House, I can take you,' Zach offered.

But even a brief car journey with Zach was more than she wanted at that moment. Not with the memory of the kiss that didn't happen fresh in her mind. 'Actually, I see Jill is serving hot chocolate. I think I'll stay and have a cup.'

'I don't mind waiting.'

'That's OK, Zach,' Lucas said. 'If Penny can't take Sharmila, I can drop her back. It's not that far out of my way.'

Sharmila furrowed her brow. Holly House was in the opposite direction from Pineford Inn. She looked from Zach to Lucas, who were staring at each other. The vibe was there again. Her instinctive feeling was their stand-off wasn't about wanting to be in her company. If anything, they acted worried about the other one being in her company.

She shook her head. Ridiculous. Why would they be worried about her? Without saying anything, she walked over to the hot chocolate.

Chapter 15

The following evening, standing in front of a house with trees brightly illuminated in red, gold, and green lights, Zach resisted the urge to scoff. Pineford and its neighbouring town, Willowbrook, went all out for their annual parade of lights competition. The five best streets of each town were entered into the contest. Pineford had lost for the last three years and was determined not to make it a fourth consecutive loss.

The group he was with had already walked past several homes with inflatable Santa grottos and snow families in their yards, reindeer on the roof, and giant candy canes along driveways. One home had a train set that lit up in a sequence to give the appearance the train was moving. Another projected images of multicoloured stars against the façade and garage door but didn't have any hanging lights. There was even one house that had all of these. It was small-town rivalry at its best.

He glanced over at the group, which included Lucas, Penny – and Sharmila. Her broad smile and rapt expression had him turning back to the decorated homes, trying to view them through her eyes.

Memories of his childhood assailed him, watching his father outside their home standing on a ladder to string the outdoor lights. His mom would try to convince his dad to allow her to add one more inflatable to their front yard. His dad would insist they had more than enough, but he always gave in to her in the end. Zach could almost taste the hot apple cider his mother traditionally made to celebrate the final decoration going up.

He pressed his lips together in a thin line. He had to focus on the goal – not start reminiscing about the past. Or become distracted by Sharmila.

For the last couple of days, he'd managed to put Monday out of his mind. Convinced himself he wasn't about to kiss her during their snowball fight. That Lucas's interruption was unnecessary. But the image of her lying in the snow, looking so beautiful with her eyes brimming with such warmth and laughter, wouldn't leave his head. She had been a constant disruption to his plans, to his thoughts. After the snowman competition, he told himself he was going to stay away and leave everything to Lucas.

Lucas wasn't showing any signs he was developing a romantic interest in her. He was friendly to her — nothing more. If anything, Zach himself was the one finding it a challenge to stay immune to Sharmila's charms.

The more time he spent with her, the more he liked her. It was becoming a big problem. He'd already come up with a simple solution to that problem — stop spending time with her. Instead of taking his own advice, he'd gone to the Chilli Cook-Off, seeking her out when he didn't need to. Now here he was at the Parade of Lights.

He should leave. He should tell Izzy he had to get back to California and that Lucas was doing fine on his own.

He noticed the group moving on, but Sharmila and Penny remained in a huddle.

He walked over to Lucas and tilted his head in their direction. 'What's happening?'

Lucas shrugged. 'I don't know. Sharmila looks upset, don't you think?'

Zach took in her downcast expression, the sparkle in her eyes more likely from tears than the reflection of fairy lights. Without thinking, he went to her.

'What's wrong? Is everything ok? Can I do anything to help?' he asked.

Sharmila gave him a wan smile. 'There's nothing wrong. I'm a bit tired. I wasn't expecting to do all this walking.'

Zach stared at her. He didn't know why she was lying. But she was. 'Would you like me to take you home?' he offered.

Her eyes widened. 'Oh, no thanks!'

He would have laughed at the vehemence of her reaction if she didn't still look sad. 'Are you sure?'

'Yes. I'm not ready to go home yet, and I don't want to miss out on seeing the lights.'

'If you're tired I'd be happy to drive you round to see the lights another evening,' Lucas suggested as he joined them. 'They're not going to be taken down overnight.'

'That's not a bad idea, pet.' Penny put an arm around Sharmila. 'Maybe we should go home for dinner. You're probably going to get hangry soon.'

Sharmila's mouth fell open. 'I don't get hangry! I am always even-tempered.'

Zach's lips quirked. He got the feeling Sharmila and Penny had this kind of conversation many times before. They had a close friendship he admired. He followed Sharmila's gaze from the lit house in front of them to the crowd further ahead. She inhaled slowly.

'All right,' she said. 'I guess I can leave the lights for another night. Penny, are you ready to go back?' At Penny's nod, she continued. 'Why don't you see whether Debby wants to come back with us?'

'Good idea,' Penny replied. 'Lucas, Zach, if you're finished too why don't you join us for dinner. We have so much food. Sharmila's been cooking up a storm.'

150

Sharmila's face went from startled to annoyed in a fraction of a second. She couldn't have made it clearer she didn't appreciate the invitation. He didn't particularly want to spend more time in her company either, but when Lucas accepted, he agreed too. He kept telling himself he needed to make sure Sharmila wouldn't use the opportunity to take advantage of Lucas.

Zach's stomach rumbled appreciatively at the aromas that greeted him inside Holly House. It smelled of home and comfort. Now the house was festively decorated in a mishmash of colours. He smiled. For some reason, he'd known she wouldn't go for a simple colour theme. Instead, the house reminded him of the elephant ornament Thomas gave her. Vivid and bright, like she was.

'I should have brought some wine or beer,' he heard Lucas say. He turned to him, watching as he helped Sharmila out of her coat, giving her a flirtatious smile.

Zach narrowed his eyes. The plan was to be friends with Sharmila, not flirt with her.

The five of them ate at the large kitchen table, not wanting the dining room's formality.

'This stew is fantastic,' Debby said. 'Are you a great cook generally, or is this your signature dish?'

'Sticky toffee pudding is her signature dish,' Lucas said with a wink.

Sharmila laughed. 'I am definitely not a great cook. I can make a few dishes well.'

'What about curry? I love curry. Can you make that well?' Lucas asked.

Penny snorted.

'Hey, come on,' Sharmila protested. 'My curries aren't that bad.'

'They were pretty awful.'

Sharmila's mouth widened. 'Charming!' A few seconds later, she said, 'OK, OK. I will admit they weren't the best.'

'Not compared with your mother's, that's for sure.'

'I was following one of her recipes.'

'Clearly not well enough.'

Sharmila laughed. 'In my defence, my mum's recipes never give actual quantities. A bit of this, some of that. It's all guess-work really.'

Zach watched the exchange between Sharmila and Penny as they continued to tease each other about their culinary abilities. Again, he was struck by how deep their friendship was. It made him think about his own relationship with Lucas. At one time he and Lucas had been as close as Sharmila and Penny. Even though they'd drifted apart a little, being here in Pineford was bringing them closer.

'My mom and sister were wondering whether you'd like to visit them for a few days before Christmas. They would love to meet you,' Lucas said.

Zach glanced sharply at Lucas. Neither Lucas nor Izzy had mentioned that to him before.

'Really, why?' Sharmila looked unsure.

'Well, I know Mom wants to meet the person who held a special place in her brother's heart and share some of her memories of him with you.'

'Of course. I'd love to hear them,' Sharmila replied. 'Why don't they come to Pineford then?'

'Oh, there's nowhere for them to stay. It's too late for them to book anywhere.'

Zach noticed Sharmila glance at Penny, who shook her head, eyes wide. Almost imperceptibly, Sharmila shrugged. He wasn't surprised to hear her next words. 'I guess your mum and sister could stay here. There's plenty of room.'

'My family wouldn't want to get in your way here,' Lucas said. 'We were all told Thomas wanted you to stay at Holly House for Christmas. They wouldn't want to impose. I would be happy to drive you to Boston and back. It's only a couple of hours.'

Sharmila's smile was forced. 'Perhaps. I don't know if I'll have time. I honestly don't mind if they stay here. It wouldn't be an imposition, and it belongs to your family after all.'

Lucas's face fell. 'Izzy and I would love to show you some of Uncle Thomas's favourite places. He may have grown up in Pineford, but he lived most of his life in Boston.'

'I guess,' Sharmila replied slowly. 'I'll think about it and let you know.'

Zach rubbed his hand across the back of his neck. He didn't know why his cousin was trying so hard to convince Sharmila to visit Boston but pushing the issue now probably wouldn't get them anywhere. He carried the plates to the sink to rinse them before putting them in the dishwasher.

'Thanks for dinner,' he said.

'Yes, thanks for a delicious meal,' Lucas said. 'You must let me return the favour.'

'Oh, that's not necessary. I was making a load of food anyway,' Sharmila replied.

'No, I insist. Why don't I take you out for dinner? Tomorrow night or the day after?' Lucas replied.

Sharmila threw a look in Zach's direction he could have sworn was mild panic. 'Time to call it a night,' he said, putting on his jacket.

Lucas frowned at him briefly then quickly smiled at Sharmila. 'Yes, thank you. I guess you'll have another busy day tomorrow, with Uncle Thomas's list.'

Sharmila shrugged. 'No, there's nothing on the list until Saturday. That's when the gingerbread competition is.'

'That means you'll be free tomorrow for Pineford's Winter Trail,' Debby said. 'I haven't had a chance to try it since I moved here but I hear it's very popular.'

'Oh, let's do that. We could be a team,' Lucas said with excitement.

'I'm not sure. I have a meeting about my Christmas party in the morning.'

'Come on, Sharms,' Penny said. 'It sounds like fun. Plus, it's a way to see more of the town.'

'I guess I can join after my meeting,' Sharmila said slowly. 'Yeah, OK. I'm in.' She smiled.

'Great!' Lucas said. 'We can be a team of four. Or five,' he added, glancing at Debby.

'Unfortunately, I'm working so I'll miss out again,' Debby replied. 'I hope you enjoy it.'

Zach narrowed his eyes but couldn't get Lucas's attention. He didn't want to spend his time doing some town trail. Not only was there a lot of work still to do helping get the parade floats ready, but he also had a growing inbox of emails to make his way through.

He waited until they had said their goodbyes and Lucas and he were inside his barn before he asked, 'Why did you suggest we work as a team on the trail?'

'Think of it this way – it gives us more chance of spending time with her, which would mean more opportunity to try to persuade her to come with me to Boston.'

'Yeah, what was that all about? Why do you want her to go to Boston?'

'Didn't Izzy speak to you today?' Lucas asked, his voice rising with surprise.

'No.' Zach pulled out his cell. There were no missed calls.

'Oh, maybe she was expecting me to tell you. I'm sorry.'

'Tell me what, Lucas?'

'She got another lawyer to look at the will, like you suggested. According to this lawyer, the will says Sharmila must stay in Pineford until after Christmas Day. But it doesn't mean she needs to return to England before then. If she leaves town overnight, we can argue she failed to comply with the strict letter of the will. Of course, the lawyer's not 100 per cent sure we'd win if Sharmila took it to court but Izzy thinks it's worth a shot. She suggested I invite Sharmila to Boston and then Mom will ask her to stay the night. I think it's a good idea to try since we're not having much luck stopping her from finishing this wish list.'

Zach was silent as he digested the new information. They only had ten days and five wishes left. He, Izzy, and Lucas probably needed another brainstorming session but now they had another option to consider. He frowned. 'If she goes to Boston, she's likely to meet my mom or see photos of the family. Then she'll know we lied about who I am. That could ruin everything.'

'If I can get her to come to Boston and stay overnight, she'll have lost the inheritance,' Lucas reminded him. 'Then it won't matter that you've been lying to her. Look, don't worry, Zach. Izzy's got a handle on everything and I'll do what she suggests.'

After Lucas left, Zach thought about their conversation. Lucas was right. He was deceiving Sharmila, he was deceiving everyone in Pineford, but it shouldn't matter that he was pretending to be someone else – he'd come to Pineford to save their family's legacy. Still, he couldn't help but feel guilty at what he had done. Even though technically he'd never outright lied to them nor denied their assumptions of him, it was still lying.

For a moment, he considered telling Sharmila the truth – explain his reasons. He shook his head. What was he thinking? He couldn't do that. It would jeopardise the whole inheritance. He wasn't prepared to risk it all for a woman. He'd nearly done that with Annette, and he'd learnt his lesson since then. The attraction between Sharmila and him was undeniable. But he still hadn't figured out why Thomas made his bequest, why his uncle would just gift this experience and leave his business shares to a woman he hardly knew. It was very out of character. Until Zach knew the full picture, he couldn't completely trust her. And there could never be any kind of relationship between them.

Chapter 16

There had only been a couple of families milling around the town square when they'd arrived at Cinnamon's for breakfast. By the time Sharmila and Penny had finished their pancakes twenty minutes later, the town square was filled with people and the closest they could get to the gazebo would be standing directly outside the diner.

Penny nodded in the direction of the window. 'Plenty of competition on this one.'

'Yes. Good job it's not on my wish list,' Sharmila replied, gathering up her coat and scarf.

They left a large tip, then walked out to join the crowds.

'I hope this Winter Trail isn't going to require me to move anywhere this morning. I've eaten too much,' Penny said, patting her flat stomach. 'I think I'm going to miss breakfast here the most out of everything when we get back home.'

'Don't talk about going home yet,' Sharmila said with a small pout. 'I can't believe we're already halfway through our holiday. And when I return, it's packing up and moving and starting my new life.'

She noticed Lucas waving in the crowd, indicating for them to head over.

'This is going to be so much fun!' he said. 'I've not seen the town so excited over an event since we arrived.'

Sharmila grinned. 'Hopefully, it won't be too hard for us tourists.'

'I was talking to Jill last night,' he said. 'She said the organising team has outdone itself this year. It's different from any previous year.'

Sharmila furrowed her brow. 'What do you think that means?'

'We'll have to wait and see. Not long now.' He glanced down at his watch. 'Have you seen Zach? He should be here by now.'

'We haven't. I don't remember seeing his truck when we left the house this morning. Do you, Sharmila?' Penny asked.

Sharmila shrugged. She wasn't going to admit looking over in the direction of the barn every time she left the house. Usually, his truck was visible through the trees. It hadn't been there this morning.

As they heard a horn, they turned to face the gazebo, where Jackie was about to speak.

Sharmila's eyes grew rounder as she listened to the rules. They had to download an app on their phones to see the Trail clues, which had different point values depending on their difficulty. Once a team completed a clue, they had to send a photo of a team member next to the item via the app and they would be notified whether they had completed the clue successfully almost immediately. There were extra points for the first team to complete a clue. The Trail would end by 6 p.m. and the three teams with the most points would win a prize.

'I can't believe it!' Sharmila said. 'That's so impressive. I can't believe they created an app for this. Who knew?'

Lucas coughed.

'Am I really out of touch?' she asked, scrunching her nose.

'I've used some of these apps before in Boston. They're mostly used for treasure hunts or scavenger hunts,' Lucas explained.

'I'm lost for words. But it does sound like fun.'

'We have to win this,' Penny and Lucas said, almost in unison.

They laughed.

'Well, I have to go meet my party squad at the house now,' Sharmila said. 'I should be done in an hour. If you two start the trail now, you can text me where you are and I'll meet you, or we can meet at the house.'

'Great. See you,' Penny replied. She and Lucas waved but Sharmila was pretty sure they were already on the first clue.

Sharmila's party squad consisted of Karen, Susan, Lydia, and CeCe, all of whom she'd met at the cookie bake, and Gayle, who couldn't make the meeting. She followed them as they wandered round Holly House, discussing furniture placement and measuring for set-up. Karen had appointed herself chief party planner, which was great for Sharmila since she didn't have the event-planning gene. But having groups for decorations, refreshments, invitations, and entertainment sounded slightly excessive when there were only six people in the squad.

Sharmila went into the kitchen to make a pot of coffee. She was getting some biscuits out of the cupboard when Karen joined her.

'I almost forgot,' Karen said, reaching into a bag. 'Gayle sent some cookies and cake for us.'

'That's really thoughtful of her.' But not surprising. Ever since Gayle helped her with the dessert competition, they'd kept in touch, with Gayle often inviting her to the bakery to taste-test her new recipes.

'She's really sorry she has to work today. But she doesn't open the bakery on the twenty-sixth so she'll be available to help on the day. She already volunteered to do refreshments.'

'Perfect.'

They worked together in silence getting the drinks ready.

'This is a lovely house,' Karen said. 'Do you know what Thomas's family plans to do with it?'

Sharmila shook her head. 'I don't know.'

'I guess they're probably selling. I can't see them moving Endicott Enterprises out of Boston.'

'I'm sure Lucas will be able to tell you what's happening with the house. It's a shame if they did sell – Thomas only bought it last year.'

'I remember seeing him round town. He was very excited about spending Christmas here with you and your family.'

Sharmila's mouth turned down. Her family never felt a great desire for an American Christmas but she knew they would have loved Pineford. Thomas had been thinking about giving her this Christmas experience for over a year but he never got to share it with her. It seemed so unfair.

'We all wish you could stay here. Everyone adores you and you fit right in. You already feel like part of the town. And it's not only because of the wish list.'

Sharmila warmed at Karen's words. 'That's very kind of you to say. I love being in Pineford and if I could, I'd never want to leave. But unfortunately, my job's in England and it's not easily transferrable. I wish I could take Pineford and Holly House back home with me.'

They carried trays through to the snug where she was updated on the decisions that had been taken. All she had to do was make samosas. It sounded like everything was going to go swimmingly. After the problems with the last four wishes, she was waiting for something to go wrong.

After the squad left, Sharmila texted Penny to find out where to meet. She got an immediate response saying they would swing by to collect her. Sharmila took a look at the app. The team had already managed to collect loads of points but were still not in the prize scorers. She smirked – Lucas and Penny would not be happy about that.

The doorbell rang so she grabbed her bag, hopping along as pulled on her boots. She was shrugging into her coat as she opened the door to see Zach.

'Hi.' He gave her a show-stopping smile and she went weak at the knees. 'Lucas and Penny decided we need to separate if we have any chance of winning. They're going to tackle the five- and ten-point clues and they want us to do the one- and two-point ones.'

'Nice to know they have such faith in us,' she said dryly.

'When it comes to competitiveness, I don't think we're any match for them.'

'I know, right? I barely recognise this Penny – the person I know is so laidback and chill in every other respect.'

'Maybe Lucas brings out the worst in her.'

She nodded. 'Probably. So are we splitting up as well or working together?'

'We can go together. I doubt we'd be much faster if we separate since most of the clues are in town.' He raised his eyebrows, throwing her a teasing glance. 'You'll be shocked to learn that the only clues Lucas trusts us with tell you exactly what you need to find.'

She laughed. 'Hope we don't go wrong then.'

She was secretly pleased Zach hadn't suggested they split up – she certainly didn't mind spending the afternoon together. She'd become comfortable with him, pleased that the awkwardness from their moment after the snowball fight was in the past. Her physical attraction to him was still there, naturally. But it was more than that. She liked him. She enjoyed being in his company.

'Shall we head into town?' she asked.

'First there's a clue about the sign at the edge of the woods near here. We can finish that then head in.'

'Sounds like a plan.'

'Are you ready then?' he asked, feeding her scarf round her neck then pressing his hand against her shoulder.

She smiled, the simple gesture suggesting he was equally comfortable in her company.

'Let's go,' she said.

'Where shall we start?' Zach asked as he held the car door open for Sharmila. They'd finished the first clue and were now in

Pineford about to look for the oldest mechanical display in a shop window.

She exhaled. 'I don't know. I feel like I've seen so many shops with mechanical displays, but I don't remember anything saying it was the oldest one. Surely there would be a notice on the building. I'm thinking our best option is to walk along Main Street until we find it. Assuming it is on Main Street. It's only worth a point. It must be on Main Street, surely.'

'Surely,' Zach repeated, with a quirk of his lips.

Main Street was crowded but no more so than on any other shopping day before Christmas. It didn't look like there were many teams peering into windows – had all the other teams already finished this clue? He glanced at his watch. It had been a couple of hours; they were probably one of the last teams to do this one.

'If you have somewhere else to be, I don't mind doing this by myself,' Sharmila said. 'I know you were forced into this.'

Zach stopped. He looked down at the top of her head, covered by a brightly coloured woollen hat. 'I don't have anywhere to be, and I wasn't forced.'

'Really? Yesterday, it didn't seem as if you were very keen on the idea.'

'Really. If I didn't want to join in, I would have said no. Lucas is used to me saying no to him all the time.' He returned her grin. 'Besides I've been hearing a lot about the Pineford Winter Trail. Don't you know? Anyone who's anyone takes part. How could I refuse?'

'Did you do these kinds of trails when you were younger?' she asked him.

'Not like this. My town organised huge scavenger hunts throughout the year. My family didn't usually take part in them though. But my parents used to make a kind of scavenger hunt specially for me inside our home at Christmas. What about you? You mentioned Thomas didn't put it on the list.'

'If a pub crawl counts as a scavenger hunt then I've done them before.' She screwed up her nose in an adorable way. 'But I never spoke to Thomas about them. They weren't in any of the films we watched and he didn't mention doing them when he was younger either. I guess there were a lot of options to choose from for my wishes. I'm just relieved he didn't put all of Pineford's WinterFest events on my list. I would need a holiday to recover from this holiday!'

Zach chuckled at her exaggerated sigh of relief.

'This is it,' Sharmila said as they stopped in front of a display with a tableau of small bears making toys in a workshop. Their arms were moving up and down as if hammering. 'See there's a plaque. Will we get a decent photo through the glass?'

'Yes. Hand me your phone. I'll take the photo,' he said, putting his hand out.

She held her phone behind her back. 'I can take it.'

'That's OK. I'd rather take it.'

She looked up at him for a moment, then she blinked. 'Are you camera shy?'

Zach shrugged. 'Maybe. I don't go out of my way to have my photo taken.'

'Really? I can't imagine you've ever had a bad photo taken with that face.'

She said it in such a casual way – had she even realised she'd told him she found him attractive. Zach smiled. 'You think my face is photogenic?'

'Well, duh.'

He laughed. 'Thank you, ma'am,' he said, tipping his imaginary hat. 'But we're doing this trail for you to get to know Pineford, not me.'

She smiled. 'Fine,' she said, handing over her phone.

He took his time framing her. The late afternoon sun cast arresting shadows across her face. Talk about photogenic.

'What kind of scavenger hunts did your parents make for you when you were younger?'

He was caught off guard by her question. An image flashed in his mind of his mother and father standing in front of a roaring log fire holding his first clue.

'It was a scavenger hunt to find one of my Christmas presents,' he said with a smile as the memories continued to replay. For the first time, he could picture his father without the accompanying feelings of guilt and regret. 'They would give me a clue handwritten on parchment paper, which would take me to where the next clue was. It was a treasure hunt as much as it was a scavenger hunt.'

'That sounds lovely.'

He laughed. 'It was. One year, the final clue took me to a pet dog. Another year it was to a car.' He smiled. He had the strongest urge to call his mom – to reminisce with her about the clues she prepared, each written in calligraphy on homemade paper. 'My parents carried on the tradition until I left home for college.'

'Well, you're never too old for a treasure hunt.'

'No,' he chuckled, 'apparently not in my family.' For a moment he was glad this Winter Trail wasn't on her wish list. He was enjoying the chance to experience an activity with her without trying to ruin it. It was getting harder to convince himself they were doing the right thing.

Turning his thoughts away from the inheritance, he pressed the button to take a few photos, then walked over to show her the images. She nodded her approval.

'Let's go,' he said.

'One second,' she replied. She went inside the shop. Through the window, he could see her talking to the lady behind the counter. Sharmila then went to the displays bending or stretching as she looked at the shelves. She picked up a few items then went to pay.

'Did you find what you were looking for?' he asked when she came back out.

'I wasn't after anything specific,' she said, looking into the shop windows as they walked past. 'To be honest, I felt bad we were using her window display for the clue without buying something in return. Luckily she has some lovely stuff in there. Thank goodness it wasn't this shop with the fishing bait.' She waggled her brows before moving on.

Zach stood still for a moment, touched by her unexpected thoughtfulness. Not many would have done what she did.

'Is something wrong?' she asked, a puzzled expression on her face as she retraced her steps back to him.

'No. Nothing's wrong.'

She inclined her head, as if waiting to make sure he was certain. Then she exhaled deeply as she looked around her. 'I love Pineford. Every time I come into town I fall in love with it a little bit more. Everything here is so much more amazing than anything I could've imagined. I don't think I'll ever get tired of walking down Main Street at Christmas.'

He stood next to her, looking round, trying to see everything through her eyes. It was a beautiful town – straight out of a Christmas card.

'I can't believe I'll be back in England in less than two weeks.' Her mouth turned down. A moment later, she clapped her hands together, her spirits clearly revived. 'Right, what's next on the list? Or do you have to head back?'

That would be the sensible option. He didn't understand his actions where she was concerned. He should go back. Keep busy in his barn. Even take her suggestion that they look for clues separately. Instead, he scrolled through the app, looking for another one-point clue they could do together.

'We could find the inscription on the gazebo.'

'There's an inscription on the gazebo?' she asked, giving him an incredulous look.

'Apparently so.' They laughed.

On the way over, they looked through the rest of the trail clues, joking about all the other things in Pineford they'd never noticed before, despite passing them several times.

The gazebo was empty for once. They walked round looking for the inscription. Finally they found it on one of the posts. Again, he made Sharmila pose for the photo before sending it on the app.

Rather than rushing to the next clue, he wiped a smattering of snow off the curved benches so they could both sit. He wanted to prolong this moment with Sharmila, where he didn't need to think about her wish list and they could simply be two people getting to know each other.

'Do you miss the snow now you're in San Francisco?' she asked.

'I'm usually too busy to notice what the weather's like.'

Her forehead creased. 'I thought you worked outside.'

'I'm mostly office-based now,' he replied.

'But I thought you did construction.'

'In a way, but I've moved over to the computerised design side now.'

'You must be a good friend to be doing this as a favour for Lucas.'

He inclined his head. 'I wanted to come too – to see where my mom grew up.'

'Oh, yes. I love it when I'm in India and I can go round to all the same spots my parents did when they were younger. It feels special. Have you been telling your mum about all the places you've visited?'

'Not yet,' he admitted. He had told his mother he was visiting Pineford but she didn't know about their plan to stop Sharmila – he didn't want to get her hopes up about keeping Holly House. He didn't want to risk disappointing her again.

He looked at Sharmila, trying to work out why he was finding it so difficult to remember his reason for being in Pineford. A few hours in her company and all he cared about was enjoying their conversation.

'Come on,' he said, standing up then offering his arm to pull her up. He moved a strand of hair off her face and adjusted her beanie. 'Let's go. We have to meet the others in a few minutes. Let's grab a table in Cinnamon's.'

Lucas and Penny were already seated when they entered the diner. He hadn't noticed them go in while they were sitting in the gazebo. He'd been too busy concentrating on Sharmila.

Penny and Sharmila moved away to order at the counter, deep in conversation.

'How did we do?' Zach asked. He hadn't checked their team score since they completed the last clue.

Lucas scoffed. 'Not even close. We were always going to be at a disadvantage not being locals.' Zach laughed at his cousin's pouting. 'Hey, I blame you,' Lucas continued. 'Your contribution was pitiful. I bet you had fun though.' He smirked as he gave a pointed look in Sharmila's direction.

'What do you mean?'

'Come on, Zach! You forget how well I know you. And I always know when you're interested in a woman.'

'It's not like that. I'm trying to find out more about her. About why Thomas would leave her so much.' He wasn't surprised that Lucas's expression was sceptical. 'Anyway, shh, they're coming over.'

'Is something wrong?' he asked. It looked like there was tension between Sharmila and Penny. Had they been arguing?

'Penny has some friends who live a couple of hours from here. They've invited her to visit and stay for a party they're hosting but she refuses to go.'

'I can't, Sharms. It's at the weekend. And you've got the gingerbread competition.'

'I know. Otherwise, I'd come with you. But, Penny, you've been working with these people online for years. It's a rare chance to meet with them in person. Tell her, guys.'

'We have to do the competition. We're a team. Maybe I could leave after the event instead of tomorrow,' Penny offered. 'I'd still get plenty of time with my friends.'

'You don't have to do that,' Lucas said. 'I'd love to be your partner for the competition, Sharmila. My sister and I used to enter one back home all the time when we were younger.'

'See,' Sharmila said, giving Lucas a warm smile. 'Problem solved.'

'Unless you want to be Sharmila's partner, Zach,' Lucas said with the barest hint of a wink. 'It doesn't necessarily have to be me.'

Zach raised his hand. 'No. You two enter. I have a lot to do this weekend.' Gingerbread houses would bring back memories of spending time with his mother; she liked decorating the structures he put together. His father often joked that was where Zach's love for architecture and design began.

Lucas clapped his hands together. 'Fantastic, that's settled. Why don't we meet for dinner tomorrow? We can discuss strategy.'

'Strategy for the gingerbread competition?' Sharmila asked. Her glance went from Lucas to him and back. 'Are you being serious? Is this like puzzle strategy?'

'You don't understand how seriously we take our gingerbread houses in the States,' Zach replied with a grin.

Sharmila grinned in return. 'I guess not.' Zach noticed with interest the smile dropped from her face as she turned back to Lucas. 'I've just realised I can't meet for dinner tomorrow. I said I'd help with parade stuff, which starts at 7.30. Liz said my costume should be ready for a fitting.'

'We could eat before or after,' Lucas suggested.

'I suppose we could meet here beforehand for a quick meal.'

'Fantastic!' Lucas said. 'It'll give me a chance to hear more about your time with Uncle Thomas.'

Sharmila gave a bright smile. 'Look forward to it.'

Why did that bother him? Everyone loved Lucas and wanted to spend time with him. He should be more worried that Lucas kept suggesting dinner to her. Was Lucas asking her out on a date or was he being his usual overfriendly self?

Zach clenched his jaw. He couldn't invite himself to their meal. He paused –thinking through possible excuses – then mentally shook his head. No, he couldn't join them. He would have to leave it and hope for the best.

Chapter 17

The diner on Friday evening was cast in a subdued light, but there was still no chance it could be mistaken for having a romantic atmosphere. Thankfully.

Not that Lucas was giving, or had ever given, her the idea he was interested in her in a romantic way. As expected, he was an entertaining and amusing dinner partner, very interested to hear about Thomas's visit to India.

Occasionally she sensed Lucas had a difficult relationship with his uncle, that Thomas could be a little frosty towards Lucas, but it did fit with the impression she'd received from Thomas. On a personal level Thomas always spoke about his family with such affection that she intrinsically knew he loved them very much, so she enjoyed listening to Lucas share stories of the pranks he, his sister, and his cousin used to play on their parents and Thomas.

Since they were getting on, she felt secure enough to bring up the snowman competition, joking that he almost cost her a wish.

Lucas's face fell. 'I'm so sorry, Sharmila. I've been so excited about being in Pineford and taking part in WinterFest, it never even occurred to me you wouldn't get a spot. You should have come up. I would have swapped Zach for you in a heartbeat.'

Sharmila briefly closed her eyes with relief. Such a simple

explanation. She'd been so silly reading more into what he'd done. Mistrusting him as she'd subconsciously started to mistrust all people.

Apart from Zach. She couldn't deny she was drawn to Zach.

And that was nagging at the back of her mind. Even though this wasn't a date, and romance definitely wasn't in the air, there was still a small part of her brain saying *Wrong Person*.

What scared her was that the image of the person she did want to have dinner with, the *Right Person*, wasn't Hari. She wasn't ready to face what that meant, so she reassured herself two weeks wasn't enough time to fall in love.

Refusing to let herself think about Hari, or love, or loss, she brought her attention back to the table, belatedly realising her name was being called. 'Sorry, Lucas. I was miles away. What did you say?'

'I was asking what other wishes you still have to do. I can't wait for the gingerbread event tomorrow.'

'I have the parade, the party, and ice skating left. Nearly halfway through and I have less than two weeks.' She gave a shaky laugh.

'Two weeks?' Lucas asked, the surprise apparent in this tone.

'Yes, I have to complete the wishes before the new year.'

'I thought you had to complete the list before Christmas Day.'

She smiled. 'I definitely won't finish by then, especially since we've scheduled the party for the twenty-sixth.'

She couldn't decipher the look on his face after she mentioned the deadline when suddenly it cleared and he smiled brightly. She followed the direction of his gaze, then inhaled sharply. Her whole body froze, tense and awkward.

Zach was ordering at the counter. For the first time that evening, she wished it was a date – Lucas wouldn't have beckoned him over then. After her earlier thoughts, Zach was the last person she wanted to see.

'Hi, guys. Did you have a good evening?' he asked as he approached their table.

'It's been great, hasn't it, Sharmila? You should listen to her stories about Uncle Thomas. She knows him better than we do.'

Zach's expression was inscrutable. 'Are you going to the parade prep meeting?' he asked her.

She nodded.

'If you're finished, do you want to head over together now?' he asked.

'Sure. Is that OK with you, Lucas?'

'Of course. It's the hot toddy competition later. I might go test out some of the entries,' he replied.

She smiled at him. 'All right. Well, I guess I might see you there. If not, I'll see you tomorrow for the gingerbread competition.'

She left the diner with Zach. Once outside, he asked, 'Did you enjoy your date?'

Sharmila looked sharply at him. 'It wasn't a date.'

He nodded, a small smile about his lips.

She opened her mouth to insist but closed it with a snap. She didn't want to make it a big deal in case Zach suspected she had reasons for making sure he knew there was nothing romantic between her and Lucas.

The community hall was already crowded with familiar faces – those from the Women's Club, some of the contestants from the chilli competition, and other people she met in town. It surprised her how many people she had got to know in such a short time.

'If all these people are in the parade, will there be anyone left to actually watch it?' she asked.

Zach's lips twitched. 'I'll be watching it.'

'You will?'

'Of course, why not?'

She shrugged. 'I thought there might be a Dr Seuss float you needed to be on.'

He rolled his eyes but grinned. 'I told you I'm not the Grinch.'

'Then maybe there's a Dickens float somewhere.'

Zach raised his eyebrows. 'I'm not Scrooge either, but I did help make some pieces for the *Christmas Carol* float.'

'Really?' Sharmila looked round the room at the various scenery pieces being constructed or painted. 'Seriously, how big is this parade?'

'I don't know. Probably bigger than the ones you had at home but smaller than Macy's Thanksgiving Day Parade.'

Sharmila smiled. 'I've only seen videos of the Thanksgiving parade online but it looks magnificent. Have you ever seen it in person?'

He shook his head. 'No. At the risk of being insulted, Thanksgiving is usually a working day for me.' He put his hand on her shoulder. 'If you'll excuse me, Bill needs my help. Did you drive in?'

'Penny took the car to visit her friends. I was hoping to get a lift from Liz.'

'I can give you a ride. Let me know when you're ready to leave.'

She watched him walk over to a group of men constructing large cut-out sweets, which were then taken to another group painting the scenery. Even among tall, well-built men, Zach stood out. He had a way of commanding attention, of being in control.

'Sharmila, you're here. Perfect.' Liz came over to her with a clipboard, looking utterly serene for someone in charge of organising so many people. 'Do you have any preference for what you want to do?'

'No, put me to work wherever I can be most useful,' she replied.

'Excellent. I don't suppose you know how to use a sewing machine, do you?'

Sharmila shrugged. 'The basics.' Her aunt who owned the teashop was an accomplished seamstress. While Sharmila stayed with her, she'd learnt how to make and repair her own clothes.

'Really? We have some hemming to do and some zippers that need to be sewn into costumes, or if you know how to read patterns, we've cut out some pieces that need to be fixed together.'

172

'I'm happy to do anything. I can read patterns.'

Liz beamed at her. 'You're an angel! I'm so glad you're here this Christmas. Lydia and Chloe are usually in charge of the sewing, but Chloe is busy with a newborn, and Lydia has more in-law problems today. You've saved the day.'

They talked about the different groups helping that evening as they walked over to the sewing machines. She would be the only one working there, which suited Sharmila, although Liz promised to send over someone to keep her company.

Sharmila kept her head down, concentrating on getting the pieces sewn. She was used to being on her own, for the last two years she'd preferred it that way. At various points, while she worked, the ladies from the Pineford Women's Club came over to speak to her. Inevitably the topic moved on to her Christmases growing up.

She worried they were assuming her experiences were the same for all Indian families. She tried to explain that wasn't the case. It wasn't the same for every Indian family, or for every Hindu family, no matter where they lived. In the same way there were differences in the British and American ways of celebrating, or even among Christian denominations.

As she saw the looks of pity they gave her when they heard how different her childhood Christmas was from a Pineford Christmas, she could tell they thought Thomas had given her this incredible gift out of sympathy, thinking her childhood was lacking in some way. They were completely wrong, but she didn't know how to correct their impression.

Instead, she asked Karen whether there had been any move-ment on the present she'd ordered and found out that Susan's plumbing had been sorted; Zach had helped. The women may enjoy a bit of gossip, but they were kind-hearted. Despite the differences in their ages, they were a close-knit group of friends, not merely neighbours. Without a doubt, Sharmila knew if she spent much time with them, they would also become her friends.

She was starting to care about these people. About what happened to them. And she didn't want that. Did she?

The entire time in Pineford, she'd been forced to engage with the town – either because of Thomas's Wishlist or because of the town's interest in his list. They were drawing her in and she was unable able to resist their charm any longer. She could be herself around them, letting her guard down a little bit more each time.

She'd finished sewing an elf tunic when Zach came over to her.

'I'm done. Were you thinking of going to the hot toddy competition?' he said.

Sharmila considered it but she suddenly didn't want to be with a crowd of people.

'I think I'm finished for the day too. If you're going back to Holly House, can you give me a lift please?'

He paused for a second, then nodded. 'I'll wait for you outside.'

She quickly cleared her workspace, then looked for Liz to say goodbye. She was tempted to offer to take some of the sewing back home with her. Something stopped her, though – perhaps her need to put some distance between her and the town.

She'd been just fine when she arrived in Pineford, exactly two weeks before, telling herself that her trip was only short and she could keep everyone at arm's length because there wouldn't be enough time to properly get to know people. Or for them to get to know her.

She had her family and Penny. She didn't want or need anyone new to care about. It came with the risk of losing them – and she was not ready to go through that again.

During the drive back, she sensed Zach looking over at her. She turned to give him a quick, tight smile.

'Are you all right?' he asked.

'Yes. There was a lot of people there tonight. It's just a lot sometimes,' she replied.

'I thought you would love the community. Isn't that part of a small-town Christmas?'

174

She gave a weak laugh. 'It looks great in the movies. And they're a wonderful group. But I'm not sure I would ever get used to everyone knowing all my business.'

'They're very curious people.'

'That's an understatement!' She exhaled. 'But they're so interested in my wish list and then they ask me about my childhood Christmases and sometimes I think they have the wrong idea about Thomas's gift. I may not have had a fairy-tale Pineford Christmas growing up, but I had a wonderful childhood. I don't need them to feel sorry for me. Obviously our celebrations in my family would be different from here. But for me, it's not just about my religion. Christmases in England seemed a world away from the extravaganzas I saw in the American films. Perhaps the difference isn't that great now. But it was the American Christmas experience I started to long for.' She laughed. For someone who had just decided to stop opening up to new people, she'd spilt everything to Zach. 'It's easy to talk to you,' she admitted. 'Maybe because you're an outsider, too.'

'Outsider?' He parked the car and turned to face her.

She looked into his eyes, momentarily forgetting what she'd said. 'You know what I mean.'

He nodded, a small smile playing on his face. 'I do.'

And she really believed he did. An image of the two of them sharing a meal in candlelight flashed in her mind – the same image she'd had earlier while she was having dinner with Lucas.

She sat in the truck outside Holly House, not yet ready to go inside. They stayed like that for a couple of minutes. Just when Sharmila thought that maybe Zach was waiting for her to leave but was too polite to say anything, he asked, 'We still need to finish the Parade of Lights. Do you feel like doing that now?'

Sharmila nodded eagerly. She wanted to see the brightly decorated houses – spending more time with Zach was a bonus.

Chapter 18

The Gingerbread House Competition was about to begin and there was no sign of Lucas. Sharmila hoped he would arrive soon – he'd been so excited about the event. Although they never did discuss strategy during their meal, she didn't want him to miss it.

Sharmila glanced at her phone. Still nothing.

She recognised a man whom she'd seen with Lucas and Zach a couple of times. She wasn't sure if he could help, but she was running out of options. She went over to ask if he had seen Lucas.

'Sorry, no, I haven't,' the man said. 'But I did hear someone saying he left town last night on business.'

'Left town?'

The man gave an apologetic smile. 'That's what I heard. I don't know much else, I'm afraid.'

Annoyed that Lucas could have left Pineford without bothering to contact her, she walked outside to call him again. Still no answer. She tapped her foot with frustration as she tried the inn. Jill answered the phone and told her they hadn't seen Lucas either. Jill went out to the car park to check whether his car was there. It wasn't. They chatted for a few moments before Jill reminded her she still needed to find a partner for the competition.

Sharmila smiled as she rang off. It was a shame Lucas would

miss the competition but she was surprisingly not concerned about finding someone to enter with her – Jackie was helping to organise the competitors and Sharmila knew if she asked her, Jackie would find a way to help her complete one of Thomas's wishes.

'Any luck?' the man she spoke to previously asked when she went back to the competition hall.

She shook her head.

'If you need a partner, I can help you for a while.'

'That's really kind of you ...'

'Pete. You probably don't remember me. My partner, Julie, was at the Puzzle and Pie Contest.'

Sharmila gave a broad smile. 'Pete. Of course. Julie saved my wish then and it looks like you're saving me today.'

'We all want you to finish the activities on your wish list. People love the annual gingerbread competition. You'll see, they take it very seriously. Besides, Julie would never forgive me if I didn't help you out. I can only stay for an hour. Let me speak to Jackie or someone, see if they can organise some kind of roster for the rest of the competition.'

Pineford hadn't let her down yet.

'Any time you can give is great.' They took their seats for the competition. 'I should warn you, Pete, I've never done this before. I don't know where we start.' She turned to look at the sheets of gingerbread behind them. 'I was expecting the house pieces to be cut already and we just assembled and decorated them.'

'Haven't you learnt yet? Pineford doesn't do simple or straight-forward,' Pete joked. 'I'm sure they try to make them more complicated each year. We have to come up with the house design ourselves. There will be gingerbread sheets of different shapes and sizes, but if we want a custom size, we can ask for it to be cut out for us. We'll also need to prepare the paste that sticks it all together. But there should be a recipe for that somewhere.'

'You're kidding me,' Sharmila said, with an uncertain smile.

'No, but you'll pick it up in no time,' Pete replied. 'I'm guessing you don't do it this way where you come from?'

'I don't even know if England has them. The movies always make these competitions look so easy because they're usually decorating a ready-made house. Apart from one film where they made life-size gingerbread houses if I remember it correctly.' She widened her eyes. 'I hope you aren't expecting us to build something that magnificent.'

Pete threw his head back as he laughed. 'Not at all! If you're happy, then we can go with the basic four walls and a roof. We won't win, but it could be fun.'

'Fun is good enough for me.'

They quickly sketched out a simple design and got the necessary pieces. Pete made the sugar paste while Sharmila spent too long picking out sweets for her decorations. She glanced around at the other contestants. She still had no idea what she was supposed to do.

'Do you think we should start with the walls?' Pete suggested kindly.

She gave him a grateful smile.

They'd glued the four walls together and were waiting for the paste to dry enough before adding the roof when Pete had to leave. He told her he would check with Jackie to find her another partner. Sharmila smiled and thanked him for his help.

'No problem. You must come round and have a meal with Julie and me. I know she would love to see you. She loves everything about England. A true Anglophile.'

'Love to.'

Sharmila concentrated on pasting the two sides of the roof together, confident Jackie would send someone over to help her soon.

'Hi.'

Her heart skipped as she recognised Zach's deep voice.

'Hey.'

'Jackie said you need a partner to finish this competition.'

'She did?' Sharmila raised her eyebrows. She'd hoped Jackie would find one of the townspeople to help her – not Zach.

The previous evening, after she and Zach had gone to see the rest of the Parade of Lights, Sharmila had realised how much she had grown to like Zach. But she didn't want to open her heart to anyone, which meant she had decided to limit the amount of time she spent with him. That was going to be hard to do when he was her partner in this competition. It wasn't like she could go round telling people she didn't want to get closer to Zach.

'I thought you had a lot of odd jobs to do today,' she said.

'I got them finished quickly.'

'Surely you have something better to do on a Saturday afternoon than take part in a gingerbread competition. Anyway, I think I could finish on my own now that Pete's shown me what to do.'

She lifted the icing mixture, testing its consistency. She grimaced – still too runny. How had Pete made it so easily? She glanced up at Zach. His expression clearly showed his scepticism about her ability to complete the gingerbread house on her own.

'What?' she asked.

He laughed, taking a seat.

'I've never seen you this grumpy about a Christmas activity.'

'I'm not grumpy. The walls don't seem to stay upright, and I can't get this glue to the right consistency.' OK, she was a little bit grumpy.

'Your construction's not the best,' Zach said, rotating the tray that held her house. 'We should fortify the foundations if we want to put all your decorations on.'

She glared at him.

'What?' he asked.

'Are you serious?'

'Yes. You've come up with a decent decorative design. You don't want a flaw in the building to get in the way.'

She looked at him without blinking, not saying a word.

179

His lips quirked. 'I can do it for you.'

She wanted to refuse, to insist she could do it on her own. But she could admit she wasn't doing a great job so far. And, this was one of Thomas's wishes. Her shoulders slumped before she pulled herself together. 'That would be great, thank you.' She left him working on the construction while she went to get more supplies. She felt completely out of depth with this gingerbread house.

She joined him at their station, taking over the mixing of the sugar glue and keeping her head down – making sure she didn't look in his direction. If she ignored him, she would technically be limiting the time she spent with him.

She blew away a strand of hair that kept falling on her face. She'd managed to get the sticky, sugary icing on her fingers and wasn't going to risk getting any of that stuff in her hair.

He gently swept her hair away, tucking it behind her ear. Sharmila found it difficult to breathe.

'Here, do you want me to fix your glue?' Zach asked.

She raised her eyebrows. Was he trying to be a white knight rushing to her aid? She didn't need rescuing. She straightened, determined to master this gingerbread house. The action caused the strand of hair to fall back onto her face. She sighed, then handed the bowl to him.

'Thank you,' she said. 'I think the walls should be sturdy enough for the roof.'

'You're going for the basic structure?'

She sighed again, then looked round the hall at the other contestants' tables. There was a variety of grand designs ranging from mansions and cathedrals to a replica of the White House.

'Zach, it took me all morning to get as far as I have.'

'It doesn't sound like you're having fun.'

'As you probably saw from the snowman and the desserts debacle, I'm not great at the practical competitions. I'm not going to lie, this one is the worst.'

'Even worse than the desserts?' Zach asked in a surprised tone.

She narrowed her eyes in what she hoped was a menacing way. Probably not too menacing since Zach laughed and put his hands up.

'I'm guessing Thomas didn't put this on your list because he knew you were dying to do it,' he said.

She scoffed and shook her head. 'No. Of course, we talked about it. Gingerbread decorating turns up in so many Christmas movies. But I don't get it.'

He smiled. 'You don't get what?'

'Gingerbread houses. I get gingerbread because of the spices, you know. But gingerbread houses – aren't they from Hansel and Gretel?'

'I suppose. I never really thought about it.'

'Well, how does a house created by a witch to tempt children so she can eat them become associated with a fun Christmas activity? How does it make sense?'

He shrugged, his shoulders shaking with repressed laughter.

She scrunched her nose. 'Do you think this means I have to hand in my Christmas-fan credentials?'

'I think you'll be fine. As long as you don't also ask anyone why we encourage children to sit on a strange old man's lap.'

She tilted her head. 'You sound like my brother-in-law.'

'He's not a Christmas fan then?'

She shook her head emphatically.

'Is that because of his religion?'

'No, it's because he's a very rational man. He suits my sister perfectly. You should hear the way they changed folktales. Even ones about runaway food like the gingerbread man.'

'So gingerbread isn't a big thing in England?'

'No, it is. There are towns famous for their gingerbread. I haven't really seen the excitement about houses there, but I've seen the kits sold in shops in the last couple of years, so maybe the craze is starting. I don't know. There's that thing where I assume it isn't big in England because I didn't notice it, but what would I know? I'm sure some families have been making these gingerbread houses for generations. Although …'

'Although what?'

'Oh, it's nothing.'

'I bet you were going to say something about how the gingerbread over there is different from the kind we have here.'

Her eyes widened. 'How did you know?'

'Lucky guess.'

They smiled at each other for a long moment before Sharmila forced herself to break the connection.

'You know gingerbread isn't a big thing in India,' she said, after casting her mind for anything to talk about. 'Which is surprising because we love sweet food and India is the world's largest producer of ginger. According to my mum, ginger can cure all ills.'

'The medicinal uses of ginger. What kind of things does it cure?'

'Enhances digestion and, of course, it's good for sickness, like morning sickness, and it can clear the nasal passages.'

'Does your mother use a lot of home remedies?'

'Surprisingly, yes.'

'Why surprisingly?'

'She's a cardiologist.'

A spoon clattered, causing Sharmila to look up from the jellybeans she was sticking to the walls.

'Are you joking?' he asked.

'No, why would I?'

'I don't know. You were painting this image of your mother as some alternative medicine practitioner, but she's a real doctor.'

'Western and Eastern medicine do not have to be in opposition to each other,' she replied, quoting her mother.

'I guess.'

'Talking of sweet food, have you ever tried Bengali mishti?'

He shook his head.

'It's an acquired taste. I have a huge sweet tooth, but even I can't handle some of the mishti. But Thomas had no trouble eating it. He loved it. You should have seen him. We walked to a mishti shop nearly every day so he could try all the different ones.'

'What are—'

But Zach was interrupted by the sound of a buzzer and the judge's announcement that they had thirty minutes left.

Sharmila looked at the house in front of her. Since Zach had taken over, it was much sturdier. He'd even extended their original design a little. It was a massive improvement but not even close to some of the other contestants' constructions. She didn't care about the quality – she was just glad she could tick off another activity from her wish list. And, despite her earlier decision to limit her time with Zach, she liked being with him. Overall, it was a good day.

It was already getting dark when they finally left the hall. Automatically, Zach followed Sharmila to the gazebo. One of his lasting memories of Pineford was going to be of this random structure in the middle of the town green.

'Is everything OK?' he asked.

She nodded. 'All good. Thanks for helping me out. It's a shame Lucas got called away for work.'

Zach looked away. He knew Izzy had called Lucas away for a pressing 'work' matter as an attempt to sabotage Sharmila in the competition. They should have realised their efforts would go to waste because the town would step in to help Sharmila. Again. Pineford had welcomed her into their community and made her an honorary member. Hundreds of people couldn't all be taken in by one person, could they?

Zach couldn't explain why he'd turned up at the competition. He knew there was the possibility he could be asked to step in. He wasn't acting rationally. He needed to put his family first and concentrate on the inheritance.

They had been unsuccessful with the wishes so far. They would need to be really creative to stop Sharmila from completing the ice skating, parade, and party activities. It would have been better if they spent their time, Lucas in particular, persuading Sharmila to visit his family in Boston.

Although, there was still one item on the list they hadn't found out. He convinced himself he was spending all this time with her so they could discover what it was.

Sharmila yawned, not even trying to cover her mouth. 'I can't believe it's only four. It feels like it's already been a long day. I didn't expect decorating gingerbread to be so energy intensive.'

He frowned. 'Have you eaten?' He hadn't noticed her have any snacks while they'd been in the hall and the competition had lasted for hours. 'Shall we go to Cinnamon's – get something?'

She wrinkled her nose in that way that made him simultaneously want to give it a playful tap and gather her in his arms.

'I think the smell of gingerbread filled me up. I couldn't face anything at the moment.' She rested her head against the railing, closing her eyes. Seconds later, she opened them, sitting up. 'If you're hungry, you should grab some food.'

He smiled. 'I'm good.'

They sat in silence, watching the town go about its day. There was something comfortable and restful being with Sharmila, so different from that first evening when everything was awkward and he was acting like a stuffy fool. Now, he was as content chatting with her, loving the way her mind worked, as he was sitting quietly as they were now. He wanted to spend the evening out there, simply enjoying the company of a captivating woman. Unfortunately, that wasn't really an option.

'Come on,' he said, getting up. 'It's getting chilly.' He waited while she groaned, stretched, then stood up. He moved in front of her, helping to tighten her scarf round her neck. 'We should start walking before we freeze here.'

Almost without thinking he bent his arm towards her. After a moment's hesitation she put her hand in the crook of his elbow.

'There are carols at the church tonight. Do you want to go?' he said.

She scrunched her face. 'I don't think so.'

'Really? I thought you'd enjoy them.'

'I do, I love carols. I just … I'm not sure.' Her mouth twisted. 'A lot of people stare at me here.'

He nodded. 'I see that. You are beautiful – I expect it happens everywhere you go. But I'm sorry the interest makes you uncomfortable.' He turned slightly when he realised she'd stopped walking and dropped her hand. She had an arrested look on her face.

'What's wrong?' he asked, moving a strand of her hair that had fallen across her eyes back behind her ear.

'Nothing.' She shook her head. 'It doesn't matter.'

'If you don't want to go to the carol service, a group of carollers are singing on the other side of town, near the river wharf. We could go there if you want to listen to some carols.'

She smiled with such delight, he felt like he invented electricity.

'I would love that,' she said. 'Lead the way.'

They walked up Main Street towards the river.

'Are these carollers dressed up in old-fashioned clothing?'

He smiled. 'Yes. I guess you've seen them in those movies.'

'I have. I was never sure it actually happened in real life though. Do they dress like that for a charity?'

She continued to reel off questions without pausing for breath. He was pleased she was back to her usual self – or at least the self she'd presented before. For all he knew, she was usually grumpy, the way she'd been during the gingerbread competition, and her happy personality was because of the seasonal activities.

Either way, either personality, he liked being in her company. Unless it was all an act.

On their way they passed a few places that had been clues on the Winter Trail. Sharmila wanted to take photos even though it was over. She persuaded him to join her in selfies. Not that he protested too much. He was enjoying the chance to huddle close to her – feel her arm round his waist, his arm around her shoulder.

He would have been happy to carry on walking arm in arm. That thought was enough to make him move quickly away from her.

They weren't a couple. They could never be a couple.

As the strong, clear notes of a Christmas carol reached them, he felt Sharmila's hand on his arm again, stopping him from walking further.

'Beautiful,' she whispered, closing her eyes as she tilted her head towards the music.

'There are already lots of people around the carollers. Are you sure you still want to go up?'

She nodded vigorously.

Almost by decree, the people parted as Sharmila drew close, allowing them close access to the singers. He was touched by their thoughtfulness – giving Sharmila the best view.

One of the carollers called out, 'Please join us in singing. You can share our song sheets if you don't know the words.'

Zach moved backwards to blend more into the crowd while people joined the singing. A brave few stood next to the carollers and sang.

'Sharmila, why don't you come and sing with us,' the caroller he now recognised as Susan said.

'You have to come with me,' she said, pulling Zach forward.

'What, no!'

'You have to. I'm not doing it alone. Coming here was your idea, remember.'

Zach grimaced. 'I can't sing,' he said.

'That hasn't stopped any of the others,' Susan said.

Sharmila giggled. 'Come on. It will be fun.'

'Do you know "O Holy Night"?' one of the other carollers asked.

'I do,' Sharmila replied.

'I don't remember the lyrics,' he said. Someone thrust a sheet into his hands.

Sharmila grinned. She wasn't showing any signs of nerves. She started to sing. She wasn't going to win any music awards, but her voice was sweet and strong. She faltered at the last line of the first verse, so he joined in with the line 'A thrill of hope', expecting the others to join too. They didn't until a few lines later.

'That was wonderful,' Susan said, throwing her arms around them. 'Do you want to sing another one?'

'Oh no, that's OK, thank you. I think we've made your audience suffer enough,' Sharmila said with a laugh.

She turned to him when they went back to stand among the crowd of listeners. 'I'm going to stay here for a while. I do love carols.'

'That's obvious. You were word perfect. You must know them well.'

'Of course.' She gave him a strange look. 'We had Christian assemblies at primary school. I loved singing hymns but my favourite time was always when we started singing the carols in December.'

After listening to a few songs, by silent agreement, they walked along the river. The lights reflected in the water and the smell of chestnuts being roasted in the open created an undeniably romantic ambience. The urge to bring Sharmila closer into his arms was strong.

Suddenly, she grabbed him and came to a halt.

'I know this place!' she exclaimed.

'You've been down here before? We can walk a different route.'

'No. I saw it in a photo. Thomas sent me a photo of him standing exactly here. I recognise that statue. He said it was of a member of his family.'

Zach walked over to the plaque. 'It's of Henry Adams. He was one of the founders of Pineford and helped develop this riverside area.' He stared up at his ancestor. His mom had told him stories about the family connection to Pineford going back centuries, but he hadn't heard about the statue. Yet Thomas had shared the photo with Sharmila.

When he came back to her, she showed him her phone. 'I don't keep many photos on my phone, but I had to keep this one. Thomas looked so happy.'

Zach examined the photo. He'd never seen Thomas look happier. 'Do you have any other photos of Thomas?'

She gave him a curious look. He'd forgotten again, she didn't know his relationship to Thomas.

'I have one more. It was taken in India when we went in March.'

The photo showed Thomas standing next to an Indian man and woman of a similar age, presumably Sharmila's parents. They were all covered in coloured powders and laughing.

'They all had powder in their hands and threw it at me as soon as I put the camera away,' Sharmila said, chuckling at the memory. She explained the Holi spring festival they were celebrating.

Zach had seen only one other photo of Thomas laughing that way. In it Thomas was in his twenties. He'd been standing next to Zach's parents and to Aunt Carla, Thomas's wife. It was taken months before she died.

Zach was more convinced the Thomas Sharmila described was the real version – or the person Thomas became in his last years. The version Zach had grown up with – the cold, sometimes aloof man – wasn't the man in the photos. This new Thomas sounded exactly like the kind of person who would be eccentric enough to leave a precious gift for someone like Sharmila.

His phone vibrated. Lucas had been sending him messages throughout the day, wanting to know what happened with the gingerbread competition, whether they'd managed to stop her completing the activity.

Zach frowned. How could he tell Lucas his attempt at sabotage had been effectively sabotaged by the town and Zach himself? Again.

He did want to help Lucas and Izzy – he believed that Thomas shouldn't have left Sharmila the shares, and he still wanted Holly House for his mom.

But at the same time, he loved watching Sharmila fulfil the wishes – her joy was infectious. No matter what she had or hadn't done to convince Thomas to leave her this holiday, she was really enjoying the seasonal events. He didn't want to take that away.

This conflict was frustrating.

Did he even need to stay in Pineford anymore? Lucas was probably at less risk in her company than Zach was. Perhaps he could leave the plan in Lucas's hands and return to San Francisco.

Why didn't that prospect please him anymore?

Chapter 19

Sunday morning was dull and grey. There hadn't been any fresh snowfall to brighten the day. Sharmila stood by her bedroom window looking over at the barn, thinking about Zach, again.

She thought back to the previous evening.

He was so easy to talk to, to open up to. She shared things with him she hadn't shared with anyone. She thought they had a moment. Then he became remote and left her without saying anything. Had she upset him in some way?

Was it when she showed him the photo of Thomas with her parents? His reaction had been unexpected. Perhaps he had been closer to Thomas than she realised. She had the sense she needed to give him some privacy, so she'd left him staring at the photo and walked over to gaze up at the statue.

She didn't mean to start crying but standing next to the statue of Thomas's ancestor, knowing Thomas had stood in the same spot not so long ago, brought so many different emotions to the surface, it overwhelmed her.

Zach was by her side in an instant.

'What's wrong, Sharmila? Please don't cry,' he said, running his thumb along her cheek to dry her tears.

She shook her head. 'I'm sorry. Thomas has given me this

amazing gift, but he should be here. He told me months ago to keep December free. I know he was planning to show me round Pineford. I think we were meant to enjoy this Christmas experience together. And we can't because he's not around anymore.' Her voice broke, and she took a couple of deep breaths to get herself under control.

'Sharmila.' He put his hands on her shoulders and turned her to face him. 'Nobody knew how ill Thomas was. I'm not even sure whether Thomas himself knew until after he bought Holly House. But I knew Thomas. And he would be happy to know that you're still getting to have this dream, even if he isn't here.'

A strange expression crossed Zach's face, and he dropped his hands. For a moment, she missed their strength and warmth. It wasn't sexual, simply comforting.

'I hope the people who loved him got a chance to say goodbye,' Sharmila said in a soft voice. 'It must be so hard when it's prolonged, but it's also hard when it's sudden.'

'You sound like you know.'

She shrugged. She didn't want to think about Hari right now. She walked on, turning to check he was following.

As they approached the town green, Zach spoke, breaking the silence that had fallen. 'I didn't get a chance to say goodbye to my father. My mother asked me to come home nearly every holiday. Christmas, Thanksgiving, Easter, but I always found an excuse. I booked a flight as soon as I heard he was at the hospital, but he died while I was in the air.'

Tentatively, she slipped her hand into his, fully prepared for him to pull away. Instead, his hand tightened round hers, accepting the comfort she offered.

'I sometimes wish I could tell him how sorry I am for leaving,' Zach said after a while, his gaze focused on the distance. 'How I never meant to stay away for so long. Maybe if I didn't leave, Dad wouldn't have been as stressed and maybe he wouldn't have had the heart attack. I carry that with me.'

'You can't blame yourself, Zach.' She shook her head at the irony of repeating the words she'd been told so often. 'I know how hard it is to stop thinking about what-ifs. I do the same.'

He turned to look at her, his expression curious but kind and encouraging.

'Hari, my boyfriend, was working in the office over one weekend. He didn't tell me where he was going to be.' She paused, taking a slow breath. 'He died from an aneurysm. I keep thinking if I had been there with him, I could have done something. Even though everyone tells me there was nothing that could have been done. It could have happened anywhere, at any time.'

'There's nothing you could have done.'

She gave him a pointed look.

He nodded, reaching out for her other hand and bringing them both up to his heart level. 'Perhaps we both need to stop blaming ourselves.'

'I will if you will.' She thought back to that dreadful time then laughed without humour. 'You know, Hari lied to me about where he was that weekend. We'd been arguing about his work-life balance of all things. I thought he was putting his work above everything. He told me he was spending the weekend with friends but he went into the office instead. I was so angry at the same time as devastated, and that made the guilt worse. I don't know why he lied. What was the point? It was a silly lie for a silly reason.'

She was connecting to Zach on an emotional level. She thought he could be feeling the same but instead he'd pulled away from her and hurried away.

Sharmila was jolted back to the present by the sound of Penny's voice calling up to her.

'You're back!' Sharmila ran down the stairs to give Penny a hug.

'I've only been gone two nights.'

'It seemed longer. This house is so huge and quiet at night without you.'

They walked into the kitchen.

'You know, if you were scared at night, I'm sure Zach would have been happy to keep you company.' Penny waggled her eyebrows in a suggestive manner.

She purposefully ignored the comment. 'Tell me about your weekend. What was it like meeting your friends for the first time in person? Was it weird? Were they like you thought online? What was the commune like?'

They took their mugs into the snug and got comfortable while Penny told her about her weekend.

After a while, Penny checked her watch. 'The Ice Sculpture Contest should be ready for judging soon. Do you want to go down?'

Sharmila chewed her cheek. 'I may just stay in the house today. I'm still tired after all of yesterday's activities.'

Penny gave her a sceptical look. 'You decorated a gingerbread house, you didn't climb Everest. What's the problem?'

Sharmila shrugged. 'Nothing.'

'Is it Zach?'

'Why would it be Zach?'

Penny's eyes narrowed. 'Are you expecting to see him?'

'Not really.'

'Did something happen?'

Sharmila scoffed. 'No. Nothing ever happens.'

'I knew it,' Penny said, clearly delighted. 'You like him, don't you?'

'I do like him,' she admitted. She liked him a lot. 'But don't start that again.'

'What?'

'Your idea I should have a holiday romance as part of my Christmas movie fantasy. It's not going to happen.'

Penny held her hands up. 'All right, all right. I won't say another word.'

'Sure,' Sharmila replied with a small grin. Penny never gave up when she thought she was right.

'If it's not Zach, why aren't you going today?'

'Ice sculptures aren't one of Thomas's wishes, so there's no need for me to go down to Pineford today.'

'Sharmila, we talked about this. You shouldn't only do the activities on Thomas's list. That's still hiding from the world. I thought you were getting better, opening yourself up again.'

'Getting better?' She recoiled, surprised at Penny's choice of words. 'This isn't something I need to recover from. Pineford people are great, but I'm not going to see them again after ten days.'

'I think you're trying to hide from the world again.'

She rolled her eyes. 'How am I hiding from the world when I've been doing all these activities? I judged a competition – that wasn't on this list. I didn't need to do that. I'm going to be in the parade, but I'm also helping them prepare for it – that's also not on Thomas's list. And I'll be hosting a party that's being organised like it's a wedding. I couldn't hide from the world even if I wanted to.'

Penny opened her mouth, then closed it without saying anything.

'What?' Sharmila asked.

Penny shook her head.

'Please, just tell me what you're thinking.'

'It doesn't matter, hun,' Penny replied. 'I'm going to jump in the shower and then head into town.'

Sharmila nursed her coffee after Penny left the room.

Hiding from the world. That's what she'd been doing for the last couple of years. And nothing had changed.

Yes, she was engaging with the town on the various activities, but it was because of the list. Nothing else. Suppose Thomas hadn't tied a charity donation to his wishes. Would she even bother completing the ones that involved interacting with the town? She probably wouldn't have, because it would mean she'd have to open herself up to the possibility of letting people in

194

once more. And as soon as she realised she was starting to care, she backed away and tried to hide. Again.

It wasn't surprising her best friend could see right through her.

Avoiding the world was safe. Knowing the Pineford residents only on a superficial level was sensible – she wouldn't risk the pain she felt at losing loved ones too soon. Like Hari. Like Thomas.

But there was a voice in her head asking her whether she was missing out. Was this how she wanted to spend the rest of her life, closed off and all alone?

She would never get another chance to experience Christmas in Pineford. If she didn't do some of the activities purely because she was frightened of getting close to people, then she wouldn't be making the most of the opportunity Thomas had given her. She'd almost be throwing his gift back in his face.

And there was Zach.

She walked through to the front drawing-room where there was a clear view of the barn. She'd spent more time at the window than she'd like to admit.

She inhaled slowly. She was only in Pineford for another week. She didn't want to get back to England and regret missing out on everything this holiday had to offer because she was scared of opening herself up.

She was waiting by the door in her coat and scarf when Penny came downstairs.

'You're coming with me?' Penny asked, with a huge grin.

'Yes. I don't want to focus only on Thomas's wishes any more. I want to make the most of all the Pineford events.'

Penny gave her a surprised look. 'I'm so happy to hear you've had a change of heart. What brought it on?'

'Nothing major. Jackie is clearly going to involve me in all things Pineford – kicking and screaming if necessary. I may as well embrace the path of least resistance. But you're right. This is a once-in-a-lifetime opportunity. I should make the most of it.'

She was still nervous, would prefer not to put herself out there, but she wasn't going to be her own obstacle.

By the time Penny and Sharmila arrived at the town green, the final touches were being put on the ice sculptures.

When Jackie had told her they used professional judges, Sharmila assumed the competition would be intense. Still, the standard of the sculptures was unbelievable. It made sense. No one was going to work with sharp tools in a competitive setting unless they were proficient.

Sharmila and Hari had spent a day in the Hyde Park Winter Wonderland one year. They'd gone around the Magical Ice Kingdom, where Christmas stories were depicted out of snow and ice sculptures. In her unprofessional opinion, what she saw in front of her wouldn't have been out of place in that attraction.

The crowds were kept at a distance while the judging took place, something about body heat and melting. Sharmila didn't know if that was true, but it gave her the chance to pop into the diner for a warming cup of cocoa, leaving Penny waiting with Debby outside.

Then they walked along Main Street, window shopping. A snowglobe in one of the shops caught Sharmila's eye. She went inside. As she finished her purchase, a claxon rang loud, making them all jump.

'Sounds like the judging has finished,' Penny said. 'Shall we go back to find out who's won or do you want to do some more shopping?'

'Let's go back.'

As they stood waiting for the ice sculpture results, she reached into her bag for the WinterFest brochure. There was a movie marathon that evening. She still needed to decide which film she was going to recreate. She was already over halfway through her wishes. There would only be the parade and the party, which were already in hand, and ice skating, which was part of Pineford's WinterFest.

A casual glance at the names of the movies was enough for Sharmila to know she wouldn't be recreating any of those. She would need to do some significant movie watching to find one that could work. Her mind immediately began to replay typical scenes from her romantic Christmas movies – only this time, the protagonists were her and someone who looked exactly like Zach.

She may have made a mistake avoiding the people in Pineford, but she wasn't wrong about Zach. She needed to keep her distance from him – she'd made the right decision on that Friday evening. For the first time since Hari had died, she started to think of love and relationships again. She was beginning to wish for a future with Zach.

She was wishing for the impossible.

Chapter 20

'She's in the kitchen,' Penny shouted in Zach's direction as she was leaving the house. He waved as she drove off. She'd left the door ajar – he pushed it open cautiously. The smell of popcorn greeted him. He frowned. Wasn't Sharmila going to the movie marathon?

'Hi,' he called out.

'Oh hi,' Sharmila said, coming to stand in the arch to the kitchen. 'How did you get in?'

'Penny left the door open for me on her way out.'

'Ah. Yes. She's going into town for the movies.'

He raised his eyebrows. 'You're not?'

She shook her head. 'Nah I have other plans.' She had a secretive smile on her face. 'Did you want me for something?'

Want her. He swallowed. Interesting choice of words. 'To see whether you want to go into Pineford together.'

'Oh. I've already watched loads of films today. Or the end of them at least. I recorded one of this year's Christmas romance movies. I'm going to watch that and then probably watch my all-time favourite Christmas romance.'

She smiled with anticipation as she poured popcorn into a large bowl then placed it on a tray next to bowls of chocolate pieces and candy, and a drink.

'Christmas romances?'

'Yes.'

'Are these the movies you and Thomas watched?'

'Yes.'

'Great, maybe I'll watch with you.' He smiled when she narrowed her eyes.

'Weren't you going to the movie marathon?'

He shrugged. 'I've seen all those movies before. I want to know what kind of movies you and Thomas liked so much.'

'I'm not sure they'd be your thing.'

His grin widened. She really didn't want him to watch with her. 'How will I know unless I watch one?'

She was hesitating. 'I don't know,' she said.

He shrugged. 'You watched them with Thomas. Maybe I'll love them too.'

'I doubt it, but it's your time to waste I guess.'

'Perfect.'

'I don't know much about the first film. It's set in a small town like Pineford though.'

'Sounds amazing. I'm dying to know what happens in the end.'

'OK, smarty-pants,' she said, rolling her eyes. 'If you're going to stay, we better set some ground rules.'

'Ground rules. You have rules about watching a movie?'

'Yes. If you want to watch with me you have to respect the rules.' She sounded like a strict school principal.

He lifted his hands up. 'Of course.'

She gave an exasperated shake of the head.

'What are these rules then?' he asked, reaching towards her bowl to grab a handful of popcorn.

'First, get your own bowl,' she said, shooing his hand away.

'Isn't it more fun to share?' he asked, the playful comment coming out slightly more suggestive than he intended.

She shook her head, batting her eyelashes. 'Sorry, I only share my refreshments with special people.'

'I'm special people,' he replied, with his most charming smile.

She laughed. 'Well, that remains to be seen, doesn't it?'

'Does it?' he asked, taking a step closer to her.

'Yes, it depends on whether you can follow my rules.' She gave him a light-hearted shove, then bent to take out another, smaller bowl, from a cupboard.

'Ah yes, your rules. OK, boss, what are these rules?'

'I like these films because I know what to expect from them. I know how easy it is to make fun of them because they tend to have recurring themes. So we can conclude I've probably already heard most of the comments people make about these films.' She paused, looking at him for confirmation he was following her. His lips quirked – the lawyer in her was coming out. He nodded. 'The rule is no commentary during the film unless you can come up with a pithy observation I've never heard before.'

'One you've never heard before?'

'That's right. You're not allowed to make fun of a cliché if your comment is a cliché in itself.'

He grinned. 'Agreed.'

She returned his grin. 'All right. That's all the rules for now. Although I do reserve the right to make up new rules at my whim.'

'Hmm, I'm not sure I can agree to that.'

'Thems my rules, take it or leave it.' She stood with her arms crossed, her eyebrows raised, waiting for his decision.

The temptation to gather her in his arms was strong. 'I'll take it. Lead the way.' He took the tray from her.

'This is the most amazing room, isn't it?' Sharmila said once they were in the cinema room.

He looked around at the large screen on one end, three over-sized theatre chairs and a two-seater sofa in front. She mentioned she'd watched loads of movies already but it didn't look like she used the cinema room. She pulled a small table up to the sofa for him to place the tray.

'Why the end of the movies?' he asked, remembering what she'd said.

'What?'

'You said you watched the end of loads of movies.'

'Oh, did I say that?'

'Yes, upstairs.'

There was a silence in the room.

'What is it, Sharmila?'

She gave him an assessing look while biting her bottom lip. 'No one but Penny knows about this,' she began.

He nodded, encouraging her to continue.

She ran a hand over her face. 'It's one of Thomas's wishes for me.'

'Watching movies?'

'Not movies. No.' She fiddled with the folds of her sweater, letting her hair cover her face.

Unable to resist, he reached out and swept her hair back behind her ear. He was entranced by her profile. 'What's wrong?' he asked.

'Nothing's wrong. It's just a bit embarrassing.'

'You can tell me.'

'Thomas wanted me to recreate the final scene of a Christmas movie. I've been watching the endings of all these movies to find one for me and Penny to do. You'd think *Die Hard* wouldn't have a soppy ending, wouldn't you?' Her tone was indignant.

He choked back a laugh. Finally, he knew what the last wish on the list was.

She picked up the remote control to press play but paused the film almost immediately.

'Remember the rules,' she said, sounding worried rather than joking.

He held up his hand. 'No talking unless I'm original. Promise.'

She nodded with approval then pressed the button to start the movie again.

He was more interested in watching Sharmila's animated face

as she watched her Christmas romance than he was in watching it himself.

The movie was as predictable as he expected but he enjoyed himself anyway. He liked being in her company. Liked talking to her. He'd shared things with her he'd never shared with anyone.

'Ready for the next one?' she asked.

'This one's your favourite?'

She nodded. 'Same rules as before.'

After the first few minutes, Sharmila let out a wistful sound and said, 'I love their coats. They always wear such wonderful coats.'

He laughed. 'Coats.'

Sharmila covered her mouth. 'Sorry. I spoke.'

He raised his eyebrows, giving her knee a gentle push. 'You broke your own rule. There should be a penalty.'

Sharmila shook her head. 'I don't think that's necessary!'

'That doesn't sound fair.'

She shrugged. 'Fairness wasn't one of my rules.'

'Oh. I see. Is your rule that you can talk and I can't?'

'And what if it is?' she asked with an impish grin.

'I suppose I have to agree if I want to stay, don't I?' he replied, nudging his shoulder against hers. He didn't mind; he wanted to hear her thoughts.

As they watched she pointed out the activities she'd done and the Christmas sets or made other observations.

'This is one of my favourite scenes,' she said when the two main characters were getting into an inflatable tube to slide down a snow-covered hill. 'Have you ever done that?'

He nodded. 'Have you been sledding?'

She shook her head. 'Sledging, you mean.'

'It's a sled.'

'I think you'll find it's a sledge.'

'You're in America, it's a sled. When I'm in England I'll call it a sledge.' She shrugged. 'Anyway, you'd probably use a toboggan.'

'What's the difference?'

'Nothing.' He laughed at her suspicious expression.

She tossed her hair and turned back to the film, continuing to point out bits she found interesting.

Her love for the movies shone through. He could imagine Thomas watching with her, sharing his views. Laughing together.

When Zach was much younger, his parents used to watch romantic comedies together. His father would gently poke fun at the plots, the way Sharmila had worried Zach would. But his mother would wave away his comments, saying the endings of his dad's thrillers were as predictable.

His mother would love Sharmila.

He took a deep breath, realisation dawning. Sharmila was precisely the kind of person his mother and his father would have adored. It made sense that Thomas adored her too.

There was nothing in what she said, or how she acted, to suggest she thought of Thomas as anything other than a close friend. Zach always had trouble seeing Sharmila as someone who was after money. Now, he no longer believed Thomas had been duped. And he knew it wasn't because Thomas's illness had caused any decline in his mental ability.

She put her hand on his arm. 'We're coming up to the ending. Look, it's just so perfect.'

He watched as the couple stood in a gazebo wrapped in each other's arms while they made their declarations of love. He glanced quickly at Sharmila. She was resting her elbows on her knees, holding her face in her hands with a dreamy look on her. His heart skipped a beat at the picture she made.

He wanted to be like the guy in the film, overcoming hurdles and fighting for love. To feel happiness and excitement over a future with someone special. And he knew he wanted that with Sharmila.

He wanted to start afresh, spend time with her without reservations, without second-guessing, without prejudging.

His phone vibrated in his pocket. A brief check showed it was

Izzy. He didn't want to deal with that now. Now he knew the final wish, he felt obligated to share it with his family. But he didn't want to, not yet anyway.

Sharmila deserved to have the Christmas Thomas wanted for her. Did that mean she also deserved Holly House and the shares? That wasn't his decision to make. If it had been, he would have said yes. No hesitation.

There didn't seem to be any middle ground.

She yawned and stretched when the movie finished. He almost suggested watching a third one together. Instead, she got up.

They walked into the kitchen, where he put the bowls and glasses into the dishwasher.

'I hope that wasn't too bad for you,' she said, 'but you did ask for it.'

'I enjoyed myself,' he replied with total honesty. 'Are you going to the Sleigh Bell Run tomorrow?' he asked.

'I'm going in at some point. To watch, not take part. What even is a Sleigh Bell Run? I'm intrigued,' she said.

'I have no idea either, but I'm intrigued too.' He answered her grin with his own. 'Why don't we drive in together? Doesn't make sense to take two cars.'

She nodded her agreement.

'Sleep well. See you tomorrow.' He walked out the door before he gave in to the urge to kiss her goodnight.

Chapter 21

'So, the Sleigh Bell Run is just a cross-country race where people wear reindeer antlers?' Sharmila asked.

'Not what you were expecting then?' Zach said.

'I didn't know what to expect. But not this.'

'Are you disappointed?'

She pressed her lips together and shrugged. 'Maybe a little.'

He pressed a comforting hand on her shoulder. 'We still have five minutes. Why don't I get us some hot chocolate?'

Sharmila watched him leave, his long strides showing an effortless grace. Her gaze roamed from his thick dark hair, cut sharp to the nape of his neck, down the length of his winter jacket, which stopped at the perfect point to draw attention to his firm backside. Suddenly aware of what she was doing, she cleared her throat, her eyes darting around to check whether anyone had noticed her appraisal.

Something had changed. She could tell he was less guarded with her now. For a moment, images from the dream she had the previous night flickered through her mind, Zach standing in a gazebo, holding her hands, staring lovingly into her eyes – like a montage from one of her romantic films.

She shook her head. A subtle difference in the way he acted

around her didn't mean there was a romance developing between them – on his part.

On her part, the attraction was as strong as ever. She'd had trouble concentrating on the films, distracted by even the slightest movement he made sitting next to her.

'Lucas called. He should be back in Pineford today,' Zach said as he handed her a hot chocolate. 'I know he'll tell you himself, but he is sorry he let you down with the gingerbread competition.'

She waved her hand. 'It's water under the bridge now. I have you and Pineford to thank, for coming to my rescue. I'm just sorry he had to miss out on some of WinterFest. He sounded really excited about it.'

'Don't worry about Lucas. He gets excited over anything. It's why everyone he meets says what a likeable guy he is.'

She couldn't help but return his cheeky grin, unable to tear her gaze away from his face. Luckily, the claxon announcing the start of the races was loud enough to distract her.

She turned to the starting line exhaling slowly. There was definitely something different in the way he was behaving around her this morning. Almost as if they were a couple. What did it mean? She forced herself to focus on the runners, cheering and waving as they ran past her.

'You seem different today,' she said as the crowds began to clear.

'I do? In what way?'

She shrugged. 'I don't know, more relaxed, I guess.'

'It's less than a week until Christmas. Perhaps I'm finally in the holiday mood. De-Grinchified.'

She laughed. 'Oh, don't remind me how close Christmas is. I still don't feel ready for the Boxing Day party. You're coming, aren't you?'

'I hope to.'

'Are you having Christmas dinner at Pineford Inn as well?'

He stood still for a moment, looking at her, but she could tell

206

he was not really seeing her. 'I don't know yet. I've been invited, but Lucas is going home for the holidays.'

'And you might join him?'

'I haven't decided.'

They watched the runners disappear.

'Are we supposed to wait here until they come back?' she asked.

'If you're not interested in the race, I have an idea about something we could do. You can ask Penny too.'

'What?'

He winked. 'Let's keep it a surprise.'

'Hmm, I'm not sure about that.'

He placed a hand on her arm. 'It'll be fun, trust me.'

She pretended to consider it. 'OK. Sounds like a plan. I'll text Penny to meet us at the house. You can let Lucas know, in case he gets back in time.'

After lunch, she and Penny were sitting in Zach's truck as they made their way to an unknown destination. She wiggled to get a little more room on the bench. Was Penny deliberately taking the space of one and a half people? Sharmila rolled her eyes. Of course Penny was – anything to push her closer to Zach. As she found herself jostled against him, he looked over at her with a warm smile. She stopped trying to move away. Perhaps this wasn't so bad. She glanced at Penny, who gave her a quick wink before turning to stare out the side window.

They drove away from Pineford in a direction Sharmila hadn't been before.

'You do have a destination in mind, don't you?' she asked. 'Driving around all day wasn't your surprise, was it?'

'Patience. All will be revealed in time,' Zach replied. 'The only thing I will say is we aren't that far from Boston.'

'We are not going to Boston!' Sharmila and Penny exclaimed simultaneously.

Zach shrugged. 'We can be there and back in a day. It's only a few hours.'

Sharmila shook her head. He was joking. He wouldn't drive them to Boston, would he? Perhaps he was doing it as a favour for Lucas's family.

He was staring straight ahead, a small smile playing on his lips. Her lips quirked in response. He was in a playful mood.

She kept her eyes ahead as he left the main road and carried along a narrow path, which led to a golf club.

'We're at a golf club?' Sharmila asked, getting out of the truck after he parked. 'We're playing golf in the snow?'

'Golf courses have some of the best hills for sledding.'

'Sledging! I can't believe we're going sledging!' Sharmila wanted to bounce with excitement.

'Yeah, you said you've never done it. At this golf club, you can also hire inflatable snow tubes.'

'This is amazing. I'm going to tell Debby where we are in case she can join us when she finishes work,' Penny said, walking off to make her call.

'Are you ready?' Zach asked, going round to the back of his truck and revealing a large sledge.

'Where did you get that?'

'It was in the barn in the yard. Either the previous owners left it behind, or Thomas bought it for you to use. I just fixed it up.'

'Overnight?'

'It was nothing.'

She put her hand on his arm. 'It's not nothing, Zach. Thank you.'

He looked at her hand, then moved a strand of hair off her face. 'You're welcome. Come.' He held out his hand. 'There's a short walk to the entry kiosk and the run, but it will be worth it.'

Sharmila already knew it was worth it. The snow in many areas was still pristine. 'What a shame we don't have any more sledges – it would have been fun to race.'

'We can hire sleds here as well if we need to. We could probably get you a toboggan if you'd prefer.' He glanced down at her, smirking.

She rolled her eyes.

'Aren't they the same thing?' Penny asked, returning to them.

'Toboggans are simple sledges mainly for little children,' Sharmila explained, giving Zach a pointed look.

'You looked it up,' Zach said, grinning at her.

'Of course I did!' She gave him a playful push. 'Anyway, the words probably are used interchangeably now.'

They'd arrived at a makeshift hut that had the rental equipment and also sold hot drinks.

'What do you want? An inflatable snow tube? Another sled?' Zach asked.

'Why don't we get one tube,' Penny replied. 'That sledge looks big enough to fit two people if Sharmila's one of those people.'

Zach nodded. 'Sure. We can always get another sled later if we need it.'

'Subtle. Real subtle,' Sharmila said to Penny after Zach was out of earshot.

'I can picture the scene now,' Penny said with an unapologetic grin. 'You share a sledge. Suddenly, accidentally, you fall off into the snow. He thinks you're hurt. But you're only winded. After he checks on you, he can't resist the sight of you lying in the cool white snow. He leans in for a kiss.'

'You've been secretly watching my films, haven't you?'

Penny grinned. 'Maybe I should be a screenwriter.'

Sharmila shook her head affectionately. 'Is Debby coming?'

'Hopefully. But don't think you can get away with trying to change the subject.'

'There's no subject to change. We're here to have fun, that's all.' Sharmila could hear the shrieks and laughter coming from the distance, out of sight from where they were waiting.

Zach returned with an inflatable snow tube. 'We can wait at the bottom of the hill for a buggy to take us to the top. The path has been cleared, but it's a longer route because it has to wind round the course. Or we can walk up the hillside. It shouldn't take too long and there's a rope to help.'

'Walking's fine for me.' Pure eagerness and adrenaline would get her to the top in no time.

Once they were ready to sledge down, and before Penny could say anything, Sharmila suggested she and Penny go together.

'I've never been sledging before,' Penny said.

'Neither have I,' replied Sharmila.

'I know. That's why I think it would be best if Zach goes with you this first time. He can help you guide the sledge.'

'Sure,' Zach agreed. 'I'll go line it up.'

Merely the idea of sitting between Zach's legs on the sledge caused heat to diffuse through Sharmila's body. She was sure her face betrayed her reaction.

'This is probably a bad idea,' she said.

'Nonsense,' Penny replied. 'Off you go.'

Sharmila blew out a breath as she waited for Zach to take his position. He held out a hand to help her sit in front of him.

He put his arms over her shoulders to adjust her scarf. 'Best to keep this far out the way. We don't want it to get caught.'

She sat ramrod stiff as far forward as she could.

'Relax,' Zach said, his breath warm on her neck. 'It will be better if you can sit further back and relax your body.'

Easier said than done when every nerve was on high alert. How could layers of sheepskin, beanies, and jumpers provide no protection from his proximity?

All of that was almost forgotten once they set off down the hill. She was secure in his arms, watching the world fly by. She let out a yell as they went hurtling down.

After they had taken a few turns on the sledge and tube, Debby joined them. They hired an extra sledge and tube so they could race against each other.

Sharmila couldn't take her eyes off Zach's handsome face as

he joked and laughed with them – more relaxed than she'd ever seen him before.

After a hot chocolate break, Penny said she needed to return to Pineford to finish off some work. Debby offered to take her so Sharmila and Zach could stay.

'Are you ready to go back home?' Zach asked after they'd been down the run a few more times.

'Sure, if you want.'

'How about one last turn down the hill?'

Sharmila nodded vigorously as they raced to the top. Once she reached the bottom, she turned to look for Zach but he was nowhere to be seen.

Thinking she'd seen an abandoned sledge a little way up, she called out his name, falling over in a rush to get to it. The panic started to build inside when she couldn't hear him answer. She clambered to her feet and managed a couple of steps before falling again. Not taking any chances she would fall again and take longer to get to him, she started crawling forward on her hands, the cold snow seeping to her knees. She had to get to Zach before it was too late. She couldn't lose anyone else.

She stopped in her tracks when she heard laughter. He was standing behind her, watching her stumble.

'What are you doing?' he asked.

'I thought you'd fallen off your sledge.'

'No, I went off course a little. But I'm fine.' He laughed again. 'Why, were you worried?'

'Not at all,' she mumbled, glad he wasn't closer or she would have hit him out of sheer relief.

'I didn't know you cared.'

His flippant reply made her pause. She did care. A lot.

It wasn't a simple attraction. She liked Zach. She cared about him. Could grow to love him if there had been a future for them. Suddenly sombre, she brushed herself down.

'I'm ready to go back home now,' she said, starting to walk away.

He reached out to stop her. 'I didn't mean to upset you.'

'No, that's fine. It's getting cold and dark. We should go.'

They drove back to Pineford in silence. Sharmila's thoughts whirring with the implications of how much she already cared for Zach.

At her request, he parked outside his barn. She could do with the fresh air from the short walk to the house to clear her thoughts. She took a couple of steps then stopped. She didn't want him to worry he'd upset her. He'd been so thoughtful, going out of his way to arrange an activity that was straight out of her favourite movie.

Turning back, she rushed up and flung her arms around him. Pouring everything she was feeling into that hug – relief, affection, joy, and ... something else she was determined not to think about.

'Thank you, Zach. That was one of the best days I've had on this holiday. Thank you.'

'It was absolutely my pleasure,' he replied, his arms tightening around her.

Her body stilled, her pulse started racing. She buried her head against the warmth and safety of his chest.

He reached to move what was quickly becoming her favourite strand of hair behind her ear, then stroked his thumb along the side of her cheek to her chin. He lifted her chin up. She stared intently into his eyes as he brought his face closer. She closed the distance between them.

Chapter 22

Sharmila sighed as she poured the brewed coffee into a mug then took the milk out of the fridge. Last night was playing over and over again in her head.

She'd been in his arms, certain as he drew her closer that this was the moment she'd been waiting for. They were finally going to kiss.

The sound of a car approaching had interrupted them before she could close the gap completely. She'd groaned, squinting as the headlights came into view. Lucas. Never had she wanted to see him less.

Lucas spoke with her briefly, apologising again for letting her down. He was apparently oblivious to the charged atmosphere between her and Zach. After telling Zach he'd meet him back in the barn, he walked off.

Zach hastily squeezed her hand, mouthing 'tomorrow', and followed after Lucas. And she hadn't seen him since.

She needed to keep busy otherwise, her mind would keep on reliving that moment. That frustrating feeling of *almost*.

This time Sharmila had no doubts about what would have happened. They would have kissed.

She took her mug into the study to check whether she had

any emails from her work. Her transfer to London had been confirmed, but she was still waiting for details for her first day.

Sharmila made a face. Even though she enjoyed her new knowledge-support role at work, the reality that she would be back in the office in two weeks was slightly depressing.

Everything about this holiday had been a perfect fantasy – down to the previous night and Zach.

And that was a problem. Despite Penny's prodding, Sharmila wasn't after a brief holiday romance with Zach. There was more to her feelings towards him than that. But they didn't have time in Pineford to explore a real relationship. She was leaving in a week, and after that there would be a literal ocean between them.

After finishing in the study, she took her mug of mostly cold coffee to the living area, curled up on the couch and stared out over the garden. There was a light snow falling, covering old footprints and making the ground pristine again.

It was going to be so hard leaving this place and returning to reality.

She expelled a breath of annoyance. She wasn't going to waste her remaining time in Pineford thinking about leaving Pineford. Liz had mentioned there was more parade prep in town. She would drive in, to see whether she could help the Women's Club.

Penny was working on a graphics project, so Sharmila drove in alone.

There were only a few people in the community hall when Sharmila arrived. Lydia came straight over to her.

'Wonderful, you're here. I heard all about your skill with a sewing machine. There are still some last-minute alterations to be made if you don't mind.'

'Always happy to help.'

Sharmila worked diligently on the alterations, refusing to let thoughts of Zach, or leaving Pineford, or returning to work, or kissing Zach enter her mind. She was concentrating on pinning a hem when she heard Zach's name mentioned. She tried to subtly eavesdrop on the conversation. Apparently he couldn't help with the parade floats because he had gone somewhere with Lucas. She'd seen Zach's truck outside the barn when she left, had even considered going over to talk to him, but in the end she'd chickened out and got into her car. Now it sounded like he hadn't even been there. All her angst had been a waste of time.

She made an effort to chat with the others there and not let her thoughts get pulled in a different direction. She quickly became engrossed in the conversation, enjoying being with the other women, not even once thinking about the ALMOST KISS.

'Oh, you'll never guess what,' Lydia exclaimed to the group, 'I have news about Kelly and her husband.'

Sharmila remembered Kelly's name from the cookie baking evening – she was the woman whose husband had been acting suspiciously. Even though Penny told her to leave it alone, sometimes she couldn't help thinking about all the possible scenarios – he was having an affair, he'd lost his job and was afraid to tell his wife, the list was endless. She laughed at how ridiculous she'd been after finding out the reason for his behaviour. He'd been working extra shifts for overtime pay and making secret arrangements with Kelly's family to look after their children so that he could whisk her away for a long weekend to spend quality time on a second honeymoon.

Sharmila chewed her inner cheek. When it came to relationships, secrets were always a sensitive issue for Sharmila – she always assumed the worst, and she hadn't been proved wrong so far. With Hari. With the clients she dealt with back at her law firm. But her eyes were being opened to the possibility that secrets weren't always harmful. If ever she needed a lesson on trusting people generally and not jumping to conclusions she'd received it loud and clear.

Penny was right. She'd been reacting irrationally, reading more into the situation and letting her past experience influence her.

By doing the activities on Thomas's Wishlist, she'd been forced to disengage her safety mechanism, leave her comfort zone, begin lowering her barriers, and face the world. The people of Pineford had helped her embrace life again. But that had also left her vulnerable to developing feelings for Zach.

They had almost kissed. That was all. It wasn't a marriage proposal or necessarily even the start of anything. Perhaps Zach was also caught up in this fairy-tale moment. She wanted to spend her perfect Christmas in Pineford with him, but part of her hoped he would spend the holiday with his mother – to reconnect with her. Sharmila could tell he really loved his mother and it sounded like he missed spending time with her.

And if he did go to his mother's home, or to Boston with Lucas, would he return to Pineford before he went home to San Francisco?

On the one hand, she could continue to dismiss her feelings, playing it safe for the rest of her life. But on the other hand, there was something special with Zach and she suspected he knew it too. Why else would he have moved in to kiss her? She could take that risk on him, live for the moment, and perhaps find true happiness once again.

If Zach regretted last night, that was OK with her. She would be able to cope. If Zach wanted to have only a brief romance while they were in Pineford, would that be enough for her? She'd fallen hard for him so quickly, her feelings would inevitably grow in the few days she had left on holiday. Or was there a chance they could try a long-distance relationship? Either way, she was opening herself up to a world of hurt – was she ready to do that again?

Avoiding Zach wasn't going to get her any answers. She decided to return home to wait for Zach and find out exactly where she stood.

Zach wasn't sure what kind of greeting to expect as he waited outside Holly House. Almost twenty-four hours had passed since he'd held Sharmila in his arms, since their lips nearly touched

– he wouldn't blame her if she thought he'd been avoiding her. Nothing could be further from the truth.

He wanted to explore having a relationship with Sharmila, but he couldn't do that while he was keeping secrets. Over the past few days, he had been leaving hints about his real identity to her – his true line of work and business. While they were watching the movies, he even managed to slip in that he would be in England, hoping she might be more open to a relationship, but she hadn't picked up on it. And there was still the biggest lie of all between them – his real name and the reason for his visit to Pineford.

He wanted to tell her the truth. But if he told her who he was, she would want to know why he kept it a secret – then the whole story about her inheritance would come out, and she would win by default. Even though he now believed Sharmila was not the master manipulator they once thought, he couldn't put Lucas and Izzy under the stress of not having full control of their company. This was his family's business at stake.

He needed to speak to Izzy and Lucas but for now, spending time with Sharmila when it had nothing to do with Thomas's Wishlist was something he wanted to do.

The door was opened by a laughing Sharmila wearing a bright green sweater with a blue Christmas tree festooned with tinsel and baubles. She looked adorable. The urge to wrap her in his arms and claim her lips the way he had wanted to do the previous night was strong. Instead, he took a step back and raised his eyebrows. 'Special occasion?'

She rolled her eyes in response, before turning and walking towards the kitchen. He followed her. Penny was standing by the hob, stirring a pan of milk. She was also wearing a tacky Christmas sweater.

'We're having a day off from the wish list and decided to have some fun. It's not Christmas without ugly jumpers, is it?' Penny said.

'We thought we'd add our own special Christmas sparkle,'

Sharmila said, getting out another mug. 'And we're making Thomas's Double Chocolate, Double Cream, Decadent Hot Chocolate Delight. Would you like some?'

'I'd love some, thanks. But I feel like the odd one out since I don't have a sweater to wear,' he teased.

'Oh, but you do,' Penny said, beaming at him.

'Yes, indeed,' Sharmila agreed, walking to a shopping bag. 'We got jumpers for you and Lucas too. Do you know where he is?'

'As far as I know he's at the inn.' He withdrew a large blue sweater depicting a snowman. 'Thank you for this. Though I don't think I'll be winning any ugly Christmas sweater competitions, especially if I'm up against you,' he said, reaching out to shake one of the baubles on Sharmila's sweater.

Sharmila cleared her throat. 'Go and put this on,' she said, indicating the bathroom.

He went to change, reflecting that Sharmila wasn't acting any differently than usual. He couldn't tell whether she was pretending everything was fine or whether she was happy, even excited, to be in his company after what almost happened between them.

He stood outside the kitchen area for a few moments, watching Sharmila as she joked and laughed with Penny. All he wanted to do was talk with her, hold her, care for her. What he felt was real – couldn't that be enough?

He joined them at the kitchen counter.

'To ugly sweaters and Double Chocolate, Double Cream, Decadent Hot Chocolate Delight,' he said, holding his mug up in a toast. 'May this be the start of a new tradition.'

They chatted for a few minutes, then Penny glanced at the time before excusing herself to get back to work. She gave him a wink as she passed.

'I can see why Thomas loved this. It *is* great hot chocolate,' Zach said, drinking up the last drops in his mug. 'But I came over to see if you want to come into town with me. The sleigh rides are already starting in the park. It could be fun?'

Sharmila nodded. 'I'll let Penny know in case she wants to go down with us.'

After the wink she gave him, he was confident Penny would be 'unavailable' and was proved right only a few minutes later when she claimed she had too much work to take a break at that moment. He grinned. He knew he could count on Penny.

The sleigh rides were taking place in Pineford's largest park, where the snow still covered the paths. They were using actual sleighs with runners, each sleigh pulled by a strong, sturdy horse.

Sharmila grabbed his arm. 'It's a real one-horse open sleigh!' she said, clapping her hands with delight.

When she didn't move, he turned to see her clasp her hands to her chest and inhale deeply. 'Is everything OK?' he asked.

'Everything's perfect. I'm just breathing in all this beauty, committing it to my memory.'

They stood next to each other without speaking. Like Sharmila, he wanted to remember this moment for ever.

'Come on, let's go,' he said, grabbing her hand, keeping a hold of it when they joined the line.

Soon they were seated in a sleigh, warm blankets placed over their legs. Sharmila was handed a muff to keep her hands warm.

'I feel like I'm in a film set in the nineteenth century,' she said, relaxing against the back where he'd placed his arm. 'This is so much more than even I imagined.'

Soon they fell into companionable silence, enjoying the cadence of the sleigh moving with the horse's trot.

'Look, is that a falling star?' Sharmila suddenly pointed at the sky. 'Do we get to make a wish?'

It was a night for flights of fancy. Zach closed his eyes to make his wish. A wish where he was a man enjoying a sleigh ride in the snow with a beautiful, intelligent, intriguing woman. And there were no company shares, no houses, or wish lists or inheritances.

She looked enticing in the moonlight. He wanted to lift her

chin with his finger, bring her lips to meet his. But he couldn't. Not yet. Not while there were secrets between them.

'You know, I never really imagined going on a sleigh ride,' Sharmila said. 'But I often wondered what it would be like to ride in one of the horse-drawn carriages in New York. Is that really touristy?' she asked, scrunching her nose. He resisted the urge to lean forward to press a brief kiss to it.

'Probably.' He paused as an idea came to him. 'We could check online.'

'For what?'

'To see if there are any carriage rides still available.'

'What, you want to go to New York?' Her voiced squeaked with surprise and excitement.

'Yes. Why not? We don't have to go on a carriage ride. You have to visit New York while you're in the States. And Christmas in Manhattan is something you don't want to miss.'

'It's a long way to go,' she said, furrowing her forehead.

'Not really. Travel's only a couple of hours – that's nothing. We could go there and back in a day if we leave early.'

'I suppose. Or … I … uh … I wonder whether we, I mean, I could try to get a last-minute hotel or apartment deal,' Sharmila said slowly. 'So we don't have to rush back. I mean me rush back, I'm not expecting you to stay. Not if you don't want to …' She trailed off.

Zach chuckled, charmed by how adorable she was when she became embarrassed. 'I know someone that has a place in the Village. I can ask if it's available. Or I can look at some last-minute booking sites if you really want to go.'

Her smile was uncertain. 'Do you really think we could? It's so impulsive.'

He nodded enthusiastically. He wanted to show her the window displays on Fifth Avenue and see Times Square through her eyes.

'We can leave the day after tomorrow,' he suggested. 'That gives us time to make the arrangements.'

The sleigh ride had come to an end, and they started walking back to the car.

'I don't know,' she said. 'Isn't it too short notice?' He could tell she was on the verge of saying yes. 'And I would need to make sure we're back in time for the parade on Friday evening.'

He smiled. 'We can take an early train on Friday morning and be back before lunch.'

'I guess.' She was quiet. 'Oh, you don't think Lucas will mind, do you?'

'Why would Lucas mind?'

'Because he's invited me to visit his family in Boston and I said I didn't think I could fit it in.'

Zach stared at her. No, Lucas wouldn't mind. It hadn't even occurred to Zach that, if their lawyers were right, Sharmila could lose her inheritance on a technicality if she spent the night away from Pineford. Even though he wasn't the one to suggest an overnight stay, it still felt wrong. 'If you're really worried, we can make a day trip instead.'

She bit her bottom lip. 'But then I'd miss the full effect of all the Christmas lights at night, wouldn't I, because we'd have to leave late afternoon to make it back in good time. I guess it would be better to stay overnight if you can get your friend's place.'

The apartment belonged to Endicott Enterprises. He was sure there would be no problem getting it.

'I'll check if Penny can come,' she said before pausing. 'I'd be missing the ice skating here on Thursday. That's one of Thomas's wishes. But I guess Pineford rink remains open until the New Year. I'm sure I could fit it in before I leave.'

He smiled, an idea starting to form. 'Don't worry, you won't miss out.'

On the drive back, they talked more about the trip, Sharmila's eyes shining with excitement at the prospect of visiting New York. 'It would be amazing if we could fit it in,' she said.

'I'm going to be busy tomorrow sorting things out and working on some projects that are due later in the week, so I probably won't see you until we leave on Thursday,' he said as he pulled up at the house.

He didn't know if helping Sharmila stay away overnight was the right move. But he owed it to his family to give them that option. And perhaps it was the best solution in the circumstances. Izzy and Lucas would get their shares, his mother and aunt would be able to stay in Holly House, and Sharmila could finish the rest of the items on her wish list, have her real Christmas experience, without any interference from Lucas or him. He expelled a breath.

He was ready to be done with the deceit.

Chapter 23

It was impossible to stand still in Times Square without being jostled by the crowds. Sharmila didn't care. The noise, the lights, the bustle were part of the experience. She wanted to throw her hands wide and sing 'New York, New York' – all versions.

They'd already visited Liberty Island and Ellis Island, walked through Central Park, and stood outside the Empire State Building but decided against going up when they saw the queues. Then of course, she had to wander around Bergdorf Goodman, Bloomingdale's, Tiffany, Macy's, and Saks Fifth Avenue – no New York trip would be complete without visiting the stores she'd seen so many times in films. Zach had followed her without complaint.

As expected, she hadn't seen him the previous day, but he was outside the house that morning as they'd agreed.

They decided to take the train in so they didn't have to worry about parking. There were no prolonged spells of awkward silence during the journey, although she couldn't remember what they talked about – and it wasn't just her doing all the talking.

He looked happy to be with her, and his suggestion that they visit New York in the first place gave her the courage to subtly drop in a few questions throughout the day about his thoughts on the future. But he was frustratingly cagey, avoiding direct answers, and she was no closer to working out where she stood or whether he was even thinking about a relationship with her.

But she wasn't going to let anything spoil her time in the City That Never Sleeps.

The sun was starting to set. They'd been walking for hours and hadn't stopped for lunch – finding something to eat was heading to the top of Sharmila's priorities. They were strolling along Fifth Avenue, pausing to look at window displays when Zach tapped her shoulder.

'Come on, Sharmila. It's time,' he said.

'Time for what?'

'You'll see. Let's go.'

Her face lit up at his relaxed, teasing manner when he crooked his finger, beckoning her to follow him. She slipped her hand into his as they hurried along.

She slowed down when she recognised a building with a large, brightly lit Christmas tree and flags flying around a rectangle.

She squeezed Zach's hand. 'Is this *the* Rockefeller Center? Would you mind if we watched the skating for a bit?'

'We can do a little better than that,' he replied, taking her in the direction of the entrance.

Her jaw dropped. 'You've got us tickets.'

'I have.'

She threw her arms round him. If they hadn't been in a public place she would have kissed him.

'How did you manage that at such short notice?' she asked.

'I know people,' he replied with a wink.

Within fifteen minutes, they were stepping onto the ice.

Zach held his hand out to her. 'It can take a while to get used to the ice. Do you want some help?'

Sharmila raised her eyebrows. She was torn between challenging his assumptions and pretending she needed him to help her on the rink. Pride won out. After testing the ice, she took a few strides. 'I think I'll be fine, thank you,' she said, skating backwards as she turned to speak to him.

He gave her a rueful laugh. 'I guess I deserved that. Sorry. I thought since it was on your list, you hadn't tried it before.'

She held her hand out, waiting for him to reach her. 'No. Thomas knew I can skate. But there's something so festive and magical about skating in the cold open air. I think that's why he added it.'

'Shall we take the photo then?'

'OK.' She skated further away from him. 'Shall I stand still, or do you want to snap me moving?' she asked, executing a three-turn.

'OK, OK,' he replied, putting his palms up. 'I completely misunderstood the situation – it's not only that you've been skating before, you're also excellent.'

She smirked. 'I used to take lessons when I was younger – my teacher wanted me to compete, but it was too much to fit into my parents' schedule. Which is probably a good thing, since we both know I don't have the competitive spirit.'

'Ready for your close up, Miss Mitra?' he asked, when they found a relatively safe spot.

'I think I'll do an action shot. Get ready,' she said, checking around her before setting up for a waltz jump.

After they took the photo, she sent it directly to Mr Bell, not wanting to forget in case she got caught up in the magic of New York.

Seven wishes completed. Only three left to do.

'What about you?' she asked Zach as he skated elegantly next to her. 'It looks like you've had lessons too.'

He nodded. 'Ice hockey.'

'Oh, Thomas told me his nephews did ice hockey. Have you ever skated with Lucas and Teddy?'

Why did he look away and avoid answering her? Most of the time, Zach was relaxed and open with her. It was only when she asked questions about family or the future that it felt as if he was hiding something. Perhaps she was second-guessing, reading into things because of her past. She'd already decided she wasn't going to let past events define her.

They went around the rink a couple of times holding hands, performing simple moves.

Zach tried to persuade her to try some spirals, but there was no way Sharmila still had the flexibility and agility to even attempt them. She resolved to start skating again once she was back in England. She'd missed it. At one point she agreed to teach him how to do some bunny hops and spins, laughing at his comical attempts.

Skating round the rink with Zach, both of them carefree and happy, was more perfect than anything she could have imagined.

After their skating session, they went into the centre to warm themselves up with something to eat and drink, which would tide them over until dinner.

'This whole holiday has been like out of some fantasy,' she said, as they found somewhere to sit overlooking the rink. 'But I would never have dreamed I'd be able to cross ice skating at Rockefeller Center off my bucket list. Thank you, Zach.'

'You have a bucket list?'

She shrugged. 'Not written down, but I have a mental list of things I'd like to do.'

'What's on this list?'

'Well, obviously I did have experiencing a US Christmas, but Thomas already made that wish come true. I'd like to travel. Perhaps hike the Inca trail or do a train tour around India.'

She'd also like to marry and have a family one day, something she'd taken off her list when Hari died. Now she was ready to put it back on – somewhere near the top. She gave a mental shake. Yet again, she was getting ahead of herself. It wasn't marriage, in general, she had on her list – it was marriage to a specific person. Heat flooded her cheeks. Hopefully, if Zach noticed her blushing, he would think it was because of the cold. 'What about you? Do you have anything on your wish list?'

'Not really,' he answered after a few moments of thought. 'I've done most things I wanted to. I guess there are places I'd like to visit so travel would be on the list.'

'What about England? Have you ever thought about visiting England?' she asked, attempting yet again to feel him out about their future.

He fell silent and she got the impression he was choosing his words carefully. 'I hope to spend time in England in the near future,' he replied.

What did that mean? Was he suggesting he wanted them to have a relationship and he was prepared to travel to England for it? Or was he trying to let her down gently, to let her know he planned to be in England but wasn't intending to see her. She was no closer to getting answers.

'But,' he continued, 'I don't think in terms of bucket or wish lists. I believe you have to set goals and take action to achieve them rather than put things onto a someday-maybe list.'

She shrugged. 'There's a difference between goals and your wildest dreams that you can only hope will come true. Like travel, I could have saved for a holiday where I spent Christmas somewhere like Pineford. That would be taking action to achieve a goal. But the experience wouldn't have been the same at all – the magic of the dream would be missing.' She looked over at the rink. 'I wish Thomas's dream could have come true and he had got the chance to skate at Rockefeller Center with Carla. I can almost picture the two of them together, going round the rink hand in hand.'

She was jostled suddenly when Zach spilt some of his drink.

'Thomas told you about Carla?' The shock in his expression was unmistakable.

'Yes. That's how we came to meet. The day he walked into the café for the first time was his wedding anniversary. My aunt's café reminded Thomas of one he visited with Carla when they came to England for their honeymoon. He looked a little sad and alone when he sat at the counter, so I started talking to him. And that, as they say, is how it all began.' Her smile faltered at the intense expression on Zach's face. 'Why do you look surprised?'

'I didn't think many people outside the family knew about her.'

'Well, you know about her.'

He gave her a cagey look. 'I'm close to the family.'

She lifted a shoulder. 'I guess I am too then.'

'I thought it was too painful for him to talk about Carla.'

'Maybe. I told him about Hari, and he started reminiscing about his lost love. Hari died too young as well. They were the same age when they died, you know? Carla and Hari. It took years for Thomas to move on from Carla, if he ever did, and he said he didn't want that for me. He said he'd made Carla his anchor and when she was gone, he was all adrift. He was worried I'd made Hari my anchor, but that wasn't the problem.' She laughed. 'The problem was I never had an anchor.'

'Thomas told you his anchor story?'

'Yes. I remember it specifically because it was unusually poetic for him.'

She watched as Zach turned away. What was going on? Was there something wrong with her knowing about Carla? Thomas hadn't mentioned any dark family secret when he brought her up.

'What am I missing, Zach?'

'Nothing.' Zach looked at his phone. 'We should go now.'

'OK. Shall we look for somewhere to eat or head to the apartment?'

'We should go back to Pineford. If we leave now, we should be back before midnight.' He stood up to gather their cups.

'What are you talking about, Zach? Didn't you arrange accommodation?' They'd planned to queue for returns for one of her favourite shows on Broadway, and if they weren't successful, walk around looking at more Christmas lights.

'We have to get back to Pineford. Tonight.'

'What is going on, Zach? Why would we leave? You're beginning to worry me.'

'I'm sorry. I need to go back.'

Her mouth fell open. That didn't sound good. 'Of course, if you need to go back, you must. Maybe I could stay here.' She couldn't hide her disappointment that Zach couldn't spend the evening with her, but she didn't want to be in the way if there was a problem he needed to quickly fix.

Hopefully, this wasn't an excuse to avoid spending more time with her.

'I don't think it's a good idea for you to stay on your own,' he replied abruptly. 'I don't even know what kind of neighbourhood the apartment's in. Penny and the Women's Club would never forgive me if anything happened to you. We should start heading back to the train station. I'll try to hail a cab but let's go in the direction of the subway.'

Slightly annoyed by his high-handed manner, she was ready to insist on remaining behind. But part of the fun of being in the city that day had been sharing the experience with someone. If only Penny hadn't refused to come because of her conviction the New York trip was part of Sharmila's holiday romance.

Sharmila snorted. So much for a holiday romance, it had fizzled out before it even started.

Chapter 24

Zach's truck wasn't in front of the barn when Sharmila walked to her car the next morning. She could get whiplash with the speed of his mood changes. One moment they were laughing, talking about bucket lists, the next they were on their way back to Pineford. He hadn't said anything on the train back. She'd made a few attempts to engage him in conversation but gave up when she got monosyllabic grunts in response. She didn't want to pry in his business – she just wanted him to know she was there if he needed someone to talk to. Instead, he'd walked away from her to make phone calls.

Once they were outside Holly House, he'd murmured another quick apology and told her he'd explain everything one day.

And that was it. There was nothing she could do. She didn't know whether he'd left Pineford, whether he would return before she flew back to England. She didn't know.

New York, even for a few hours, had given her such beautiful memories, she wasn't going to spoil them thinking about Zach anymore that day. Or for the rest of her stay.

It was Christmas Eve. The day of the big parade. Although the parade wouldn't begin until the evening, Sharmila had offered to be around for last-minute sewing emergencies or if Liz needed a hand with anything else.

Everything about this holiday had been a perfect fantasy. In a few hours, she would be finishing one of her last wishes and in just two days she would have completed the penultimate wish. After that there would be only one left. The scene from the movie. She decided to shelve that wish until she was back in England on Tuesday and concentrate on making the most of her last few days in America instead.

Later that evening, Sharmila was in the town hall changing into her costume for the parade when she received a text from Penny asking to meet by Santa's float.

'Everything all right?' Sharmila asked when she got there.

'Fine, but there is one Christmas tradition you've yet to do.'

Sharmila was confused by Penny's words, until she followed Penny's gaze up to the float. 'Oh no, I'm not sitting on Santa's knee,' she laughed, the words evoking memories of Zach setting up the grotto.

'Come on, it wouldn't be Christmas without a visit to Santa!'

'Ho, ho, ho, merry Christmas, Sharmila. Why don't you come up here and see what present Santa has for you today?' Santa called out.

Sharmila had no idea who was under the full costume and beard. 'Is that OK?' she asked. 'We're not too old for this?'

'Never too old, step up. There is one condition, however. You must tell me what you wish for this Christmas, ho, ho, ho.'

They laughed as they took the two steps onto the float.

'I want peace on Earth and goodwill to men,' Penny said, as she took a seat on one side of Santa. 'And a new drawing tablet.'

'Same for me. Apart from the tablet,' Sharmila said.

'Nothing else, Sharmila?' Santa asked.

'No. Everything I wished for has come true already.'

'Everything?' Penny and Santa questioned at the same time.

'Everything,' she repeated.

There was something precious about the simple childhood activity of telling Santa her wish. Secretly she made another wish, one she couldn't say out loud, hoping Santa would know anyway.

They thanked Santa, accepting a small, wrapped box, then moved to find a good place in the crowds that were lining Main Street. Originally Jackie had suggested Sharmila should ride in the mayor's car next to her but changed her mind when she realised it would mean Sharmila would miss out on seeing a lot of the parade. Instead, Sharmila was now in the penultimate float, before Santa's sleigh – that way she would be able to watch the parade go past before taking her position.

The first band in the parade was starting to warm up when Lucas came over. 'I'm about to leave to spend Christmas in Boston but I wanted to wish you happy holidays first and find out about your trip. How was New York? Was it everything you imagined?'

Sharmila nodded.

'Did you do any shopping? I remember my first time in New York. There's something about that city that isn't like anywhere else,' he continued. 'By the way, I haven't seen Zach. Is he coming down soon?'

She frowned. 'I haven't seen Zach since last night.'

'Last night? Didn't you come back together this morning?'

'No, we had a change of plans. We came back last night instead. I think Zach had some kind of emergency,' she told Lucas. 'I don't know what happened. He's not in Pineford though.'

Before lunch, Zach had sent her a message apologising again for the abrupt change of plan. He told her he would be back in Pineford in time for her party. At least she would get the chance to see him again – even if it was only to say goodbye.

She'd tried to put Zach out of her mind, but the knowledge that their time together would soon be over meant the memories kept replaying. Building a snowman together, watching movies with him, skating hand in hand round Rockefeller Center … laughing with him … falling for him.

Lucas briefly touched her shoulder, bringing her out of her

thoughts. He excused himself, moving away from her as he took out his phone. He came back a few minutes later. 'OK. I'm heading off. Hopefully, I'll be back in time for your party on Sunday.' He leaned forward to press a friendly kiss on her cheek. 'Merry Christmas, Sharmila.'

'Merry Christmas, Lucas.'

Sharmila watched him go before turning back as the first band set off, starting the parade. She smiled, waved, and cheered as they went past her, followed by baton twirlers. Next came people walking on stilts or riding unicycles – part of the float organised by a local gym club with a winter circus theme. There were floats based on Dr Seuss, *A Christmas Carol*, and Narnia, princess floats, a snowscape float with icebergs and penguins. Between each one were people on the ground, either in a band or a dance troupe.

Although Sharmila had sewn many of the costumes and helped Zach get some of the props ready, she's only seen them as individual pieces. She hadn't imagined how they would all come together. The crowds were cheering, singing, and dancing along to the music booming from the loudspeakers. Nobody seemed to mind standing in the chilly night air. It was loud and bright and colourful and spectacular.

Finally, she could see the German Society's float about to head their way, which was her cue to get to her float.

Liz had added her to the one showcasing 'The Night Before Christmas'. She was wearing a mouse costume with a long tail, pointed ears, and a warm fake-fur coat. She went to lie on a bed resembling cotton wool, where she would represent the mouse who wasn't stirring the night before Christmas. From her position, she could see the people dressed as the eight reindeer led by Dasher and Dancer and the ballet dancers in glittering purple, round costumes, the vision of sugar plums.

As the float came to a halt, Sharmila looked behind her at the road strewn with streamers and glowsticks.

Another wish crossed off Thomas's list. Two left.

The moment was bittersweet. Two wishes also meant that her time in Pineford was coming to an end. Her dream holiday would soon be over.

Chapter 25

The Boston home he grew up in looked exactly how Zach remembered from previous Christmases, decorated like the movies Sharmila loved so much. But there was an energy missing. He knew what it was – the presence of his father. Ever since he'd passed away, Zach's childhood home felt empty and no longer like the one he knew. One of the reasons he'd only visited a few times in the past few years.

One of the reasons. Not the main reason.

He'd avoided returning home while trying to deal with his own grief, mingled with a massive dose of guilt. He couldn't deal with his mother's grief as well. He'd been a coward and a bad son – another thing on his list of regrets of ways to disappoint his family.

And now he was going to add one more disappointment.

'Zach!' His mother's cry interrupted his memories, and he turned to her, gathering her in a hug – a hug to make up for all the hugs he should have given her over the years.

'Mom, you look very well. How have you been?'

His mother held onto his hand as they walked into the living room and sat on a couch as if needing his touch to convince her he was real. He pressed his lips together. He had a lot of apologising to do, but he would find a way to make it up to her. He simply couldn't do it at Sharmila's expense.

'I'm well, Zach. I couldn't believe it when Helen told me you were here. Why didn't you let me know you were coming?'

'I wanted it to be a surprise,' he replied. It certainly had been a surprise for the maid who'd answered the door. She was new since his father died and had been unsure whether to let him in.

'A wonderful surprise,' his mother said, keeping his hand in hers. 'Have you eaten? I was going to have dinner soon. How long will you be able to stay?'

'I was hoping to stay until the day after Christmas.'

The joy on her face struck a flash of heaviness to his heart. He should have been here for her, spent the holidays with her. They used to mean so much to her when he was younger.

He always knew it was wrong to avoid coming home after his father disapproved of his departure from the family business. He would always regret those lost years with his father. It had been selfish of him to continue to stay away from Boston when his mother was on her own, grieving. He should have been there for her.

'That's wonderful, Zach. I was going to have Christmas lunch with Carol tomorrow. Do you want to join? Lucas should be there. Izzy is spending Christmas with her partner's family.' Worry creased her face. 'Or I can tell Carol I won't be able to come and we can spend the day together.'

He placed a hand over hers, trying to reassure her. 'I would love to join everyone for lunch. Like old times. And perhaps after lunch we can do a family jigsaw.'

'That sounds perfect. Now tell me what you and Lucas have been getting up to in Pineford. What did you think of the town?' Now was the perfect opportunity to explain to his mother how he couldn't get Holly House for her. He opened his mouth to begin when his phone rang. Lucas. He excused himself and went into his father's old home office.

The call couldn't wait. This was the first chance he had to speak to Lucas since he'd returned from New York. He'd tried to contact Lucas before he left Pineford but hadn't got through. He'd arrived in Boston that morning and gone straight to Izzy's office, knowing she'd be working on Christmas Eve, even though it was a public holiday this year.

The conversation with Izzy hadn't been easy. She didn't care that Sharmila knew about Carla or that Sharmila must have meant so much more to Thomas than they'd thought if he had shared something so personal as his anchor story with her. It didn't change anything. Izzy didn't accept his decision that they should respect Thomas's wishes. She accused Zach of being taken for a fool, again. Told him he was abandoning his family, again. She walked away from him. He was under no illusion that she was going to give up.

In contrast, the conversation he was having with Lucas was much easier since there was always a big part of Lucas who was against the plan in the first place. It sounded as if Lucas was relieved that all the scheming and games would be over with.

After his call, Zach wandered aimlessly around the room. He hadn't been in there since the evening he told his father he was breaking with family tradition to start his own business, thousands of miles away.

If he had known he wouldn't get the chance to spend Christmas with his dad again, or with Uncle Thomas, he would have come back. Now all he had was regrets. Seeing Sharmila revel in the spirit of Christmas helped Zach remember some of his childhood joy of the season. How important his family and his traditions were. How lucky he was to have such a close and loving family growing up.

The maid called them for dinner, which was served at a table in the kitchen rather than the formal dining room they used when he lived at home.

'I didn't like eating at that grand table when it was only me,' his mom explained, with a small smile. There was no accusation in her tone.

They chatted generally about Pineford for a few minutes, sharing places they'd seen, comparing differences, swapping stories about people they both knew.

'And Sharmila Mitra, you haven't mentioned her yet. What's she like? I've been dying to know ever since Thomas went to India with her family. She must be special for Thomas to think of her in his will.'

He smiled, picturing Sharmila running through the evergreens as she looked for her perfect Christmas tree, carolling in public, becoming irritated with the disaster of her gingerbread house. Then, inevitably, he brought up the memory of her face moving closer to his as they stood outside his barn. He could almost feel her breath on his cheek as their lips nearly touched.

'She is special,' he admitted. He put his cutlery down. 'Mom, I need to speak to you about Thomas's will.'

'Of course, sweetheart. I'm sure it can wait until after we've eaten though. Tell me about your move to England, is everything going ahead still?'

He wanted to get it off his chest as soon as possible, but he was pleased to have a temporary reprieve so he could enjoy a normal meal with his mother. The first one after a long time.

After Christmas, he would have to fly back to San Francisco to pack his things for his move across the ocean before the end of January. If everything worked out as he hoped, would Sharmila be part of his new life in England?

'I'm so happy your work is going well. Your father would be so proud. He was so proud.' She looked down at her plate for a few moments, collecting herself. 'Let's have cocoa in the living room.'

He followed his mother. It was wonderful spending Christmas Eve with her. If only he hadn't left everything so late – he barely had any time to spend with her.

But he couldn't extend his stay in Boston – he had to see

Sharmila before she left. He didn't want to wait until they were both in England to tell her the truth.

'So, Zach, what did you want to tell me about Thomas's will?'

He reached out to take her hand. 'I'm sorry, Mom.'

'Should I be worried?'

'No, Mom. It's just I know how much you were looking forward to living in Holly House. Lucas and I went to Pineford to try to get it for you, for the family.' He gave her a summary of their plan to stop Sharmila from collecting her inheritance.

His mom laughed at the way the town prevented all their plans. 'I wish I could have seen your attempts. They sound pitiful.'

He smiled. 'They were.'

She put her hand on his knee. 'But sweetheart, I never wanted to live in Holly House. This is my home,' she said, gesturing round. 'The home I made with your dad and where you grew up. I would never move.'

'Mom, you said after the will-reading you wished you had a chance to spend Christmas in Pineford again.'

'Yes. I did. And I'm sure I will go to Pineford. Sharmila's inheritance won't stop that. I understand Izzy and Lucas were worried about the business but there was never anything inappropriate behind Thomas's gift to Sharmila.'

'I don't think she did trick Thomas. She isn't like that.' He couldn't interpret the expression on his mom's face.

'I'm so happy to hear you say that. I know you've been wary of women after your experience with that dreadful Annette. You let her affect you for too long. I'm pleased you didn't let it get in the way when you met Sharmila.'

Zach expelled a breath. He didn't want to tell his mother how suspicious of Sharmila he'd been. 'Sharmila's nothing like Annette or any of my ex-girlfriends. I trust her. I don't know why Thomas left her anything but—'

'I know why.'

Zach reared back. 'You know?'

239

'Yes, Thomas told us when he was writing his will. He told us about his plans for Holly House and the shares. Carol and I have always known his reasons. If only you'd asked us.'

'Then, why did he? They weren't …' He couldn't finish his sentence.

His mother burst into laughter. 'No, there was nothing romantic or sexual between them. Thomas never said it out loud, but I think he loved Sharmila as the daughter he never had. He loved all her family.'

Zach listened intently as his mother recalled what Thomas had said about his time in England and India with Sharmila and her family. Although Sharmila had mentioned bits of what they'd done, she'd been evasive. At the time he thought she was dishonest. Now he realised she was being modest about how much her family had done to include Thomas, even without knowing about his illness.

He felt calmer after speaking to his mother, certain everything would work out. As long as Sharmila gave him a chance to make things right.

He glanced at the time. The Pineford parade would be over now. He could almost see Sharmila in her mouse costume – she would look adorable. He made a silent wish that they'd find a way to be together.

'What's wrong, sweetheart?'

He shook his head. 'Nothing's wrong, Mom.'

'You look worried only a moment ago.'

He smiled. How could his mother read him so well, even after all this time? 'I was thinking about Pineford.'

'Pineford or a certain lady who's on vacation there?'

He didn't reply.

'I knew it! I knew you like her!' his mom said, sounding delighted.

'Mom!'

She put her hands up. 'Fine. I guess I can't expect my adult son to tell me about his love life.'

He rolled his eyes. 'Am I always so obvious?'

'I'm your mother. It's my job to notice,' she said, covering his hand with hers. 'All I will say is I hope I get to meet her one day. Hopefully soon.'

Zach nodded. He hoped his mother and Sharmila would meet too. But first, he needed to tell Sharmila the whole truth.

Chapter 26

Pineford on Christmas Day. Finally.

Sharmila stood at her bedroom window, watching the fresh fall of snow. A white Christmas in America, just as she'd always imagined. She laughed at herself – there had been snow for the last few weeks in Pineford, but there was something magical about it on Christmas Day itself.

It was still early. The sun had barely risen.

Her phone pinged. A message from Zach wishing her a merry Christmas. She sent him a quick reply, trying not to spend time thinking about whether his sending her a text so early in the morning meant she was on his mind. She hoped it did. He was never far away from her thoughts. She couldn't help worrying about the reason he had to leave New York so abruptly – whether it would mean he had to return to San Francisco to sort it out. He always sounded so busy she hoped he would find a way to celebrate Christmas this year.

And she hoped he would come back to Pineford so she could see him one last time.

But she wasn't going to spend the day pining over a relationship that she wasn't even sure was a relationship. She remembered what Thomas had written in his letter. Only joy on Christmas Day. That was going to be her mantra.

She wrenched herself away from the view. Her sister's family were going to call her for a video chat in an hour and there were still some things to do for the Boxing Day party.

Had it really only been three weeks ago she'd spoken to Jackie about the need to host a party? Her squad had given her constant updates but made sure she didn't worry about a single thing. They had already prepared most of Holly House in advance, all she needed to do was the basic set-up for the party. She didn't even need to cover the cost because Thomas had left a 'party' budget for her. She wanted to finish her tasks before they left for Christmas lunch at Pineford Inn.

She'd been overwhelmed by the number of invitations she'd received from people in Pineford, inviting her to share a Christmas meal with them. But neither she nor Penny wanted to intrude on a family celebration, so they agreed to join Jill and her family, since they were already preparing food for the rest of the guests at the inn anyway.

She got ready then started to pack some of her things up. But the realisation she would be back in England in a few days threatened to put a damper on her determination to enjoy the day, so she abandoned that task after a few minutes.

No thinking about Zach. No thinking about the end of her holiday. Only joy on Christmas Day.

As she walked down the grand staircase, Sharmila could make out a brightly wrapped package under the tree. She and Penny had agreed not to buy each other presents – their holiday in Pineford was enough of a gift for both of them. It looked like Penny had ignored their agreement.

She picked it up and carried it to the kitchen, where Penny was pouring them mimosas.

'What's this, Pen?' she asked, holding the present up.

'I don't know. Why don't you open it and find out?' Penny replied, with a grin.

Sharmila unwrapped the present to uncover a watercolour rendering of Holly House with a small figure in a red coat near the door, bending to gather snow.

She swallowed a few times, trying to compose herself. 'Oh, Pen,' she said. 'This is wonderful. Thank you.' They hugged.

'Enough,' Penny said, with a catch in her voice. 'If I'd have known it was going to turn you into a puddle, I wouldn't have painted it.'

Sharmila laughed. She couldn't have asked for a more perfect gift. Tears of joy were OK on Christmas Day.

When the doorbell rang, Penny got up to answer it, giving Sharmila more time to compose herself before Debby joined them for breakfast. Since Debby lived alone, Penny and Sharmila had invited her over for the day before the three of them went to the inn for their Christmas meal.

Penny preceded Debby into the kitchen holding up two stuffed Christmas stockings. 'Look what Debby brought for us,' she said.

Sharmila clapped – it was her first Christmas stocking. Debby laughed and Sharmila realised she'd spoken aloud.

'I thought Christmas stockings at the foot of the bed were a British tradition,' Debby said.

'Not in my family,' Penny replied.

'Not in mine either,' Sharmila said. 'But I think everyone knows my family didn't do Christmas.'

'Have you put an orange and a ha'penny in here?' Penny asked Debby, pulling out the contents of the stocking.

'No, but there may be a lump of coal for you,' Debby replied, giving Penny a playful shove.

Sharmila laughed. Penny was always happy-go-lucky. She got on with nearly everyone she met. But her friendship with Debby had been instantaneous. Sharmila knew Penny and Debby would keep in touch.

Would Zach do the same with her?

Penny clapped her hands.

'What?' Sharmila said with a quick shake of her head.

'You were about to go into pensive mode,' Penny said. 'We don't have time for that. The party squad sent me the final list for tomorrow's party. We are already hours behind.'

Sharmila smiled to herself as she set up the table for the potluck supper and the drinks table.

After the party the next day, there would only be one item left on Thomas's Wishlist. Not for the first time, she imagined completing this last activity with Zach, recreating the end of one of her Christmas romance movies.

A few hours later, she was at Pineford Inn, trying to adjust to the noise and festivity. Jill and Graham had gone out of their way to offer their guests a traditional family Christmas, believing that just because their guests couldn't spend Christmas at home didn't mean they should miss out.

On the table in front of Sharmila was the most amazing spread of turkey, prime rib, and ham, served with mashed potatoes, roast potatoes, sweet potatoes, corn, green beans, glazed carrots, and cauliflower.

One of the guests mentioned that her Christmas meals would usually consist of meatballs and pasta because of her Italian heritage, which started a conversation around the table about everyone's Christmas traditions. No one seemed to celebrate the season in exactly the same way.

Sharmila realised that every family had their own traditions or created new ones as families blended together. She had, over the years, romanticised what a perfect Christmas would involve but, although her family didn't celebrate the festival, until her parents retired to India they had always spent the winter holiday together. And that, she recognised, was a big part of the season – spending time with loved ones, filled with love and happiness.

Sharmila caught Penny's eye and nodded towards the carrier bags they had stashed to the side. When she and Penny had booked their holiday, they thought they'd be spending Christmas at the inn, probably having Chinese takeaway for lunch but, so they would have some festive spirit on the day, they'd packed crackers and mince pies in their luggage, which they had brought with them to the inn. Now, she would get to share a small part of an English Christmas with those round her.

She brought out the box of crackers and started handing them out. They would have to share but that could be part of the fun. The guests were holding them as if they were fragile, uncertain what to do with them.

Sharmila took one side and offered the other side to Elaine, the person next to her. 'Now we both pull.'

Elaine jumped as the banger went off.

'You got the main part,' Sharmila said. 'So you get the prize.'

Elaine looked curious as she searched inside the cracker chamber, pulling out the tissue crown, a piece of paper, and some dice.

'This is the prize?' Elaine asked, holding up the dice.

'Yes, the prizes are dreadful but part of the fun, I promise. Now you have to read out the joke on the paper.'

Groans were heard around the table as Elaine read out the cheesy joke.

'Truly bad jokes are part of the fun too,' Penny said.

Soon the others were paring up to pull at their crackers, fighting over who wouldn't have the prize and reading out their jokes.

'The person who got the bigger part also has to wear the crown,' Sharmila declared. She helped Elaine put hers on.

She looked round the table as everyone laughed and ate, some wearing the jaunty paper crowns, and her heart filled with joy. She couldn't have asked for a more perfect Christmas meal.

After lunch, there were party games. All Sharmila wanted to do was get into some elasticated-waist trousers and nap but she joined in the charades and drawing games, happily chatting and getting to know people.

How different from the day she arrived in Pineford, when she still wary and guarded, preferring to avoid meeting anyone new. How much she might have missed if Pineford and its people hadn't worked their magic.

They left the inn in the early evening when the guests were breaking into smaller groups for board games, too full and tired to do anything other than curl up in the entertainment room and watch movies. There was still some set-up for the party left to do, but it could wait until the morning.

Christmas in Pineford had never been about one day, although the day itself had been perfect in every way.

Christmas had been pure joy.

Chapter 27

On the evening of Sharmila's party, Zach walked to his barn, which had felt more like a home to him in the three weeks he'd spent there than the apartment in San Francisco he'd leased for the last three years. Soon, he'd be moving thousands of miles away to a different country with a new apartment that he would have to make a new home.

He laughed to himself. If he'd learnt anything over the last few weeks in Pineford, it wasn't the furniture, the décor, or the soft furnishing that made a place a home, it was the people.

He was at home in Pineford. No matter what happened between him and Sharmila, he was certain he would be back to visit the town with his mother one day.

His phone rang. He reached into his pocket, then glanced at the caller ID with a frown. Lucas.

'Have you heard from Izzy?' he asked before Lucas could say anything.

'I've left messages but she's not taking my calls. She's meant to be back in Boston. I was waiting to see her but she's not here so I'm heading to Pineford. Zach, I'm worried about what she's going to do. She doesn't care that Uncle Thomas had good reasons for leaving Sharmila the shares. I knew he would have. If only he'd told us about them from the beginning.'

'Yes. It could have saved all of us from coming to Pineford in the first place.'

'Come on. You have to admit you enjoyed Pineford and everything that's happened the past few weeks – the WinterFest activities, the people, especially a certain someone …'

'You're right. If we had known the reason, we wouldn't have come up with our ridiculous plan, and I wouldn't have met Sharmila.'

They were both quiet. Zach couldn't imagine how empty his life would be if he hadn't come to Pineford and got to know Sharmila.

'You haven't told her yet,' Lucas said.

'No. The party's still going on.'

'Everything's going to be fine,' Lucas said, in his most optimistic tone. 'You two are meant to be together.'

Any other time, any other person but Sharmila, Zach would have scoffed at the idea that two people were meant to be together – that someone could fall in love in three short weeks. Now, he could only hope and wish Lucas was right.

It had been a strange Christmas. For him, it had been his first time celebrating with his mother without his father. For all of them, it was their first Christmas without Thomas.

Before this vacation, having spent so many years living far away from his mother and Lucas, he didn't have any concerns about his transatlantic move. Now he knew he was going to miss them more than he realised. He was determined that he would fly back to the US to spend the next Christmas with his mother, no matter what happened with Sharmila.

His flight to San Francisco was first thing the following morning. Luckily he hadn't brought a lot with him, and it didn't take him long to pack up his belongings and tidy the barn. There was a chance he would never be back at Holly House, but he had to remain hopeful that a future with Sharmila was possible, even after he told her the truth.

The last thing he had left to do was take the decorations off the silver Christmas tree. He stood in front of it, reaching out to touch a branch, smiling at the memory of his visit to his friend's place to pick out Sharmila's tree.

It had been a long time since he cared about Christmas. This year, a large part of his enjoyment of it had been seeing everything through her eyes, experiencing it like it was his first time too. He'd known instinctively, as early in the holiday as that first week, that she was someone special – even though he hadn't wanted to listen to that instinct. Now he needed to know whether what they had could be real – something worth fighting for.

He wasn't deluding himself. She wasn't going to fall into his arms. But there was something special between them, the kind of thing that could grow into something permanent if they gave it a chance.

He expelled a slow breath. He wanted to see her. He had to go over to the party and hope for an opportunity to speak to Sharmila in private. He grabbed his jacket.

On the short walk across he was stopped by several people who were leaving the party. They all wanted to know about his Christmas. After chatting with them briefly, he watched as they went to their cars. It wasn't only Sharmila who was owed the truth. He'd been lying to everyone in Pineford as well. He made a wish they would understand and forgive him when they learnt the truth too.

She was standing in the foyer by their tree when he saw her, her face flushed with happiness. She looked stunning in a green dress that emphasised her figure. His heart flipped, his hand flinching with the urge to touch her, move that stray piece of hair off her face.

She disengaged herself from the people around her when she saw him.

'Hi,' she greeted him, her smile wide and warm. 'You're back. I hope everything got sorted out.'

'Pardon?'

'The reason you had to leave Pineford.'

'Oh, I'm sorry about that. I didn't mean to worry you. I went to Boston to speak to someone. After that I went to see my mother. I wanted to spend Christmas with her.'

'Really? That's brilliant. I bet she was so happy.'

He nodded. 'I wish I hadn't left it so late.' He looked around the room at the other guests. 'Can we talk soon, in private?'

'Sure. I think we should be finished here soon. Do you want me to find you when I'm done?'

He was in a hurry to have no secrets between them but he couldn't be selfish. This party was part of her wish list, and the number of guests who had turned up showed how popular she'd become in Pineford.

But one thing couldn't wait. 'I have something for you,' he said. 'A Christmas present.'

'For me?' She gave him a brilliant smile. 'Really? I have something for you too.'

He followed her to the fireplace in the snug, where a stocking was hanging on the mantelpiece.

'It's only small because I know you're flying back to San Francisco,' she said, handing him a box.

She'd bought him a small snowglobe. Inside was a rolled-up scroll of parchment and a quill.

'I know it's probably Santa's naughty and nice list,' she said, 'but it reminded me of the clues your parents made for your scavenger hunts.'

He nodded, unable to speak beyond thanking her. Deeply touched by the gesture.

'Oh wow, you shouldn't have, Zach,' she said, holding up the charm bracelet with the snowflake, tree, and sled charms he'd chosen for her. 'Thank you, it's perfect.'

He'd picked it out the day before they left for New York, wanting to give her something that was small enough for her to take back to England and that would remind her of this holiday. And him.

Their eyes met and held for a few moments before Zach looked away.

'The party looks like it's going well,' he said.

'Yes, finally. It's been such a day – a catalogue of disasters. At one point I didn't think I was going to be able to host the party. We lost the heating!'

Zach straightened. Meddling with the heating was one of Izzy's ideas for sabotaging Sharmila's party. That and tenting the house for termites.

'Have you seen Lucas?' he asked.

'Not yet. He said he'd try to get back. Oh, but Izzy's here. Lucas's sister. Oh, you know that,' she said with a laugh, brushing her hand in front of her. 'She came this morning. She should be here somewhere. You should look for her.'

His heart started to race. 'I do need to speak to her. I'll come find you later?'

'OK,' she replied with a smile.

He reached out to cup her cheek. She pressed her lips to his palm – a feather's touch. 'Later.'

He was dialling Izzy's number as he walked out of the house towards his barn, where Izzy showed up minutes later.

She went straight to his couch, sitting with her legs crossed, her expression unrepentant.

'I don't want to hear it, Zach,' she said, holding her hand up. 'I expected this of my soft-hearted brother but I was trusting you to be sensible. She must be something special if she managed to fool both you and Uncle Thomas.'

'She is. But not the way you mean.'

'You have feelings for her!' Izzy scoffed. 'I didn't want to believe it when Lucas's message suggested you might care for

Sharmila. But it's true. Never send a man to do work you can do yourself. If you and Lucas can't get the job done then I'm here to sort it out.'

'And how successful have you been? The party looks like it's going well. That's the ninth wish.'

'People from town helped sort everything out.' She shook her head. 'I almost didn't believe you when you said Pineford always finds a way to help her. How did she trick a whole town? It's fine. There's still one more wish. I plan to find out what it is and stop her.'

He looked away.

'You know what the wish is,' Izzy said. 'Tell me.'

'It doesn't matter, Izzy. I'm going to tell her the truth today.'

'She'll never forgive you for lying to her.'

He grimaced. 'That's a risk I'm going to have to take. If she hears it from me, at least there's a chance,' he said, trying to convince himself.

Izzy narrowed her eyes. 'Perhaps if you're going to tell her anyway, I should tell her first.'

Zach stared back. Would his cousin deliberately ruin any chance of a relationship between him and Sharmila? He couldn't believe she would go that far.

'I'm sorry, Izzy, but she deserves Uncle Thomas's gifts. The house and the shares.'

'You can say that because it's not your business.'

'My family name is still on the company.'

'What about if we give her Holly House? Please, Zach. Don't tell her the truth. Help me stop her and we can keep the shares but ask our moms to let her have the house. You said yourself she loves Pineford. She should have the house and we should have the shares. Doesn't that sound fair? Please, Zach. This is my life. Endicott Enterprises is my life.'

Zach paused. 'I don't know, Izzy. I trust Uncle Thomas made the right decision giving Sharmila the shares. And, more importantly,

I trust Sharmila will make the right decisions when she exercises her voting rights.'

'I'm not going to change your mind, am I?' Izzy said, her shoulders slumped. 'I hope she's worth it.'

'She is.' He looked out the window, which gave him a view of the courtyard. Most of the cars had left. Only one remained, parked near the garage. He narrowed his eyes. 'Is that Lucas's car?'

Izzy came over to him. 'I wonder what he's doing here. He didn't tell me he was coming back.'

'He wanted to say goodbye to Sharmila.' Zach hoped that was all Lucas was doing. He strode over to Holly House, not waiting for Izzy to keep up with him. He needed to tell Sharmila the truth. Now.

Chapter 28

Sharmila blinked slowly as she tried to understand what Lucas was saying. What inheritance? Lucas's mouth was moving but the words seemed to be crossing through cotton wool as the muffled sounds reached her.

There was a gift from Thomas. Something about shares and his business and Holly House and an inheritance. And a plan. Zach, Lucas, and Izzy's plan to stop her. Stop her from doing what? And how?

A movement at the doorway caught her attention.

'She knows,' Lucas said as Izzy and Zach hurried over to them. 'I told her. She had a right to know the truth.'

Sharmila looked at Zach. The guilty expression on his face told her that everything Lucas had said was true.

Blood rushed to her ears and the room moved, swirling round her. She barely heard her name being called, then suddenly Zach was near her, lifting her, and carrying her to an armchair, holding her head between her knees. A few moments later, a glass of water was thrust into her hands.

'Are you OK?' Zach asked, the concern in his voice evident. Lucas and his sister weren't anywhere to be seen.

She lifted a hand, keeping him from getting any closer to her. 'I'm fine. I'm not going to faint.'

He took the glass from her, placing it on the low table at the side of the armchair.

'Did Lucas say …' She broke off, the words too unbelievable to say.

'Thomas left you Holly House and shares in Endicott Enterprises, the family business.'

She stared at him unblinking, still not fully able to process what she was hearing. Even though it was exactly what Lucas had told her. It didn't even make sense. Why would Thomas leave the house to her? Why leave her shares?

'It only amounts to two per cent of the company, but they are voting shares,' Zach said.

'I don't understand what you're trying to tell me.'

'Thomas left you shares in his family business. The type of shares you have will give you the deciding vote if Lucas and Izzy can't agree on something.'

That couldn't be true. 'I didn't know. Nobody told me anything.'

'The shares were conditional on your staying in Pineford for three weeks and finishing Thomas's Wishlist.'

'But I haven't finished the wish list. You know that. I still have to …' She didn't want to mention her scene from a film. Didn't want to be reminded of her fantasy of completing the wish with Zach. 'It doesn't matter. I haven't finished the wishes, so I guess the shares go somewhere else.'

'That's not the case. Now we've told you about the condition, you automatically inherit.' He reached out to touch her hand.

She flinched and moved it away. 'Lucas told me about the condition. Not you. I don't want the shares – Lucas and his sister can have them. He didn't have to tell me any of this.' She ran her hands over her face. Was she in some surreal hallucination? 'It doesn't make any sense. What was Thomas thinking? Why would he leave this house to me? Why would he leave me the shares?'

He opened his mouth, but she put her hand up. She wasn't sure she could take anymore. There was too much to process.

She still couldn't grasp what Thomas had done. She'd spent time with a charming older man who was interested in her culture and shared her love for romantic movies. She'd never questioned whether their friendship was unusual – they had a lot in common despite their generational difference, including losing a loved one at a young age.

But none of that explained what he'd done. The holiday in Pineford had been more than generous – the wish list and the charity donation had been a huge bonus. She didn't need or want anything else.

It was too much.

No wonder Lucas and Zach had come to Pineford. It took her a while to absorb the implication of that. 'Lucas said you had a plan to stop the inheritance. All three of you. Is that true? You didn't think I should get the house or the shares.'

He pressed his lips together. 'We didn't know you. At first, all we knew was Thomas had left this house to a woman he met briefly in England. I don't live in Boston, so I never heard your name mentioned until l was told about the will. Of course, Lucas and Izzy had heard of you and knew that Thomas had joined your family for your cultural festivities, but it didn't sound like a good reason to leave you such a valuable inheritance.'

'You went to a lot of trouble to help your friends,' she said. Zach couldn't meet her gaze, and silence fell between them. She could feel the frustration rising. There had to be something more for him to still be so cagey. She narrowed her eyes, trying to stop the tears from slipping out. 'What is it?'

Finally, he spoke. 'There's something else I didn't tell you. About who I am.'

'Who you are?' She laughed, the sound bordering on hysterical.

'Lucas is my cousin. My mom and his mom are sisters.'

Sharmila blinked a couple of times, letting his words turn

over in her brain. How was that possible? 'But Lucas's mom is Thomas's sister,' she said, not making the connection.

'Yes. Thomas was my uncle. I hadn't seen him much since I moved to California. We weren't that close. Not as close as you and he were.' His eyes were still avoiding hers.

'You're Thomas's nephew,' she said slowly. 'How can that be? No, Thomas told me about his nephews. Lucas and Teddy.'

'I'm Teddy. I mean Teddy was a nickname from my surname. When I was young, my family used it to distinguish me from my father – it stuck.'

'How is Teddy possibly a nickname from Lawrence?' Her mind was reeling. She felt safe asking unimportant questions about minor issues – anything to avoid the big questions like, why? Why had he lied to her about who he was? Had anything he told her been true? Or had they all been silly lies for silly reasons?

'Lawrence is my middle name. My full name is Zachary Lawrence Endicott. The Third.'

'Zachary Lawrence Endicott?' She took a few calming breaths. She hadn't even known his real name. She furrowed her brow. 'So you lied to everyone. Not just me. You lied to everyone in Pineford. Nobody knows who you really are.'

'You have to understand, in this area, the Endicott name is well known. My father's reputation goes before him. Because we share the same name, it goes before me too.'

'The third,' Sharmila echoed.

'Yes, I've always been expected to follow his footsteps and take over the business, even though Lucas and Izzy have loved it more than I have.' He raised his hands. 'But the point is when people know my name, there's an expectation. When I moved to San Francisco, most people didn't care who I was or, more importantly, who my father was.'

'You wanted people to get to know you for you, not for who your family is,' she said slowly, hoping she followed his logic.

He smiled. 'Exactly. I didn't want people to treat me a certain way because of my name.'

'And you couldn't trust me to know the truth before now?'

He grimaced. 'It's complicated.'

She threw her hands up. 'What's complicated about it? You're Thomas's nephew. How hard would it have been to admit that once we got to know each other? Did you think I would treat you differently once I found out?'

'There was a risk,' he admitted.

'What risk? Were you worried I would tell everyone else the truth – you didn't trust me?'

He looked away again. 'Put yourself in our shoes. We didn't know you.'

'But later, when …' She broke off. 'Oh, the inheritance. You were trying to stop me getting it.'

She was a fool. She thought Zach was her friend, even thought they could be more. But all this time he'd been working with Lucas and Izzy, with his *cousins*, to keep her away from the inheritance. She had trusted him. It hadn't even occurred to her he was hiding something. She'd been suspicious of Lucas but Lucas was the only one who hadn't liked the plan, the one who told her the truth.

She was a fool.

'I trusted you. But everything you've said to me has been a lie. Everything.'

'It may have started off that way but—'

Sharmila nodded as she worked things out. 'You didn't know me. You were lying to me all this time. Instead of getting to know me, you've been pretending to be my friend.'

'I haven't been pretending. We are friends. I do like you. I more than like you.'

'You like me? Don't insult my intelligence.'

He hung his head. 'You may not believe that right now, but it's true.'

'I don't believe a word you say. You've been trying to sabotage

259

the wish list. It all makes sense. The puzzle pieces going missing. The desserts. Did you do something with them? Lucas going to Boston instead of doing the gingerbread competition. You were trying to sabotage me.' Her breath caught as she remembered what else he told her. 'I had to stay in Pineford until Christmas Day. That means if I left even for a night, I'd lose everything.'

'Sharmila, I—'

'No. I'm still talking,' she said, putting her palm up and straightening. She wasn't going to cry in front of him. 'Lucas invited me to Boston. When that didn't work, you suggested we go to New York.'

He avoided her gaze, staring at the floor instead. She wanted to be sick. Everything between them had been a lie.

'And if Lucas hadn't told me the truth today I would never have found out.'

'I was going to tell you today. I came back to talk to you.'

'Why should I believe you? It's easy for you to say that now I already know.' She wanted to cry. She pinched her thigh through her dress to stop the tears. The man didn't deserve her emotions. 'I'm such a fool. You even pretended to be attracted to me as part of your plan.'

'I wasn't pretending. It's real, the attraction is real. I didn't make any of that up. I never lied about how I feel.'

She drew a blanket over herself, wrapping it round her. 'I think you should leave now.'

'We should talk.'

'No. I think you should leave.'

Zach nodded reluctantly. 'All right. Maybe we can speak more tomorrow.'

'No. I don't want to see you again.'

'Sharmila. Please.' He held his hand to her. 'Let's talk about this.'

She recoiled. 'Just go, please.'

She stared into the flames until she heard the door close.

Chapter 29

When the sun eventually rose on Monday morning, Sharmila had long been awake – she hadn't slept much throughout the night. She told herself it was the anticipation of returning to England. Told herself it had nothing to do with Zach and the revelations of the previous night.

Penny wasn't awake yet so she silently went downstairs into the kitchen to make herself a coffee. She carried the mug with her as she went round the ground floor from the kitchen to the great hall to the formal living room, the formal dining room, and the snug – all rooms that had become so familiar to her. Were these really hers now?

Why? Why had Thomas left it to her? It would be amazing to live in Pineford, but she couldn't move to the USA. Her career, her life, was in England. And Holly House was too special to be left empty for rare occasions when she could visit the States.

She glanced at her watch – 6 a.m. She quickly made the time conversion to England and from there the time conversion to India. Her parents should be free to talk – she could always rely on them to give her sound advice.

For the first time since last night, Sharmila felt happiness when her parents' familiar faces appeared on the video. They were eager to hear how her Christmas Day and Boxing Day party went. As usual, her parents had spent their weekend volunteering at the nearby clinics.

She told them what she'd found out and what Thomas had left for her. To her shock, they showed no signs of surprise.

'Yes, Thomas told us about this. He wanted to make sure we didn't have any problems with his leaving something for you in his will,' her mum said.

'But why? Why would he do that and why didn't you say anything when I told you about this holiday?'

'Thomas asked us not to.'

Sharmila shook her head. Was everybody keeping a secret from her? 'Did he tell you why he left me so much?'

'He didn't give us his reasons, not fully. Your Thomas was a kind and generous man. He liked you a lot. All we know is that he wanted all of us to spend a Christmas with him in Pineford. When he found out about his illness, he came up with the idea for the holiday wishes and leaving you the house instead.'

'But what about the shares? And why didn't you tell him not to?'

Her parents laughed. 'Of course we told him he didn't have to give you anything but it was his decision in the end. Who are we to tell him what to do with his possessions?' her mum said, her voice gentle but firm.

'I can't keep it, Ma,' Sharmila said. 'It's too much.'

'Sharmi, beti,' her father said in Bengali. 'Thomas wanted you to have this gift. You can't just turn it down.'

She bent her head. 'Ha, Baba,' she acknowledged.

They finished the conversation shortly afterwards. She understood where her parents were coming from. But she couldn't keep the house. It was too much.

And she didn't want the shares. She had no desire to be the decision-maker between Lucas and Izzy. There was no way she wanted to arbitrate between a brother and sister. She only had a vague idea what Thomas's family business did – something in construction.

Penny came into the room, her arms moving as she yawned. 'You're awake early. Didn't you sleep well?'

'Not really. Too much nervous energy, I guess.'

'Zach left early yesterday. I thought you'd want to spend all your free time with him.'

'No. Zach was lying to me. To all of us.' She told Penny about Zach's relationship to Thomas. She wasn't ready to tell her about the inheritance yet – she needed to decide what to do about it first.

'I can't believe Zach is Thomas's nephew. That's amazing!'

"Amazing? Did you miss the part about him lying to us?"

'No, I didn't, hun,' Penny replied, putting her arm around Sharmila's shoulders. 'And I know how you feel about lies so I understand why it would upset you. I really do. But I think it's great that Zach's another connection to Thomas for you. And it was a small lie in the whole scheme of things. Zach couldn't fake the kind of person he really is.'

'It doesn't matter how big or small the lie was. It was a silly, unnecessary lie. He deceived the whole town.' Sharmila was sure if Penny knew the full story behind Zach's deceit and the inheritance, Penny wouldn't feel the same about Zach and his *small* lie. She waved her hand in a gesture of dismissal. 'Anyway, it doesn't matter. We still have a lot to do today.'

'I know. It's gone so quickly. I'm going to be sad to leave. Debby and the Women's Club will be round before lunch to help clear up from yesterday and tidy the house away.'

Sharmila nodded. Hearing about the kindness of the people in Pineford no longer surprised her.

'I would love to move to Pineford, I think,' Penny said.

'Really? A couple of weeks in a small town was enough to change your big-city soul?'

Penny shrugged. 'I don't know about any small town. But Pineford is special.'

Sharmila couldn't agree more.

'Thanks to Thomas and his wish list I don't think there's a single Christmas or winter activity we haven't covered. Which reminds me, you still have the final wish,' Penny pointed out. 'But you've got until New Year's Day to complete it haven't you?'

'Yes, but I don't want to think about it. I'm not sure I'll even finish it to be honest.'

'Never say never,' Penny said.

Sharmila shook her head at Penny's optimistic outlook. Too often, when she'd thought about doing the final wish, Zach had been part of it. But right now she didn't want to think about Zach at all. She had to concentrate on getting the house back to normal.

The Women's Club arrived and helped clear up the last remnants from the party and put away the other decorations, leaving Sharmila to undress the tree. That was the hardest part. Taking off all the baubles Thomas picked out for her. She carefully packed her elephant ornament – that one was coming home with her.

The ladies had to leave shortly after they finished – unlike in England, it wasn't a national holiday so many of them had to return to work.

She bit her lip as they came up to say goodbye. She wasn't ready. She'd arrived in Pineford expecting to leave without letting anyone get too close to her. She hadn't anticipated these ladies' absolute refusal to let her remain aloof – hadn't expected them to adopt her into their community. In just three weeks, these ladies, who had started as acquaintances, had grown to be probably lifelong friends.

After Hari passed away, she'd wanted to protect herself from caring too much because she didn't want to risk getting hurt, so she'd gone to the opposite extreme of not letting anyone in at all. But not allowing herself to care wasn't a solution to caring too much. She knew that now. There was a balance, and Pineford helped her find that balance again. She would always be grateful for that. She wasn't ready to say goodbye to these new friends she'd made. Not forever.

Which brought her back to Thomas's will and Zach. She could tell Jackie and Jill had found out who Zach really was, but they were careful not to bring it up around her. Did they feel the same way Penny had? Maybe it was easier for them.

He hadn't pretended to care about them. Hadn't held them. Hadn't made them wish for a future. Hadn't broken their heart.

She took a shaky breath and turned back to packing the decorations.

Once the rooms were cleared, the last boxes were closed and put into storage, and the house was bare again.

Christmas was officially over.

Chapter 30

Zach had never been more nervous than he was at that moment, two days before New Year's Eve, standing at the door to Sharmila's apartment in Birmingham, waiting for it to open. He'd pulled every string he could to get a flight to England at short notice. Even though he would be moving to London in a few weeks, he didn't want to wait to speak to Sharmila – to explain himself and apologise again.

He swallowed as the door began to open.

'What are you doing here?' Sharmila said, when she saw him. There was no welcome on her face.

Zach was expecting Sharmila's hostile reaction. What he hadn't expected was the way his heart warmed at seeing her again. This wasn't a brief holiday romance for him. He would do what he could to prove his feelings to her.

'I was in the country and thought I'd drop by,' he replied.

She rolled her eyes at his attempt at humour. 'You were in the country. Sure. OK.' Her eyes narrowed. 'How do you know my address?'

He cleared his throat. He didn't want to get any of her friends into trouble.

'Don't tell me. Penny?' She raised her eyebrows.

'And Jackie and Jill and Liz and others offered it to me.' A range of emotions crossed her face but he couldn't read them.

'They told me you spoke to them before you left Pineford,' she said. 'They didn't tell me they'd given you my address.'

'Don't blame them. They're all hopeless romantics at heart.'

'Hopeless is right.' She huffed. 'I suppose you should come in, I guess. Do you want something to drink?'

He walked into the warmth of her flat. In the hallway were packing boxes.

'You're in the middle of moving?' he asked, following her into a small living area. Her place was vastly different from the open-plan living space of Holly House.

'I'm transferring to my firm's London office.' She indicated for him to take a seat. 'That was the only reason I could have the three-week holiday. The timing happened to work out.'

'You're going to be in London?' His mouth widened in a beaming smile. He was never one to believe in fate but it had to be a sign that Sharmila was moving to the same city as he would be in. 'That's great.'

'Why?'

'I'm going to be living in London.'

'What do you mean?'

'Remember I told you I hoped to spend time in England in the future? My company has set up an office in London as part of our international expansion and I'm going to be running it. I'm moving in the middle of January and I'll be here for at least three years.'

She stared at him for a few minutes. He wished he could tell what she was thinking. Was she pleased to hear they'd be in the same country, in the same city?

'How do I know this isn't another one of your lies?' she asked.

He grimaced, closing his eyes. 'I'm sorry you don't trust me anymore. Believe me, I know what's it like when you trust someone and they betray you.' She didn't say anything. 'I came to

267

England ahead of my move for the chance to explain everything fully to you. Please.'

'What is there to explain? You lied to me. You lied to everybody. I can't believe they forgave you so easily.'

He pressed his lips together. He couldn't believe it either. Although they were initially upset when he told them who he was, they had forgiven him quickly – prepared to base their judgements on the person they got to know while he was in Pineford. He was immensely grateful for their understanding – it gave him the smallest hope Sharmila would forgive him in time too.

She shrugged. He took that as an indication he should speak.

'You didn't tell Mr Bell you know about the house and the shares.'

She shook her head. 'I never asked for them.' She waved her hand. 'As far as the lawyers know, I haven't completed Thomas's Wishlist.'

He looked away. 'That's not exactly true. I told them.'

She'd been facing away from him but turned suddenly at those words. 'Why? Wasn't the whole reason you were in Pineford to stop me from inheriting?'

He grimaced. 'I'm sorry we weren't able to tell you about the terms of the will. And I'm sorry we tried to stop you finishing your wish list.'

'You decided I shouldn't get what Thomas left for me without even getting to know me first.' She arched her eyebrows.

He held his hands up. 'All we knew was our uncle met a woman abroad when he was unwell. The next thing we hear, not only has he arranged for her to have a dream holiday, but he's also left her shares in the family business and in a house he just bought – his childhood home. Wouldn't you question why?'

She was silent for a few minutes, sitting back in her armchair. 'You thought I was after money?'

He gave an embarrassed nod. 'Yes. It was the only explanation that made any sense at the time. And based on my experience …'

He rubbed his chin. 'But it was wrong for me to judge you based on my past. I know that. I'm sorry.'

She didn't say anything.

'You'll have what you rightfully deserve now,' he said.

She shook her head. 'If the lawyers contact me, I'll tell them to transfer the shares to you or Lucas and transfer the house to your mum. That's the way it should be.'

'No. I thought my mother wanted to live in Holly House. That's one of the reasons I was ready to help Izzy. My mom grew up in that house and she mentioned how much she wished she could move back there. She's been so sad since my father passed away, I thought having the house would be good for her.' If only Zach had taken the time to speak to his mother properly, he could have prevented the hurt he caused Sharmila. 'No member of my family will accept the house or the shares. Thomas wanted you to have them.'

'It doesn't matter. I'm not going to accept it. I can't,' she said, wringing her hands in agitation. 'He shouldn't have left them to me. I know you won't believe me, but I didn't know about the house and I didn't ask for it. And I didn't trick him into leaving it to me. I didn't even know he'd bought Holly House until I was told about the holiday.'

'I do believe you. I do trust you. And I know why Thomas left you the house.'

'You do?' She looked up. 'How? Why?'

'My mother told me at Christmas. Thomas already told her his plans once he decided to stop treatment. He gave you the shares because Lucas and Izzy disagree on a lot of things. He didn't want to let them have half the company each because the company would never grow, because they would never come to an agreement. He knew leaving shares to anyone else in the family could cause problems with loyalty so you were the best option to force Lucas and Izzy to come to a mutual agreement. With your empathy and legal brain he was confident you'd make the right choice if they couldn't.'

It had made perfect sense once his mother had explained it to him. Even Lucas and Izzy acknowledged their disagreements could affect the business. There was no point giving the shares to another family member – that would cause too much tension and conflict. Sharmila probably hadn't realised the annual income from the shares would cover the expenses for Holly House. Thomas had thought through everything – it couldn't be clearer that he'd made a conscious decision to leave so much to Sharmila.

A range of emotions crossed her face as she worked through what he said. 'And the house?'

'Not everything Thomas did may make sense to us even if he had a reason for doing things. He wanted to make your dream come true.'

'Giving me the chance to spend Christmas in Pineford was more than enough to make my dream come true. He didn't need to leave the house to me too.'

'When Thomas knew he wouldn't be able to show you around Pineford like he hoped, he still wanted you to have that chance. Thomas told my mom that your parents were worried about how you'd closed yourself off from everything after Hari died.' He stopped speaking, wanting to check her reaction. She clasped her hands together and looked down at the floor.

'Thomas never told anyone outside the family about Carla or used his anchor metaphor. When you mentioned it, I knew then you meant a lot to him.' It was that moment in New York he knew, without a shadow of a doubt, Sharmila deserved everything Thomas left her. 'He worried you were going down the same path he had and you were floating out to sea. He wanted you to have an anchor. Holly House could be your anchor.'

'My anchor? Holly House. He gave me it as an anchor,' she repeated. She crumbled at the revelation.

He rose to gather her in his arms. Initially, she flinched but a moment later she wrapped her arms around him. He held her close to him, stroking her back, offering her comfort. He placed

270

a tender kiss on the top of her head, regretting it when she immediately moved away.

He had to make it right between them. Sharmila belonged in his arms and he belonged in hers. They may have only known each other for three weeks but that was enough.

'I am so sorry about our deception, Sharmila. So sorry I hurt you. I honestly was going to tell you the day of the party. I know that's too late anyway. I wish I could make you understand a little of where I was coming from.'

She raised her head, looking at him as if she was receptive to listening.

'I told you people have pretended to be interested in us only because of our family name and wealth,' he said. 'The main person was my ex-fiancée.'

'Your ex-fiancée?'

'It's not an excuse—'

'No, it isn't. You judged me based on what a completely different person did.'

'It wasn't only her. It happened all the time.'

'Oh, please!' Her tone was extremely sceptical.

'It's true!'

'I think if someone was after you for shallow reasons it would be because of the way you look not the amount of money you have.'

He raised his head, arrested by her lighter tone. 'You think I'm good-looking?'

She tossed him a look of exasperation. 'That's not pertinent to the discussion.'

He chuckled. She was still angry – understandably so. But there was definitely a thaw in her behaviour since the last time they saw each other.

'I am so sorry for the way I acted in Pineford,' he repeated. 'I'm going to do everything I can to make you trust me again. I may have lied about who I am—'

'May have?'

'I did lie about who I am. And we did try to stop you finishing Thomas's Wishlist. And we did try to get you to leave Pineford.'

'Thank you for your confession.'

His lips quirked at her snark. 'But that changed as I got to know you. I found myself looking for ways to spend time with you and help you finish the list despite my loyalty to my family. That's why Izzy was in Pineford. She knew I planned to tell you. Lucas only got there first because he thought I'd already told you everything. Please believe me. I'm going to show you that you can trust me.'

She stared at him. He tried to remain still under her scrutiny. 'It doesn't matter. Look, I understand why you felt the need to lie – you already told me you find it hard to trust people. Obviously, with your past, I can understand why you wouldn't want to tell me about the inheritance but I will never know how much of what you've said is a lie.'

'I never lied about the way I feel about you. I care about you a lot.'

There was silence. He held his breath.

'Maybe I don't believe you,' she said.

Although he had expected that response, it still crushed some hope inside him. 'That's fair,' he said. 'But I'm not going away. You can't get rid of me that easily.'

'Really? You're planning to take up stalking as your next vice?'

His mouth twitched. 'I'm not going to stalk you. I'm not going to pester you. I'm not going to text or call you all the time. I'm not going to send you expensive gifts. But I'm not going anywhere. Now we're going to be in the same city it's going to be even easier.'

'London is a huge city.'

'It's closer than San Francisco.'

She sat back in her armchair. 'It won't be easy to win back my trust,' she said finally.

'Nothing worth having is easy.' Something had changed – he could sense it.

272

'We'll see.' Again she stared at him unblinking. After a few minutes, she said, 'If I were you, I wouldn't completely rule out sending me extravagant presents.'

He couldn't help the huge grin that crossed his face. He knew she had no interest in the monetary value of gifts. If she was making jokes, she was definitely less angry now. There was hope.

He left soon after, driving to a nearby hotel where he started finalising his plans to make another wish come true.

Chapter 31

'I'm not sure about this, Penny,' Sharmila said in Penny's car two days later.

'About what?'

'A big New Year's Eve party. Perhaps a quiet night in would be better.'

'You missed my New Year's party last year. The first time ever. I don't plan to let you miss this one.'

Sharmila couldn't believe less than one month ago she'd been getting ready to travel to Pineford. Already that day, she'd received messages from several of her Pineford friends, wishing her a happy new year in advance since they wouldn't get a chance to speak to her on the day itself. She'd also had video chats with Liz and Jackie.

They'd found out about Thomas's will and were excited that Holly House would be hers. They made her promise she would try to come out there soon. None of them sounded surprised by the legacy.

They also brought up Zach and had only kind words to say about him. They easily got over his small deception, explaining to her what the Endicott name meant. For them, the white lie was nothing compared to everything he'd done to help the town, the way he treated everyone with kindness, the way he fit in with the town the same way Sharmila had. If Zach ever needed a cheerleading squad he had one in Pineford.

It was the same thing Penny had said back when she heard about Zach's deception – he couldn't hide the person he was inside.

'Besides,' Penny continued, 'I was worried you'd spend the day moping in bed.'

'I don't mope! What do I have to mope about?'

'Zach.'

'Zach? Why would I be moping about him?'

'Because you miss him and because you love him,' Penny said in an exaggerated lovey-dovey tone.

'How can I miss him? He's going to be right here.' She wasn't going to talk about whether she loved him.

'Where?' Penny gave her a startled look.

'I mean in England. But you must know that. You gave him my address.'

'Oh, that's what you meant. Yeah, I did give him your address. I thought you needed to talk. And it did help, didn't it? You're not as angry anymore? You wouldn't mind seeing him again?' Penny sounded worried, which was unusual.

'The thing is, I get why Zach and Lucas were concerned about the inheritance,' Sharmila replied. 'And I believe Zach now when he says he was planning to tell me the truth. It's the hiding his identity I'm struggling with most – even though I know he had to do that because of the whole inheritance thing.'

Although she hated that Zach had lied to her, she could understand his reasons. She would also do anything to help her family. Yes, it hurt that he hadn't trusted her. But she did believe him when he said he cared about her.

And she cared about him. She would no longer deny it.

She wasn't going out of her way to tell him but she wasn't going to push him away if he meant what he said and would work to get her to trust him.

'If we hadn't talked the other day, if he hadn't explained things, I'm not sure I would want to see him but I think I'm ready to give him a chance,' Sharmila said.

'That's good to hear,' Penny said, as she pulled up in front of the building that housed her work studio.

'Why are we here?' Sharmila asked, getting out of the car. There were no other cars and the place looked dark.

'Come on,' Penny said. 'It's inside.'

Sharmila followed her friend. There were no signs of a party anywhere. Penny opened her studio door.

As Sharmila walked in she could hear Christmas carols coming from speakers. Straight ahead of her was a small metal trellis arch that was resting against a small pop-up canopy. Garlands, strewn with fairy lights, were interwoven through the makeshift structure. The ground underneath her feet and in front was covered with a blanket of material resembling snow. It must have taken hours to set it all up.

Open-mouthed, she turned to Penny. As the overhead lights came on, a movement to her side caught her attention.

Zach. Looking gorgeous as always but nervous.

'Happy new year, Sharmila,' Penny said, kissing her cheek. 'I'll call you tomorrow. I want to hear everything.' She closed the door behind her.

Sharmila walked forward slowly. 'What's going on? What's all this about?'

'Your last wish. Recreate the last scene of a Christmas movie.'

As she looked again at the arch and canopy, Sharmila's chin quivered, and she raised her hand to cover her heart. It had been set up exactly like the gazebo from her favourite Christmas movie. From the final scene in that movie they watched together. Zach was offering to help her recreate it. A scene that ended with a romantic embrace.

When she'd imagined her first kiss with Zach, and she'd imagined it more times than she could count, it had never been a

276

prosaic peck for a photo. She couldn't help feeling a little disappointed. But perhaps it was better that way. There would be no pressure, less awkwardness. Hopefully.

Zach came to stand in front of her, reaching for her hands. 'Sharmila, I wanted to say sorry, again, for not telling you the truth about the inheritance and who I am.'

'I understand why you did it. If someone in my family gave a generous bequest to a stranger I'd be concerned too,' she told him in earnest.

He brought her hands to his mouth and placed a kiss on each one. 'I meant what I said, I'll make it up to you.'

'You don't need to do that.' She meant it. Everyone had told her to look at Zach's actions, at his genuine kindness and warmth.

After Hari, she thought it would be safer not to risk relationships. She never thought she would find someone who could open her heart up to love again. Zach had burrowed his way in so completely, she wasn't going to turn her back on what they could have together.

'It's the new year,' she said. 'Let's start over.'

His bright smile of relief made her heart skip a beat. It was the perfect way to begin again. They had a lot to talk about – he still had a lot to explain. It wasn't going to be easy but she wanted Zach in her life.

'I would love to do that,' he said. 'But first shall we take the photo. Are you ready to finish your list?'

'You've gone to so much trouble, Zach. This looks perfect. But really, we don't have to do this. Thomas was already too generous. I can't accept the charity donation, not when your family are refusing to take the shares or Holly House.'

'What donation?'

She widened her eyes. 'You don't know?'

'About what?'

'If I complete Thomas's Wishlist, a donation will go to a charity of my choice.'

'That must have been a separate condition,' Zach said, shaking his head. 'I didn't know anything about it.'

'Then why?' She tilted her head at the gazebo.

'I wanted you to have all your wishes come true.'

She pressed a hand to her mouth, the tears welling at the realisation he simply wanted to help fulfil her final wish. She now knew, without a shadow of a doubt, he cared about her – they did share an emotional connection – it wasn't guilt or a sense of honour behind his gesture. She took a deep breath.

'I'm ready for the photo.'

'Here, you'll need this.' He handed her a carrier bag.

She opened it and drew out a pink winter coat, similar to the one she admired in the film. He'd bought her a coat!

'Zach! What are you doing to me? At this rate, I'm going to look completely red and blotchy for the photo.' She laughed through her tears.

'You're going to look beautiful, as always,' he said, handing her a tissue.

She went to put on the coat, stroking her fingers against its warmth. Zach was also putting on a winter jacket – like the one worn by the hero from her film. He really had thought of everything.

'Ready?' he asked.

She stood in the gazebo. After he set the timer, he walked towards her and put his arms around her – exactly like the final scene from her favourite Christmas movie.

Zach mouthed a countdown as their heads moved closer, leaning in for a kiss. Finally.

Sharmila was vaguely aware of a flash but that was nothing compared to the heat that seared through her at the lightest touch from Zach's lips. There was nothing prosaic about their first kiss.

Within seconds they were kissing greedily. As if they were each other's oxygen source. He gathered her closer.

She fit perfectly in his arms – where she wanted to be always.

Perhaps Thomas wanted her to have Holly House as an anchor, but in Zach's arms, she already knew what her anchor was. Or who.

'I've wanted to kiss you for such a long time,' she said, resting her cheek against his chest as she made her admission.

'Me too. A long time. But I couldn't. Not when you didn't know who I really was.'

'I think I always knew who you really were, even if I didn't know your real name. You couldn't hide the person you are inside.'

Unable to resist they kissed again. She didn't know how long they'd been kissing before they broke apart. A couple of deep breaths later, Zach gathered her back in his arms. She put her arms around his neck, lifting herself onto tiptoe so she could bring her mouth up to his.

After a few more minutes, Zach said, 'Before we get carried away, we should check the photo and send it to Mr Bell.' He moved away reluctantly.

Sharmila murmured a protest but knew he was right.

'So that's it,' she said, turning to him once she emailed the photo. 'Thomas's Christmas Wishlist is done.'

'How do you feel?' he asked, drawing her into his arms. 'Now, all ten wishes have come true.'

'Twelve actually.'

'What do you mean?'

'Twelve wishes. I had twelve wishes of Christmas that came true.'

He tilted his head, a warm but curious expression on his face. 'How were there twelve wishes? What were they?'

'My first wish came true right at the beginning of December. I always wished I could spend Christmas in a small American town. It's been one of my biggest dreams for a long time. Thomas made that wish come true with my Pineford holiday. Then, of course, there was his Christmas Wishlist.'

'Which had ten wishes. That's eleven. What was wish number twelve?'

279

She smiled, sure he could already guess. She was a romantic – always had been, always would be.

'You,' she said, reaching to put her arms round his shoulders, drawing his head towards hers. 'I wished for you.'

Acknowledgements

Firstly, a huge thank you to my lovely editor, Melanie Hayes, who helped me shape Sharmila and Zach's story into the best book it could be.

Thank you also to the team at HQ Digital who saw my premise's potential from a few early chapters. On that note, I think I must give thanks to Hallmark for all their movies I've watched – those movies truly were the inspiration behind this book when I asked myself what a Hallmark Christmas story would be like if the heroine was Indian.

Thanks to the Romantic Novelist's Association. Without the 1-2-1s at their 2020 virtual conference, none of this would be happening.

Thank you to the RNA gala dinner gals who inspired me to get writing and particularly Stefania Hartley, who persuaded me to keep going when I really didn't want to.

My special thanks to Donna Fasano. Our friendship was instantaneous and proof that oceans can't keep people apart. Thank you for our chats and for playing 'Do they say this in America?' with me.

Thank you to my parents and siblings who nurtured my dream of being a writer.

And finally, thank you to Gareth for your unconditional, endless support, and to D & E who brighten up my days.

Dear Reader,

We hope you enjoyed reading this book. If you did, we'd be so appreciative if you left a review. It really helps us and the author to bring more books like this to you.

Here at HQ Digital we are dedicated to publishing fiction that will keep you turning the pages into the early hours. Don't want to miss a thing? To find out more about our books, promotions, discover exclusive content and enter competitions you can keep in touch in the following ways:

JOIN OUR COMMUNITY:

Sign up to our new email newsletter:
http://smarturl.it/SignUpHQ

Read our new blog www.hqstories.co.uk

https://twitter.com/HQStories

www.facebook.com/HQStories

BUDDING WRITER?

We're also looking for authors to join the HQ Digital family! Find out more here:

https://www.hqstories.co.uk/want-to-write-for-us/

Thanks for reading, from the HQ Digital team

If you enjoyed *The Twelve Wishes of Christmas*, then why not try another heart-warming story from HQ Digital?